WHERE LIFE IS EASIEST FOR MEN

D.C. Emery

This original edition was independently published by the author as an electronic and physical book in 2024.

For those we have loved and lost

'As for your own end... You shall not die in Argos, but the gods will take you to the Elysian plain, which is at the ends of the world. There men lead an easier life than anywhere else in the world, for in Elysium there falls not rain, nor hail, nor snow, but Oceanus breathes ever with a West wind that sings softly from the sea, and gives fresh life to all men.'

HOMER, THE ODYSSEY (4,500-6,000 BC)

CONTENTS

DISCLAIMER

The following work of fiction contains depictions of violence, self-harm, substance addiction and suicide. Reader discretion is advised.

If you or anyone you know has been affected by any of the issues raised in the following work, please reach out and get the relevant help that you require;

(UK)

Samaritans:

(+) 116 123
www.samirtans.org

(US)

Suicide & Crisis Lifeline:

(+) 998
998lifeline.org

A NOTE FROM THE AUTHOR

I, myself, have never been particularly fond of grandiose prefaces or introductory notes of a self-indulgent nature (especially so for debut novels by debut novelists who may only be adding to the word count of a piece that may never be widely read). However, on this occasion, I feel compelled to add a few supplementary points for the readers' attention that ought, in my estimation at least, to add some deserved and perhaps necessary context to the following story that I have spent the past five or so years working on.

'Your lifetime will always be referred to collectively by the biggest tragedy that you were present in' (or something to that effect) is a phrase I recall hearing in my early adulthood, although I neglect to recall the source or the dramatic context which brought about its utterance. Honestly, it might have been a drunken family member or a celebrity from what I recall. And, it certainly is a rather macabre proposal *prima facie*, albeit one I deem worthy of certain considerations, particularly so in contextualising the background of the book you are about to read. In my interpretation of this statement, I do find it to be somewhat accurate (depending on the degree to which you treat it literally), for a couple of reasons that I briefly wish to entertain.

In school, I vividly recall learning in great depths of WWI and WWII, of the bubonic plague, the Great Fire of London, The Holocaust, etc. I am not proposing there is no virtue or value in educating oneself upon the aforementioned nor do I question it happening for any reason, but rather suggest that, on the contrary, one thing I do not recall ever learning about, (aside from when it was glanced over in brief to aid an alternative counterpoint), are the grandiose achievements such as those by the founding fathers of Western Civilization in the Ancient Greeks, the works of Michelangelo or Da Vinci, the splitting of the atom, the foundations of modern medicine or engineering, or the moon landing. I suppose the disparity in these occurrences' counterposed timeline may make my point redundant but, rather than give concrete examples or evidence to essay any validity for the aforementioned claim, I simply wish to engage with the idea that, a simplistic analysis of this supposition may dictate that a period of time is indeed best noted for the worst of all horrors that it entailed and as such, so are the people who belong to it. I do not know whether, (although I would not outrightly dismiss any postulations pursuant to a similar articulation), there is an innate and perhaps evasive human desire to associate with those things morbid and frightful. Perhaps this is why rubbernecking accidents are one of the biggest causes of motorway traffic, why the gory horror genre persists to boom, or why preceding message disclaimers regarding 'graphic content' make us all the more likely to click continue. I am not advocating this as a fact, and ultimately I accept that the opening assertion conveys a point fundamentally consistent with incontrovertible subjectivity. However, I entertain the predilection that it is or certainly can be the case for what I hope should soon be apparent

As an example I construe to be in accordance with my point, a fascinating person I once knew in brief had a great-grandparent who landed on the beach of Normandy on July 6th, 1944. He survived, no doubt had an infinity of tales to tell, and lived until an old age. Amongst his family, of whom there were numerous grandparents amongst its wider extension, he was referred to colloquially as the 'war grandad' or 'grandad Norman(dy)'. From my presumptuous outsider understanding, this was not done out of mockery or cynicism or indeed for any conceivable motive on the part of the phrase's numerous participants, it was just a status quo term of reference, and that is what he was called up until he died and afterwards in perpetuity. I suppose my point, should it not be lost in translation, is that no one ever called him the 'tall' or 'short' grandad, nor the 'kind' or 'mean' grandad, nor any name that made some indication to any of his characteristics or idiosyncrasies as a man who lived and breathed. I find it odd and even amusing that this was the case and I dare to suggest that was not the only circumstance, ever, of it happening. I do not know whether what funds such an affair is inherent patriotism, respect, a subliminal desire to recognise adversity, or a testament to one's strength in superseding it. Ultimately, I am not a sociologist, this is not a study and the reasoning behind such a conception is, to my end, irrelevant. What I believe is pertinent, however, is the following consideration it shall lead into.

Having been born in 1999 in suburban Sheffield to a mechanical engineer and a counsellor, it always seemed to be the case that indeed I never had one or was going to have one of these conflicted, worldwide events that may dictate my inherent outlook on life and render vulnerable my capacity for torment – and I make no mistake about it; what a rarity and a privilege of a life that is. Occasionally when my mind wandered back to that phrase for any multitude of self-absorbed philosophized reasons, I often wondered, are we going to be known as 'those who escaped?' 'The lucky ones'? As generation 'no-mishaps?' I recall once being told by an elderly lady on a train, (seemingly as a result of being involuntarily a part of a demographic she bore a grudge with); '*You lot* (my generation) *don't know you're born.*' I may add that she hissed it with such dire conviction as to sound like she was advocating a personal tenet. It wasn't quite, in both form and execution, the most graceful supposition nor one I would lay claim to being the rightful recipient of, but was it in any way accurate and what exactly did she mean? At what point, precisely, is one 'metaphorically' born or at least sentient enough to develop a self-awareness pertaining to this fact? It certainly sounded in that case that, (by virtue of inference) it is when and only when one has become afflicted - when their character is forced to endure or be subjected to unspecified displeasures and only when such things have occurred can one's character develop accordingly. And crucially, if this were to be the case as I suggest it, was she right to any degree? The answer is that I do not know. At the risk of manifesting myself into a pseudo-masculine cliché, is there any utility to the idea that we are 'the middle children of history, with no purpose or place, our great war is a spiritual war and our great depression is our lives' as Tyler Durden once claimed? (See: Fight Club; Chuck Palaniuk, 1996). Conversely, if there is no utility to it, whether one deems it pretentious or whiny or an inadvertent admission of dire naivety, why does it leave a sour yet familiar taste on the tongue? Is that how the history books are making us feel? Is it what elderly people on trains are hinting at? Are we, fundamentally, missing or craving something we don't actually want but feel inclined to need?

And if, to any wavering extent, such statements about my generation are true, then what does it subsequently mean for us, as participants of society and executors of our own free will and soulful desires? Does it (or should it) make our lives rudimentary; uneventful, unimposing, uninspired? I wish not to embark upon a further tangent and confess that the reason I believe such thoughts have presented themselves to me in such a way is because I always dreamt of being a writer from a young age. (I do not, hereby, mean a writer in a commercial sense, but rather in one where I am permitted to execute such existential discussions effectively). As I grew, among my favourite writers of prose, albeit for different reasons, and on who I had written numerous essays, were Dostoevsky and Hemingway – two men who, although as dispersed as seemingly possible in terms of environment and afflictions had, *inter alia*, a truly remarkable aptitude and comprehension of the human condition – of its most wicked complexities, its anomalous oddities, and its effects on social anthropology. And, although I won't chronologise their lives or their misadventures, I think it would be a stretch to suggest they had it 'easy', at least certainly not so by modern parameters. It would seem, in my mind at least and in alignment with what I am alluding to, that the imposition of difficulty was the most mutual companion they shared (should it be deemed appropriate to draw any correlation whatsoever).

I suppose my fundamental point hitherto, although I divulge it is one I find difficult to articulate, is not that I *wanted* to suffer or be subjected to anything of such like, but rather I wondered, can I write 1/1000th as well as they wrote (or even endeavour to try) if, from a fundamental perspective upon the unfolding of my unwaveringly placid life, nothing has happened to me? A relatively well-educated, moderately bland societal output unable to boast of traversing true struggle or being moulded by it, inadvertently filled from the boots to the eyeballs with the tendencies of modernised corporate culture, bureaucracy, consumerism, and pretentious social media inflictions, how can I reach into the despairs of the soul, of the intermittent wretchedness of the human being and mind; how can I be one who understands on a grand scale what it means to be who I am and to be here at this very moment... Henry David Thoreau once wrote that '*the mass of men live lives of quiet desperation*' (see Civil Disobedience and Other Essays; 1866) and, in terms of the sentiment to which he was expressing in full, I wholeheartedly agree with him. However, he wrote that quite some time ago and, what if our lives manifest themselves into ones which are no longer desperate or quiet? Why of course, I might be happier or more content, but to what end could I be a sensualist or a nihilist or an atheist? How could I be successful or intellectual? How can I love or be loved or be taken seriously, or how can I write truly and honestly, from the heart, if I have not done anything and do not know what it means to suffer? And as my old man used to say (humorously albeit with intonations of sincerity) '*You know nothing, boy*'. I believe the issue is not knowing nothing but not knowing what it is that you don't know.

Surely, the quintessence of an advanced, cultured and harmonised society would be one where people indeed live their entire lives without being subjected to a grand-scale tragedy or something that threatens to change the world they live in. Therefore, I aim to make it clear that I am in no way stating I wished to partake in such ailments for all of the rational and salient reasons one may deduce; only naivety would lead someone to such a wholeheartedly advocated thought. I also duly appreciate that this condition is one representative of the natural, progressive order that humans have been striving to achieve for millennia. And up until around 2017, I rested my case and concluded that that was indeed that... That I should drop all of my pretences as a self-deprecating, hopelessly romantic writer with delusions of grandeur and accept my place in the world as a little cog in need of lubrication. Then, COVID-19 hit.

Now, I do not mean to imply, nor am I drawing what would be futile comparisons between the COVID-19 pandemic and any event which went before throughout history in terms of its franticness, consequences and ensuing difficulties. However, it seemed that all of a sudden, we were living in one of those times somewhat capable of being categorised in such familiar terms; namely a terrible and unprecedented time that we would always be referred to amongst by way of its effect on the population and modernised society, and of course, the number of people whose lives it sadly claimed.

With the aim of being candid and transparent, its initial uprising led to me spending prolonged periods of time asleep, in bed, or drinking alcohol amidst the summer sunshine with nothing but a half-written legal essay to finish in the way of occupying my mind. Resultingly, this is not a declaration of sorrow nor an aim to attract sympathy... I make no claims that I was the worst one afflicted nor do I wish to say anything without due humility. However, as was inevitably the case, soon a year had a past and me and my university flatmate found ourselves locked away in a tiny, two bedroom, third-story flat in Nottingham with only a kitchen, a TV and some bar stools to watch away the days and months. This is where things became a little more tricky, and ultimately quite sinister. At the start things were easy, we can be fickle creatures so a television show or some tomfoolery normally satisfied to keep the existentialist within far enough away. Gradually, things became worse; increasingly desperate, unstimulating and miserable by all accounts. Soon, we began spending many days and many nights drinking into extreme excess, without any cause or purpose for which we could do anything or feel alive – entirely devoid of any tangible purpose for which we could act or indeed do anything. On the worst occasions, we did not leave the house for a couple of weeks at a time. On a few occasions, a sense of normality reinstated itself when the regulations were lifted and we spent some time pouring pints at a pub on North Sherwood Street in Nottingham City. One day when the sun was out, we went to the Arboretum Park and both felt dumbfounded at being in the presence of other actual people. Soon after, however, things had once more declined and we were back to square one. Some days it was fun and games, others were actually, really quite horrid – and I will spare the details for my own and my good friend's sake. COVID-19 claimed the life of an untold number of people and I write this admission with due respect for the fact that many others had it far, far worse than us.

However, amidst the chaos and the loss, there too was another pandemic (and one under-addressed in my opinion by mainstream media and communal interest) taking place beneath the surface. This pandemic was, in my opinion, equally as horrid – and that was the number of people, primarily men between the ages of 25 to 40, who were taking their own lives on a daily basis. I was, at this point, growing somewhat numb to dealing with unimaginably horrid cases of suicide during my short stint working as a legal intern in the Nottinghamshire Coroner's Court prior to the first lockdown. Some of the things I saw and was privy to during my time there will haunt me until the day I die. However, nothing came close, statistically at least, to what was being reported daily during those lockdown periods. I will not recount a precise figure at the risk of unfairly misdocumenting it but, I will add that I checked those figures religiously, and it was, for lack of a more sincere phrase, a hell of a lot of people. I am assured that every single one of those accounted for in that statistic was loved widely and dearly and who by all rights, still ought to be here, but lost their battle to a war very few talk about. Looking back candidly on some of those lockdown occasions, especially those at the darkest times, I believe there were occasions when I was very close to adding one more to that figure. However, I am one of the lucky ones and, if you are reading this and you knew one of those people who were affected as such, this book is more theirs than it is mine.

When I digressed earlier into the point regarding a person's lifetime often being referred to by its biggest catastrophe, its relevance is on account of my writerly nature and the idea for my first novel that I had been trying to conceptualise many years prior and up until that point. I had developed and subsequently became obsessed with an innate desire to construct a story surrounding the torment of someone locked in just a singular room. In doing so, I was endeavouring to shine a light on a peculiar irony in the sense that, regardless of whether one is confined (or not) in a physical sense, their mental condition is indeed the most totalitarian form of oppressive imprisonment should it be that way inclined. Maybe this was brought about by a creative or philosophical urge, a struggle to 'fit in' or a general difficulty in the intellectual and existential nature required by this peculiar life we all share. Nonetheless, this idea was frighteningly insistent and was one I could not shift no matter the passing of the years.

Of course, the primary issue was that to write such a story, that is to say, one without any narrative structure or indeed happenings of any nature whatsoever, would have been almost impossible and if I had done so, it seems it would have been either a seemingly monumental literary achievement or failing that, exceedingly dull and worthy of the dusty bin in my university room where I would have thrown it. Alas, a prison setting was the most reoccurring internal suggestion but it didn't quite cut it for reasons which still evade me and failing this, my story had no grounding – no way one could relate to it nor a dimension in which its expositions felt necessary or relevant. Consequently, I refused to acknowledge this burning, innate desire and wrote it off. And then, on one monotonous evening whilst watching the sunrise during a 12-hour bender over Nottingham City through cigarette-smoked-stained windows, my dreary flatmate turned to me and said, 'Imagine if this went on forever.'

I am not sure how earnest this ponderance was and as we were both extremely drunk, he may not have even remembered saying it at all. However, for me, there was this euphoria – a beautiful irony discovered amidst an alcohol-induced epiphany. It felt as though, everything had just fallen together with mathematical precision; the premise of a story I had obsessed over but never came to fruition finally had the context it needed, a world now presented itself in which people could relate to it, and I had finally experienced the kind of turmoil I always, for some morbid and pompous reason, deemed necessary to fund the great writing I was trying to achieve. In other terms, it felt as though, *I had finally been born*. The next day I began working on the following piece that you are about to read.

I would like to emphasise that this note and the following book is, in no way shape or form conceivable, intended to be a criticism or satire upon any of the socioeconomic or political activities, conduct or ramifications during and proceeding COVID-19 by any organisation or body. Nor do I wish (in fact, quite the contrary) for the book to be considered a 'COVID book' or acquire any such associated generalisations as it was and I hope is so, so much more. Indeed, it is quite a monumental tale of entrapment and resurrection and the pandemic-induced world it is set in is not, via my greatest efforts at least, primary to the holistically creative vision or artistic intentions behind it. I may also add for the sake of balancing any unintentional sombreness, if it was not for COVID hitting and its ensuing tribulations, I may well have never gone on to ditch a deceptive career of 'glamour' in law, filing letters and issuing semi-automatic summons beneath a senior who didn't even know my name until he hired a more befitting replacement, and pursue my passion by studying a Creative Writing MA, or ever have written this story at all.

I add these considerations as I publish this book, purely and solely because I am fully aware that it is, well, rather an odd story, and with odd stories questions naturally ensue, some of which will no doubt be worthy of a suitable response. At least, I doubt people will have seen something directly comparable to date (written the way it is and told how it is) and I don't say this arrogantly or pretentiously. I suppose my biggest fear is for a prospective audience to be detracted from the narrative they are otherwise engaging with on account of insistently pondering over what the f*ck is going on... It is of course, impossible to gauge the reception as such and if in the completion of reading this piece, the preface felt redundant I sincerely apologise. However, having reread it on my final editorial run prior to release, it simply felt like the righteous thing to include. Perhaps I add this note out of sheer cowardice and anticipation, or as a prelude to thoughts not shared or appreciated by the general consensus. After all, I have spent, quite literally, years staring at this story on a Word document and such a condition certainly takes its toll. Perhaps I also preface this book to appease some hidden angst generated from an early dissertation comment by one of my tutors who felt this story was simply 'too soon' and drew issue with the inability to distinguish precisely 'what is real and what isn't.'

Therefore, I wished to make certain declarations regarding the nature of its publication and its preceding background before one indeed makes their own mind up on it, as I would fully and wholeheartedly encourage one to do in the most unliberated sense. Ultimately, it is fiction and nothing more, but I have often found that sometimes fiction can be just that little bit more magical when in it is, metaphorically speaking, tangible. Or, failing 'tangible', it feels as though it is never quite out of reaching distance or never truly operates as a stranger.

I would like to add that if you are reading these notes it means you have paid to access this - my debut book. The literary world is a beautiful one but far from easy to enter, no matter your experience, efforts or passion. I have seen a few great writers and many great people devote large portions of their lives to trying to 'make it' in return for little or no avail. Truth be told, even now I have spent years studying, writing and attempting to accomplish a certain level of the remarkable art that is short stories and novels in an attempt to 'crack' the industry, and have had no assurances as of yet that I will come anywhere near or achieve any such descriptions, and I have made my peace with this. A lot of novels which I had completed or almost completed I have binned entirely. I have some short stories sitting in my computer that I can hardly remember writing and refuse to reopen. What is more, I almost scrapped the following book numerous times over the years, and even considered burning it dramatically in an empty metal bin rather than face putting it into the public eye where it is at the mercy of its (and my own) reception - perhaps this is what people mean when they talk about the fragile ego of a writer, and in my own case, it would be hard to disagree. Ultimately, when I made the decision to dedicate my life to doing this many years ago, I didn't do so with the aims of a being a best seller - I did so in the hopes that my stories may mean something to someone, no matter who or where there are. If I can do that just a couple of times, it will be in my mind, mission complete.

In my final digression, I simply wish to *thank you,* as deeply and genuinely as I am capable, for parting with your hard-earned money and time in taking a chance on me and what is, in its purest and most genuine form of expression, my heart's fervent passion and my mind's unsatiable obsession.

I hope you enjoy and please do leave a rating or a
review if you have the time, I'd love to hear from you.

Yours,

Dan.

CHAPTER I - ODYSSEUS ALONE

I believe the present year is now 2038, although there is no way to establish factual certainty and no one to argue to the contrary for I am alone and my imperious solitude is all. As for the current date itself, I estimate that to be somewhere between the rise of June and the fall of August. This may seem inaccurate and excessively broad by most civilized time-keeping standards but I can assure one that it is not due to an absence of reason (that will soon be clear). In case one was wondering as a judicious mind might, I did also attempt to keep track of the individual days themselves but have long since conceded as they are not deserving of it and no one or nothing thanks me for my *sacrifice*.

I for one am able to approximate the date solely because I took it upon myself to manually track it with some degree of accuracy. I do this using an old calendar that hangs lifelessly from my tattered wall. I manually replaced the previous years that were documented upon it with the future years that had not been accounted for and can no longer be accounted for. However, this does present numerous issues, primarily because I am limited by the amount of calendars I own but also because in different years the days of the week fall anomalously, hence the difficulty in now being able to ascertain precisely what day it is. Naturally, I cannot attribute blame to the producers of the calendar for their lack of forward-thinking and intuition. This is because no logical calendar-maker or indeed logical person whatsoever could fathom the state of life within which their product now drearily exists. What is more, it is inconceivable that they would have been able to foretell all that is left in the new world which is nothing other than immortal tedium and persecution of the soul. It is an admissible testament to how fickle the old world was that we only felt the need to mass-produce calendars a year in advance of it coming to fruition. Had one known what was going to come, they would have made them hundreds, if not thousands of years forward and even this may not have sufficed as no equitable predictions could endeavour to encompass the extent and duration of my anguish.

There is no one around to force or manipulate me into doing this task, in fact, it is almost irrefutable that nothing would care if I didn't and as such, no ramifications would present themselves as a result. I try most heartily to pretend that this is not the case but no amount of emotional conviction or subjectivity can override what is otherwise a certitude. Alas, the crux is that it is only I who forces myself to track the dates out of duty to maintain some normality in a world entirely devoid of it. My motivation for doing this erroneous chore lies within the absence of any common authority over anything that warrants such command. I am aware that our conception of time is a man-made construct and it is possible, if not probable, that I am the last man alive. The irony of this is not lost upon me but I retain that if I ceased to do it then time would be forgotten altogether and ultimately, this would be my fault and my fault alone.

Although I have never had much control over the world, let alone my place within it, timidly forfeiting the opportunity to keep track of the one thing that sustained our humanity is not something that I could bear the responsibility (and ensuing guilt) of. I suppose there is a contradiction in this thought process; devoutly preserving something for the sole purpose of it not being forgotten is superfluous if there is no one around to forget it anyhow. Moreover, if I am sure of one thing, it is that the earth will continue to spin in blissful ignorance regardless of what day or time I think it to be as my ubiquitous insignificance is not something which I cease to appreciate. Quite contrarily, it is something I am perpetually reminded of as all other paltry distractions have long since absconded. It could be the year 7000 as far as the world minds and somewhere amidst the intricacy of this hopeless desolation lies my fundamental point; the fact that nothing extrinsic cares and anyone else who once did no longer exists means that so *surely* someone must. It is without a reluctant saviour such as myself that nothing is stood for and this is one thing that I just cannot abide, even if I am ultimately my own adjudicator and persecutor. Besides, it is well within my ability to do it and I would be unjust in proposing that it is a task for which I have to set aside other priorities in order for it to be completed. I rest assured that if this was not the case, if indeed this fixation became physically immoderate in any sense, I may well have surrendered my obligation to do it long ago. However, what I feel compelled to add is that, although I make no request for sympathy on the matter, its completion is something which takes its toll upon my mental well-being; with each day I record the previous one that has passed, the less providential I am about what is promised by the one that follows. As true and pertinent as this is, it is not an errand that offers any pragmatic challenge. If I were to do it in the most simplistic terms, without weighing up the philosophical connotations of its completion, all it would take would be to cross a mark off on a certain box once a day. However, I must emphasise that it is arduous to delineate the worldly context at present so that my readership can appreciate it for the benefit of my expositions. As such, I do not doubt that for most this timekeeping exercise sounds like something that is so tedious it requires a reminder just to prompt its completion and that a certain level of difficulty (in the form of monotony) would arise as a result. Howbeit, as a direct outcome of the new world's way I must insist that the concept of a 'task' is one that has since departed; a task is something that one does not want to do on account of having other things more important or favourable superseding it. Unfortunately, in this world, there is nothing significant to do whatsoever, let alone there be a multitude of tasks for which we could allocate a hierarchy in order to accommodate them. In the new world, wherever and whenever there is anything asking to be done, regardless of how peripheral it may or not may not seem by situational contrast, it becomes extremely effortless and rather than it being a duty it feels more like something that one should be grateful for.

However, I try not to indulge in the negativity that my timekeeping burdens me with. I still am able to humour things where possible or indeed necessary. For example, I do take some satisfaction when envisaging a hypothetical argument with another timekeeper, should there be another one out there in this indigent plane, especially if we were to come together and discover discrepancies with our individual recordings. Although an odd situation to propose, it is one I have envisaged incessantly. Perhaps because it is as perplexing as it is deprecatingly humorous; it is a scenario whereby we could argue until we turned to dust and still neither of us would be any the wiser, because there would be no way to be objectively sure of which account is correct. There is something haunting about such a proposition; about living in a world where there is no way to be certain about anything that dictates a level of certainty is required, let alone the very things which keep our lives structured and intact. When there is no way to be objective over anything then everything is assured to fall apart and the current world is, if nothing else, a testament to this morbid fact.

Perhaps I still keep track of the time because I have a subliminal need to self-deprecate; only by doing so am I able to document exactly how long I have been suffering. This may sound like a vindication of sorts, as if it is a way to tell others in order to extract sympathy or justify my irrational actions but this could not be any further from the truth. The need to do this is one which lies deep within me and as such, must be honoured out of an obligation to my own sanity and well-being. The concept of being subject to this torment infinitely, without having any way to know how long I have actually been experiencing it just seems the slightest bit more hopeless, if at all possible.

Unfortunately, I must accept the fact that someday very soon I am going to get to the final page on the final calendar, and with there being no way of acquiring a new one, I am certain to lose the ability to continue doing this. This is a fact and as with all facts, it is one that I must accept because regardless of how I feel about it, it will continue to exist nonetheless. Indeed, that final page may well prove to be the final page of all human timekeeping for eternity, until something or someone comes along and creates their own version once more. Further, it is inevitable that this will, at some point, occur and although I dejectedly accept this, I just cannot cease to continue doing it – I suppose (in absence of any other forthcoming rationale) it is a compulsion, an addiction, an obsession of a strange variety. I presume that one could question why I would even bother keeping track in the first place if the day was certain to come when I would no longer be able to carry on. The truth is that I never thought it would go on for so long, nor did anyone else as there was no means to do so. I thought that one day some godly being would arrive at my doorstep surrounded by a backdrop of golden light and tell me that everything has become passable and that I can leave my home once more. In slowly returning to some state of normality, where crowds gather in the masses to hear the words spoken by a figurehead behind a podium, I could just foretell someone asking;

'It may seem most deviant and ambitious to inquire and although I highly doubt it, I don't suppose anyone knows what the date is, do they?' Only for me to put my hand up from the back of the small crowd and rejoice in my glory. What could only follow would be the world's remaining occupants to engulf me in celebration for being the person who saved time itself despite having no logical reason to nor expecting any kind of reward. The lack of motivation and or self-gain from having done so would increase my heroic status because only the most altruistic of acts are done in such a capacity. I welcome this optimistic and somewhat egotistical envisagement for what it is but one can be assured that my delusions of grandeur have been duly punished. This is because I now realise, as I should have all along had I tuned into a sense of grounded humility, that this will never occur and all my efforts will fade into unrecognised obscurity. I would endeavour to think these elucidations have been adequate and although I wish to contextualise the background of my suffering, it is difficult to explain something which I do not fully understand myself. Alas, I do not have any further reasons which may validate why I do what I do. However, I certainly would disagree with the aspersion that I do it because I am wanting of what once was. If anything, I do it out of hatred for whatever now is.

Despite matters that one can be certain about having become an entirely scarce commodity, one thing I retain confidence over is that the present day is no shorter than the one before it, nor will it be any shorter than the one which follows. In fact, if the sun ceased to rise and the moon didn't bother following its setting, there would be no way to distinguish one day from the next. It is a difficult concept to illuminate one to, that of a day being so nugatory it is hard to recognise its passing other than by astronomical indicators and the imbuement of light and dark, but I aspire to do so nonetheless as its reality is my own. The requirements of naming days such as 'Monday' as we once did has dissipated as the days no longer warrant the recognition, nor do the months or years. The passing of time and our place within its confines is more irrelevant than it has ever been and ever could be. The biggest atrocity superseding this is that I have nothing to distract myself from what is my own mortality because no tedious tasks within the day offer me such relief.

One thing I wish I had appreciated more in the old world was that whilst work and chores seemed so burdensome (and although this was undeniably so), there was still a purpose to them being completed and to this end, they were necessary and insistent. However, it is only when their requirements no longer exist and a typical day is diluted down to being trapped within the mind that I crave the need to go to some corporate office or indulge in social etiquette by mowing the lawn and nodding to the neighbours that I despise. Anything which distracts one from considering the hopeless ruminations of their existence is something which deserved more respect than it no doubt acquired, certainly so from me if no other.

When I divulge the redundancy of time that has now become persistently prevalent, I do not do so due to the lack of trains to catch or meetings to make or social occasions to be punctual for. Contrarily, I do so because the days no longer offer any remnants of identity in the form of joy or laughter for their memories to cling incessantly to the back of the mind, as they otherwise might under certain parameters. Sometimes all it took in the old world for one to remember a time they would otherwise forget was a unique situation in which a short-lived laugh or cry was provided. Now, there is nothing to remember and there is nothing to forget. There is no warmth of a newborn child's laughter, the crack of a joke by a drunk friend or an affectionate look of a lover with whom one shared a moonlit tryst. There is no joy to be had in sharing the company of another because there isn't anyone from which one could take it. There is no way to socialise, no way to holiday, no way to work or oblige, no way to escape. The misery of this world and life within the remit of its expiration is now constant and seems to enjoy its untouchable state of perpetuity.

Albeit, I accept that misery is not exclusive only to the new world. It was too present in the old one, indeed in a large way. However, the two are not even closely comparable and I would dare anyone to say otherwise as to do so could only be negligent or intentionally ingenuous. Even in the old world when I found myself in a slump or an emotional decline, I was always able to find the means within which it could find itself. What I mean by this sentiment is that contextual misery is not *true* misery, something which through the affordance of hindsight I wish I was aware. For example, I could always recall my first lover's given name, which was 'Mia', and how much she despised it when people would mistake 'Mia' for 'Mya' when pronouncing. However, I never made that mistake other than deliberately to irritate her. I believe my point is that it was not the tedious correction that made me remember its importance or lack of it, but rather the memories and the person associated with it. When these trivial amalgamations become void, everything else loses its place in the world as there is nowhere they can be set. It may seem that the resulting loss of such a thing would be nothing other than trifling but as if to illustrate my point, I can assure one that I now no longer recall with any degree of certainty how 'Wednesday' is correctly enunciated. At one point I was assured it was pronounced somewhere in the verbal remit of 'Wensday' - but having seen its written form a multitude of times, and having heard it being pronounced so sparsely (there have been no other attempts that I have heard beside my own), my brain can no longer fathom how a verbal form of a word could be so disloyal to its written companion. Perhaps the reason for this assertion lies in my indefinite acceptance that nothing seems loyal to anything anymore. I believe this is because nothing is significant enough for anything else to offer its loyalty to it. Loyalty results from offered conditions that eventually, by way of consistent continuation and mutual gain, become assurances that one relies upon. Nothing of the sort can any longer be offered and as a result, I have now decided that if a future Wednesday ever did enough for me; if it were to pierce just a minute hole the size of a sand grain in this veil-like state of banality, and as a result of I was capable of remembering its events, I believe I would say it was a 'rather interesting 'Wed-nes-day'.

My calendar, amongst other dwindling practices of the old world, allows me to feel habitual and reminds me of what it means to have a routine because now there is no such thing, and whilst our conception of time never did exist from any extrinsic perspective of space and beyond, it is only when it has faded into obscurity that I feel the unnerving effects of its abandonment. I do not believe people of the old world ever extracted pleasure from the utilisation of a calendar nor of alarm clocks or reminders, and I certainly did not. However, I now crave the things that I once had but have no longer - not because I enjoyed such things when they were in my possession but only now they are out of my reach to reclaim, as is often the nature of entitlement and oversight. The need for routine arose in the old world from the need to allocate time to different tasks. Of course, things used to be required of us and under such constraints, we were required to organise these tasks, not for the satisfaction or benefit of the tasks themselves but rather to uphold our own capability to deal with them. It is odd that I felt so trapped and unnerved by things which indeed offered enough to make them worthwhile. Now I am left wondering which is worse; for our existence to be wholly intolerable or for there to be nothing in the world that is worth us not tolerating.

Today is a very significant day because I endeavour to begin documenting my experiences and my story, not for the pleasure or dismay of any other, nor to make a statement of any kind, but purely to satisfy the inherent need to retain my rapidly dispersing sanity. Only by digressing into the deepest parts of my mind am I able to make any sense of my plagued thoughts which get more sinister with every passing day. As aforementioned, my calendar is running out of space and soon I will run out of paper too. When someone or something finds my corpse rotting in the same room I spent the last few years of my life, if they ever do, I do not want the only thing they find besides my body to be a worn calendar as this denotes nothing of my character. I want it to be something much more explanatory and cathartic, something which allures one to the condemnation incumbent with my pathetic life and all it had become. Of course, I do not wish to die here rotting in this derisory room, but to convince myself that anything else is possible let alone likely is gruelling. What is more, I do not want my suffering to go to waste, I want it to be known to all those intrigued by it. The ringing of these depraved thoughts which sounds as I reread them alone in the dark remains to be the only reverberations I have left to hear. However, I have now surpassed such vain considerations because I no longer care for or about myself as I know I will soon perish. Therefore, before I do so, I want to tell my wretched tale; I want to tell the story of how the world came to an end and then carried on some.

* * *

In 2020, when the world was how we all knew it to be, with governments and laws and economies and a functioning society, a deadly virus broke out in a small city that was very far away. I shall not name that city because I have no desire nor intention to blame or assume. At the time when this first happened, it was not something that anyone gave any thought to, it was just another read-over subtitle on page five of the newspapers, another issue amongst a variety of others that was too distant for us to entertain. In the first publications that alluded to the outbreak, the story of it was superseded by a footballer's affair and a corporate tax scandal. Unless one was paying due attention and capable of reading the fine print, as was I, it was easy enough to miss the story in question altogether. The issue with the prominence of the media and the mass amount of information that it relayed to us only sought to desensitise the population from the information that we needed to be more thoughtful towards. I do not attribute blame for this matter because it is completely natural. The more people talk, the less important what they say becomes and the less people listen.

I always thought it to be problematic in the old world that people were completely obsessed with the comings and goings of their own lives and before they knew it, they became the centre of the universe in their own minds. The ability to perceive themselves in relation to the grandness of the population (as opposed to individualistic means) and all things pursuant to this, was one that seemed particularly evasive. This was more commonly known as egocentrism, the problem being that everyone was, to one degree or another, a narcissist, most just weren't very good at it. When such characteristics harbour in an individual, as was increasingly becoming the case, it creates a partition which protects itself from oncoming information that can't get past the protective wall that has been put up. The irony of this is that the unwanted and useless information is that which is stuck behind the walls and the useful information is that trying to work its way in. I am not trying to declare that I was far more superior or intelligent to my fellow man, in fact, this could not be any further from the truth. I just wish that, even on the most simplistic level, if we had sought to discuss less nonsense and think a little more beyond our station, there is a chance we may have treated the matter as the grave one it was and perhaps we could have begun looking for a solution sooner. By doing so, one may well have been found. It was only when the weeks and eventually months passed by that it slowly crawled its way into the mainstream and this is when people began to take notice. Unfortunately, the virus had already begun causing havoc at this point and it was much too late for such a delayed reaction.

As for the nature of the virus itself, no one was sure what its causes or contributors are because the ensuing efforts were focused on discouraging its spread. Naturally, attempts were made to investigate it so that a vaccine could be created but there simply was not the time. Many conspiracies grew about how such a dangerous and unprecedented virus just popped into existence, particularly as it is the nature of one's mind to wander away from what can be the inconceivable horrors of reality. However, whether such alternative theories were born truthfully, negligently, or incorrectly remains unclear. One thing that is for sure is that they were most unproductive.

At such a dire global time, it would have made far more sense for us to come together as a collective and turn our efforts towards the virus as one. Unfortunately, this was not the case. It has always seemed that people find it much easier to blame and digress than to accept and address because the latter often is entailed with the acknowledgement and acceptance of responsibility. I am not, of course, proposing that everyone around the globe no matter their merit should have become a scientist overnight and fought against the virus, nor was I expecting everyone to become a hero or a martyr or exercise any efforts for it. Only a foolish man indeed thinks that he can solve the world's problems. Rather, I am suggesting a view more aligned with the old saying that he who saves one life saves the world entire. All it would have taken was to reach out to a neighbour or a friend or even an enemy, just to make sure they are surviving and have things that they need, to show a little more time for others as we all began to struggle. Such an attitude, if spread wildly and believed deeply, could have changed the outcome for the better and is something of which I am certain.

I for one never did have any time for nor indulged in conspiracies and just ignored all the ones that I reluctantly saw as they took over the internet. The number of dullards that came out of hiding to advocate the next greatest theory on social media or boards outside their houses started off with the few and finished in the millions. The issue with such things always is that one is entitled to their opinion, as was always the social mandate. I understand, within reason why this was a popularly accepted view. However, problems inevitably arose and when two fools agree with each other about a foolish statement, and no one their rightful wiser is allowed to take away from their right to do so, they only become more foolish. The irony of this was that there was so much hysteria that the voices of governments and officials and more importantly scientists became drowned out in the uproar. In the following weeks, there was of course the given desultory guidance; to stay inside and not to leave or socialise, to wear masks when going outside and such. Needless to say, there were also the reassurances not to panic and the rest of the foreseeable platitudes and truisms. Soon after this, things took a sour turn. Rather than the widespread panic and aggravation culminating, the opposite took place. Instead, things just became more and more quiet. It was apparent that things were going on behind the scenes as it is not the nature of government to be quiet in times of heightened public tension but the less they spoke the less people seemed to worry. The newspaper and media outlets were still going at it aplenty, but it is hard to know how much of the information is given out of virtue and how much is given for the desire of profit. For the most part, people eventually got bored of the 'distant virus concerns grow' narrative and just carried on with their daily lives in joyous ignorance for as long as they could.

As this record will seek to be mine and mine alone, one thing that

I would like to be documented in no uncertain terms is that I do not think there was any involvement or foul play by humans in this virus. In fact, quite the contrary. I think what caused this virus to be was nothing other than a completely natural occurrence; an inevitable progression of a biological phenomenon. Viruses mutate and can do so very quickly, all it takes is for one species to catch something in their habitat and wander into another for it to pass and before we know it, a new strain has fought its way into existence that we know nothing about. It is arrogant and entirely foolish to presume that, just because humans were as advanced as they were, that they knew everything about the planet and could foretell all of the potential threats that may have come to be. Just because this one specific strain was something that we were unaware of was not something I found shocking or unbelievable; there are millions of subatomic things out there that our limited minds ceased to understand. I do not think this is the case because we are not clever enough or because we have not got around to it yet, I just think that some things are far beyond our intellectual grasp. What is more, there is nothing to be ashamed of about this fact. We should strive to accept our place in the world and embrace the limitations conferred upon us rather than trying to fight them. Human beings have been around for a long time, and prior to this, we avoided all other mammoth endangerments to our existence including those which were posed by ourselves unto ourselves. Our annihilation was not a case of discrimination or of choice, it was nothing other than what everything else in the natural world is assured of – a beginning and an end. I must accept for the sake of impartiality that there was a surprising lack of officiated medical literature and reports about the virus which confirmed what I suspected. There were a few, of course, that were published in the immediate aftermath but I found them to be rushed and arcane. However, I just allocated this to my obvious lack of medical expertise; I do not think it shocking that it flew over my head as most works of this nature probably would have done the same and as such, rejected any claims which suggested the virus was anything other than previously stated.

As for the people who may disagree with what I believed had happened, my stance is unwavering and I hope intelligible. However, I do not wish to be nor to purport the idea that I am a proprietor of fact, this is my story and I will tell it as so, withstanding all the commonplace facets (including that of exposition) of such an account. I do not think that any of the widely accepted and proven rules of the universe changed just because this strange virus came into the world. I take pride in being a man of pragmatic ideals. I believe that nothing has an explanation nor does anything have a right to one. I never gave any acclamation to the sentiment that everything happens for a reason or any such aversions that are closely void. The rationalization for this is simple, there is no such thing as a reason, other than the one which we humans on earth gave it. The universe and everything greater does not know what a reason is. What happens is not guided by a conscience being, provoked by empathy and understanding of the human condition, which weighs reason into its decision-making process, should there even be one.

Even those who are religious and believe in a singular higher power must surely have accepted it preposterous that one singular entity is evaluating the thoughts and feelings of every individual at every moment. It could only do this practically if had the time to do so or logically if it was empathetic enough to care. It is nothing other than indulgent for us to think that conceptions which do not exist outside our finite and minute existence would influence things so grand and beyond us. The advancement of modern life led to us surpassing the basic need for things such as food and water, which the majority of other beings still have to fight for. The result of this over a long enough period of time is that we started thinking above our pay grade. We start getting ungrateful and needy. I have never understood those who feel that way; people guided by vague notions of destiny and fate, of a higher purpose. There is nothing to suggest that any of these conceptions are true, and no evaluation of the human condition which is true to its cause would rightfully advocate them. The only way I can see such things appealing to an individual is if they are too scared to accept the fundamental hopelessness and insignificance of life. There is nothing wrong with feeling this way, and I do not intend to berate those who do. However, we should not seek to divide our intentions and allegiances towards illogical resolutions such as this. I mean, what do we do that grants us such a level of otherworldly significance? The way in which I have always interpreted life on earth is simple and need not be anything other than this; things happen in the world and we know this simply because they do, just because we do not understand how or want to know why does not change this. We can surrender to this condition or suffer in trying to fathom the way in which it makes sense; the latter is ensured to lead to disappointment because it simply doesn't.

* * *

Alas, I return in prose to the story from my digression, which is unfortunately the natural ordinance when the only thing I have to consult with is my own thoughts. The backstory of this virus, as already alluded to, is perhaps very unimportant when compared to what happened next. It was not before long, perhaps a month at most, that the small city where the virus originated was totally consumed by it. Every two in three people had it at this point, one of which was slightly ill and becoming worse and another on the brink of death. Soon, every one in two people who had it were dying from it. I should also comment on, out of respect for the victims, what took place when one contracted this virus. However, for a lot of what I now discuss I am trusting in the reporting evidence from other sources, as I cannot honestly attest to whether exactly this was the case... Firstly, the symptoms were mild and easily brushed off. There was nothing present in its initial invasion into the body that would have distinguished it from a common cold; a dry cough, a runny nose, a slight fever and also headaches and nausea. A large contributing factor to its spread, in my opinion, was that when the first carriers contracted the virus they brushed it off as minor and continued to go to work and about their daily lives. Infected people who surrounded themselves by others also naturally assumed that it was nothing to be frightened of and through this understandable ignorance, it progressed throughout the inhabitants of the city.

Unfortunately, this was just the start of its advancement. Soon after, perhaps a few days, all of these symptoms got gradually worse, dry coughs became bloody coughs, headaches became those which bound one to bed, and the body struggled in almost all cases to fight it. Soon, the virus entered the lungs and in putting so much strain on them, other organs also struggled to cope. Once this had happened, the carrier was as good as dead. Their now pale skin began to flare up and then tighten, presenting itself as a blackened, tar-like texture that pulsated throughout a person's appearance and consumed their being. Their now thickened and purple veins, which struggled with the pressure and lack of oxygen, began to protrude through the surface of the skin. The bloody coughs gradually got worse, leading to thick showers of pasty and discoloured blood as it filled the lungs like shoddy paddling pools before being spat out of the mouth at the body's disdain. I never actually watched or studied a person as they went through all of these stages, but I had heard many accounts of which this sounded to be the case, or at least a somewhat truthful rendition of what did indeed happen. Whether there was some misleading information about the progression of the condition is uncertain. Howbeit, one thing that all can be assured of is that the victims of this virus did not die well.

Nonetheless, at this point, the rest of the world was still watching this happen on the televisions, grimacing with a look that was more likely disgust than sympathy, before proceeding to turn over the channel to watch something more appealing whilst eating their evening meal. However, things did not end here. After the first month, when the majority of the population was becoming zombie-looking, bedbound, and coughing up a third of their body's blood, the city began to panic. Despite the obvious advice that the government gave to stay at home and not travel, I suppose it is very difficult to tell a family of any composition that they cannot go anywhere when death is lurking around the corner. Their natural reaction, albeit a foolish and selfish one, was to flee as far away as they could as soon as they could and by any means necessary. The problem with this is that most people did so knowing full well they had contracted the virus already, and a lot probably did whilst carrying it unknowingly.

The entire city became consumed by terror; those who were fortunate enough to own a car had since driven as far as it would take them. The few economic elites who had boats and yachts had long since disappeared, perhaps on account of getting advice from people in powerful enough positions to have inside knowledge. However, by all accounts, the state (which was not particularly advanced) was built on manufacturing industry; on blue collar, working class labour, and not many were rich enough to own private transport. Therefore, train stations began to crowd so quickly that people often fell onto the railway tracks before seeing the distant lights of a train as it ploughed towards them. I do not doubt that some people just jumped in front of the trains on purpose. People pushed so hard to get into the stations that some even suffocated on the platforms or on the staircases. The police patrolled the areas trying to instil some sense of calm even though they did not appear to be talented mediators and anyhow, they never stood a chance. Soon, the trains began to come to a halt as the drivers and operators also became ill and the government tried to clamp down on people leaving (no doubt for diplomatic purposes). There was footage of people hoisting their children above their heads in tears and begging for someone to take them away with them. They closed the stations down eventually and had armed patrols blocking all the entrances just to make sure people didn't try and run down the tracks.

Before long the police had begun shooting people under dubious circumstances, claiming that they were advocating violent means for a peaceful end. Then, riots began in the streets and violence of the most barbaric kind ensued. Molotov cocktails were thrown through threw buildings although it is unlikely that there was any left in them. Rogues began burgling homes and stores. People in the street became subjected to muggings and assaults. The remaining police and military presence engaged in all manner of tyranny. Huge increases in all manner of violent and none violent crimes spiked across the city. Even those of righteous means had began hoarding resources and as things continued to spiral into pandemonium, it was evident that there was to be no ensuing refuge.

Once the trains became hopeless sources of escape, people turned their attention towards airports and fought in aeroplanes for seats that did not exist and space that was not incumbent, begging to be let into the hold or any way possible for them to board. Any of the private planes that were in the airports had either disappeared long since or were destroyed by those angry at the more fortunate. Public planes were overfilled and incoherently navigated amidst the bleeping dots of chaos that no doubt began to surface on radar systems. There were stories of good Samaritans, of pilots flying planes against orders just out of sympathy for the masses. However, the supply of fuel was not enough and no more was coming. There also was an insufficient amount of ground crew to maintain the plane, traffic controllers to oversee their flight and towards the end, pilots who were able of operating them. Soon the planes began to plummet from the clutches of the sky before even having left the country's border. They came cascading down into the mountaintops or oceans before becoming balls of hellfire. When people around the world began realising the seriousness of the virus and more importantly, the efforts that people went to get away from it, it became treated with the gravitas that it deserved from the outset.

About two months had passed at this point and those from the original city (or those who managed to leave) were scattered all over the globe. It did not take long before what happened in that city was happening everywhere else. Albeit, the scale was much, much greater but this did not prevent the same scenario from beginning to once again unfold with minimal amounts of deviation from the original. What was even more sinister about the virus, aside from its effects on the host, was how easily it was spread. I do not know exactly how it is transmitted aside from the obvious coughing or sneezing. However, it seemed as if there were some other way that it was managing to transmit around people - the rate at which it spread was simply unfathomable. Although humans had survived for thousands of years and in greatly adverse scenarios, I believe it is fair to say that this was one hell of a foe, and perhaps deserving of its title as the entity that finally won.

One may assume that although the virus had spread across countries, the greater power administered when combined may have been enough to help control it and fight back. This could not be any further away from the truth. The outbreak could not be contained despite desperate worldwide attempts to do so. Diplomats, scientists, and experts alike all came together in unison to try and figure something out but whatever as done was wholly insufficient. Even for all the committees and boards and organisations, no one seemingly knew enough to implement any effective strategies. It may be undue to phrase it in such a way as to attribute blame or by specifying particular failings, as it is unlikely that even a room full of the greatest genius to ever have breathed would have been able to do any better.

No measures, vaccines, or efforts were ever close enough to even remotely challenge the temperament and ferociousness of the virus. It spread like wildfire from city to city, country to country and then continent to continent. It killed indiscriminately, and despite the human race being the most evolved intellectual beings to date by all accounts, it tore through everything we have ever known and achieved in any regard. It only took around a year before economies collapsed and infrastructures fell or were torn down. Sometimes it was down to the effects of the virus and people no longer being able to work or surpassing this, starving or dying. Sometimes it was due to protests and people taking advantage of the situation for their own benefit. Sometimes it was opportunistic anarchists who saw it as their time. People did not leave their houses for days and months and although this seemed radical at the time it was indeed the most sensible thing that anyone could do. Hospitals became so full that they could not cope and eventually, the admitted patients were abandoned and left to die within them. Of course, with no functioning economy or methods of funding, no one working to pay tax nor no one spending to be taxed, soon the governments began to fall. They very quickly lost all of their power and influence once the money began to drain away and people were so fearful for their lives that they did not care about such establishments. Once the standing order had perished, everything else began to follow it. Buildings fell apart, cars were left to rust in the streets as there was no fuel to put in them, rivers began to flood their neighbouring towns, no one came to collect the bins, and there was no police or military on the streets. There was nothing to stop anyone from doing anything and based upon the reaction it seemed that some degenerates preferred it this way.

Soon many lifetimes, a long-standing heritage, a rich and varied cultural history, a society and an international ecosystem of human beings had been completely torn from existence. It is remarkable the rate at which something can be torn down, no matter how long it has stood for or how established it is. Destruction is always quicker and easier than creation. In my humble opinion, perhaps the scariest part of this experience was when the news stations stopped airing and as the shops were all closed, so too was access to a newspaper. The most surprising part about this is that there was no forewarning, no explanation as to why this happening. Of course, in hindsight it was obvious; things were beyond dire and those who knew it had already begun with their own contingency plans. They did not care about broadcasting the news because soon enough there would be no one around to hear it. I accept that I earlier criticised the media outlets and such bodies for their shortcomings and profiteering ambitions, but I must say that to suddenly be plunged into informational darkness was terrifying. One minute everyone was going mad about the world ending and the next there was nothing, not even a radio message or a meagre street sign. I did not have a clue what was happening in my country or anywhere else around the world. Foolish I was to still be thinking that people were focusing their efforts elsewhere because they weren't.

About three years had passed by this point and the only thing that remained afterwards was those who were trapped inside their houses. It was at one point the advice given to do so, but perhaps more importantly, it seemed like the most logical thing to do and those who managed to do it successfully were indeed able to survive the longest. I believe that I am an example of this fact. The more profound (and indeed inferential) query that I cannot resist but ask myself is was it worth surviving this long? I think back to the first people who caught the infection and died a nasty death; of course, they suffered and in all likelihood, they did not want to die. However, did anything subsequent happen that would have made them want to keep on living? The only thing that followed was destruction and death and now the worst of all mortal curses - eternal isolation. I lust to ask someone who had died in those first few weeks if they would swap places with me and although they may have said yes, I contest that they would have been a fool to do so.

There is not much else that need be said. I suspect one may be enticed by the question of where was I when I very first heard of the outbreak. Well, I was sat in my house, in the very room in which I now continue to sit. All of this happened fifteen years ago. The year now is

2038, and I only know this from looking at my tattered calendar which continues to hang lifelessly on my wall. I have not been particularly sure of anything in these past fifteen years as I continue to cross off the days as they pass, aside from one thing and one thing alone, which is that no amount of physical proximity, no matter how constricting, crushing or claustrophobic, could ever be as entrapping as the place inside my head.

CHAPTER II - HE WHO SAVES HIMSELF

I envisage my life to be similar to that of whoever else is left, assuming (without a basis to do so) that this is the case at all. There is very little to be done apart from what one can occupy themselves by doing within the wearisome confines of their own home and there is no other greater purpose or diversion. Sometimes I crave nothing other than the opportunity to correspond with another person in my position, to inquire about exactly what it is they do with themselves and how they cope and what they make of it all. In doing so, I imagine my own life and its incumbent difficulties would seem much more rational.

I never was one to compare myself or my own way of thinking to others but there is a subliminal need to do so and a certain logic behind it that is inexpedient to assess. It is hard to contextualise your own life in the sense of what is favourable and what isn't when you have no other life to compare it to. Even if one were to say that their life was indeed happy and permissible, that they are grateful to be alive and enjoy the safe space that is their home, at least this would give me something that I could consider or aspire to achieve. Alternatively, if someone were to say that their life is absolutely horrendous and they spend every day wishing they were dead, then I probably could relate to that too. It may not help my sanity to have my own position rectified but the reassurance that I was not alone nor alien in feeling such a way would be an emotional revolution. For all I know there could be a group of people bathing in some tropical, clearwater cove down the road having the time of their lives and I would be none the wiser. I believe my point is that in either hypothetical situation, there would be something to be taken from it and something to operate with regardless of its affordances or hindrances. Life is about attitude and the degradation or acclamation of it can affect all else that we do. What is more, the power that our inner attitude has over our emotions and nature is extreme and establishes itself as a worthy adversary once it has manifested negatively. Such a state, as having now materialized, is no doubt aided by the fact that I am perpetually alone and have no one around to prevent my decline into madness.

Whether there is anyone left is not something I can be certain about but is also something that I try not to dismiss the possibility of for the sake of my own sanity if nothing else. It seems inappropriate to tell the rest of my story without providing enough contextual information regarding the personal state of the world as it currently stands. Without it, I do not believe the rest of my story would be provided with the gravitas that it deserves. My greatest fear would be for someone to read this account only for them to pass it off as dramatic or unsubstantiated nonsense, for them to think that I was making it up or exaggerating. It would be unfair to blame another for doing this because I too probably would have thought my own story preposterous had I not been the one who was subject to it. Resultingly, I believe that only by being forthright can I prevent this from occurring. True it is that I have not seen or heard anything from a human in what I estimate to be three years according to my calendar, which I confess is becoming less reliable by the day. Nonetheless, one thing I can be sure of is that I have not seen anyone walk past any of my windows, nor have I heard any footsteps or the sounds of anybody's voice.

This was not always the case. Even when the new world had only existed a short while and although people were trapped inside, they would often be seen to wander the streets for undisclosed reasons. Of course, this number decreased over the years but to begin with, it was quite common and its decline was, logically speaking, most likely due to their being a smaller population over time. Nevertheless, there was all manner of people from all different walks of life, just stumbling confusedly through the apocalypse none the wiser. Fitfully, there would be people who would look so disorientated and bemused it was as if they had been transported there in some kind of machine without any disclosure. At other times, people would look entirely at home, as if they knew everything about the current state of affairs and that they could not care less about any of its afflictions. It was as if they were taking a recreational Sunday morning stroll with the dog down a country path.

Sometimes there would be men in suits or groups of people, sometimes all men or all women and sometimes a mix, with a vast variety of different complexions and auras strolling in unison. A lot of them dressed casually as one might have done in the old world and spoke nonchalantly about indistinct casual topics as if nothing was amiss. As time went by, the fewer people I would see or hear from my window. Oddly, the ones that did sporadically appear thereon became increasingly abnormal. Some of them muttered what sounded like demonic chants to themselves or convulsed and moved erratically as they went, as if they were being controlled by something else or they were in the final stages of consumption. It was these types of people that made me somewhat content that I still had the safety of my own home to rely on. However, not all presented themselves with an unorthodox spirit. On occasion, there would be families, sometimes even with small children, who would wander the streets wearing their masks pleading for help from anyone that could hear. I presumed that they had run out of food or simply could not go on living as they were any longer. I occasionally watched them through the thin cracks in my boarded-up windows, lumbering up and down the desolate streets, crying and praying and begging.

I speculate that a question could be (and indeed should be) posed to me as to why I did not seek to help the people of the desperate sort. I find this a difficult question to answer. Perhaps this is because I know full well that it is a question one would be justified in asking and one that I do not have a morally satisfactory justification for. I find myself quite fortunate that I am in a position where there is no one left to interrogate me about such activity and my motivations which led to their enactment, aside from my own thoughts which linger insidiously inside my head. As much as people have the capacity to scorn, there is nothing quite as inescapable as one's own conscience. However, I aim to provoke myself into being held accountable for my actions and the only way I can do this effectively is to force myself to address such affairs. My prolonged and persistent failings to do so is most likely the reason why I cannot sleep at night nor can I bear to be alone for much longer.

The truth (with regards to my being) is that I never was a brave man, rather I have always been a compliant person with a meek disposition; I did not need to be asked twice to do as I was told nor was I one to question any sense of authority. I never fought for myself and I never stood up for what I believed in. This is a certitude I have tried to escape as its acceptance is one which only adds to my terminal sadness and generalised notions of all personal failings. The occurrences whereby this aspect of my nature arose to the detriment of others are only a testament to this unavoidable fact and thus I felt it apt to address them forthrightly.

With the objective of being candid, I shall address my failings sincerely, with interjections of justification and reason only where I have deemed them necessary. I suppose the truth behind why I never sought to help anyone is not merely because I didn't want to break any rules but rather because I was too frightened - this is the naked fact of the matter and an admission that I do not make nonchalantly nor whilst upholding any sense of good dignity. Surely, it may sound like a solo, self-sufficient man living slightly beyond his means would be the ideal candidate to elicit sympathy and assist such families but I never did, and although this is part of the reason why I have survived for so long it is too why I am damned. However, what one ought to consider before being inclined to express indignation on the wanderers' behalf is this; how could I possibly trust them, or how could anyone in my position endeavour to do so? I did not know who these people were or what their intentions were destined to be. If one had willingly entered the dangers of the street, given all the context and general mandate as to why one should not do so, there could be no doubt that they were already seriously desperate. This is something I do not speculate over but rather a conclusion that I take as fact, as no amount of subjective discussion could arrive at any other reasonable assertion.

Even though I never had children, I am eternally grateful that I did not because the extent to which I would go to feed them would be endless. This is the sort of knowledge that derives from the ability to be empathetic which is a scarce resource in this wasteland. What is more, such awareness becomes more advantageous when coupled with the ability to then ignore the emotions which naturally ensue. This aided me in making informed decisions about how I would live to see another day. Ultimately, there are two choices when life becomes as dire as this. The first choice is to be the hero, to help whenever and whoever one can, to let emotion and sympathy overrule rationality and in doing so, a swift death is sure to follow, as honourable as it may be. The second choice is to do whatever one must to ensure their survival, no matter the requirements. Sometimes I wish I had chosen the first but the more I consider it, the more I conclude that this is actually something that is decided for us and that consequently, we must accept. An omission does not equate to an act and therefore, the guilt which accompanies each cannot be equal. I did not cause their suffering, nor was I in a position to cure it of its ailments, therefore I cannot be (from all manner of moral implications, so surely) held responsible for not leaving my comfort to come to their aid.

What is more, and perhaps most pertinently, how was I to know that these people were not looking to slash my throat and rob me the second that I opened the door and offered my benevolence? How could I even be assured that these wanderers were indeed families and not just bandits holding sacks of sand beneath their shirts, pretending to be mothers or fathers or innocent God-fearing men, only to attack anyone in whatever way they could given the opportunity? I admit that this is a cynical mindset and certainly a presumptuous one at that, this I make no mistake over, but it is the case for good reason.

For example, let me advocate from a different perspective by proposing the best case scenario - that these people were devout, honest, family-loving people and I did choose to offer them their deserved refuge. Then what? I did not have the space for another two people let alone another four. I could not feed them or clothe them, I barely was able to sustain my own existence and it was a miserable one at that. What would happen when the food supply eventually expired and I told them that what was left was for me? Imagine looking a mother and a father in the eyes and telling them that you are effectively going to let their child starve at your own behest - what is the most beneficial outcome? For them to say thank you or that they understand? This is now a cruel world, a lost world - one which can only be understood by experiencing it and all of its varied horrors. Platitudes are non-existent, as is politeness and the nature of all well-mannered social interactions that once governed human behaviour. There is only one thing left in this world now and that is the means of and reasons for survival. Any effort to help others, regardless of how benevolent they may have seemed, would not end well no matter the circumstances. I accept that I am not a noble man, I accept this with all due assurance, but one thing I am not is stupid.

These initial considerations do not even remotely cover the full extent of the issue regarding whether or not I should have helped, and all of them are ones that I have deliberated over wholeheartedly. I mean, what if one of the people that I took in had the virus and infected me? Then what? All of this time I had spent surviving and looking for a way out for myself, only to die by not following the most simplistic of all rules, one which was so supreme and salient even in the long-since perished world before this. What if things were satisfactory for a while, only for it to reach the inevitable point whereby I told them that they must leave now, having grown tired of carrying their burden on my resources, and on my conscience? What if they were simply detestable, what if their conversation was dull and trite? What if the children screamed all night long, what if the adults fought, or the food was not enough? I cannot imagine them walking out of the temporary comfort that I had just offered without a fight or at the very least, a stern complaint or attack on my character that would rattle in my mind until it or I ceased to exist. And at the very worst, what if, pursuant to their preordained eviction, the desperate father caved in my head with a pipe wrench, or the mother slit my wrist as I slept? Only an idiot would be this idealistic in thinking such things are feasible and ideals in this depraved world are for fools. Helping any one of these people, no matter how noble or righteous it may have seemed, would have only ever ended in one way and it would not have been desirable in any sense. I thought over every possible situation which may have arisen and its incumbent resolution and for all of them, an impasse is reached, no matter the case. Logic and rationality must defy all, it is the only way. The reality of the matter is that eventually, we would be back to fighting for our lives all over again and they would have done what I or any other person would do when they are struggling desperately to survive - whatever it took.

It would be grossly misleading to suggest that these were not crucial postulations, ones that I did not think about, that I did not care about, or that the burden of such sinister thoughts did not affect me or appeal to my deepest felt vehemence. I am not a sadist or a monster, I am a good man – an honest man, and I think about these people most often. I have nightmares about them, too. I have dreamt about them getting torn apart or gunned down just moments after walking past my door and me rejecting their help, screaming my name or cursing me to the devil as their guts are ripped out or as they hold their dying beloved in their arms. I have had feelings that whatever could have happened to them was entirely my own fault. I am many of varied terrible things but of them all I am foremost a survivor. For this, I am most guilty and my punishment is my prison.

Unfortunate as it is, being alone is the best and perhaps the only way to live in such conditions, even though at times I cannot be sure precisely why I want to and this is a complex and multifaceted matter in of itself. Sure, I have lived to see another day, which is something the people I refused help to probably never had the chance to do no matter how much they craved it. However, at what point of omnipresent suffering does this fail to be satisfactory? What is the profitable essence of living when all there is to do is survive, and nothing further on the back of this is promised? What is the objective when there is nothing to live for, nothing to do, nothing to see or feel or experience? These are questions I should have answers to as my survival makes it apparent I subscribe to whatever ideology their answer promotes. However, as sure as the day is long, I have nothing to offer by way of response.

I do not understand my motivations more than anyone who may read this. I suppose, all I can suggest is this; there is something very instinctual about the will to survive, which stands tall and strong even when everything else suggests that the alternative is the better option, even when death seems peaceful and inviting, and living appears nothing but the opposite. It often occurs to me that saving a life is the greatest thing I will have ever been able to achieve in this wasteland and in all likelihood, the thing that I will never have the chance to do again. It is, out of all my inadequacies during the course of my miserable life, the one thing I regret above all, and the one thing that will no doubt bind my soul to perdition in the afterlife. I can only hope that those I did not help and no doubt proceeded to perish, do not berate me for my inaction and that instead, they take solace in the fact they have made it to a better place long before me, should I ever reach it.

* * *

It was not just civilians who used to wander the streets, there used to be para-military and self-proclaimed security groups that would do so too in groups. They wore body armour and helmets and carried rifles, handguns, and knives. These groups began to form and were most populous during the immediate collapse of the old world. It was hard to decipher whether they were approved by or exercising their duty on behalf of the government when it existed and proceeding to carry it on after it ceased to. If they were, it seems ironic that the final act of an established government was one of monumental tyranny - using soldiers to force people to stay indoors. Of course, this may not have been the only reason why they were instructed to exist or failing this, felt the need to. I may interject at this point by stating from the outset that whilst the existence of these groups is a matter I can attest to, I am reduced to mere speculation regarding their methods and means.

I cannot see any reason why such groups would exist, should there not have been some form of commander or activist behind it that rallied the groups up on the basis of some kind of principle or cultish design. Maybe one might suggest it was to deter banditry or any other decadence, but at this point in time, there was very little of either, and having armed soldiers in place on residential streets to stop these things also seemed to be rather eccentric. Perhaps the most bizarre factor about these measures was that most people who were told to stay indoors did so without arguing or thinking. A lot of the time, especially in the old world where the powers that be were rife, it is very easy for people to be convinced to do as they are told and I was no exception. A false threat made in a formal manner or the mere insinuation that failing to do as told would result in some kind of social punishment or, superseding this, moral penance seemed to be enough for the masses without the use of physical intimidation.

What is more, and perhaps most pertinently, there was a plethora of fucked up people doing fucked up things in the old world, and such measures were never enacted, in fact, quite the opposite it so often seemed as the bureaucracy associated with such systems was prioritised much before all else. Utterly bizarre it seemed to me that it was only now there was little to no one left in the world that such extreme lengths had been reached. Of course, there is always the possibility that I am wrong and no such groups were instructed to do any such thing. Maybe they just did it off their own backs, because they thought it was the right thing to do or did not care if it wasn't. They could well have been virtuous, or they could well have been malicious, it was hard to tell, as was all else.

The majority of the time I would just watch them from a window as they patrolled up and down the street in unison. One thing I noticed, which struck me as particularly odd, was that they never seemed to say anything, never made any announcements through a megaphone and never held up any boards. Also, it seemed like they never spoke to each other. All they seemed to was march, up and down and back and forth. As they never interacted with anyone else that I could see, it was hard to deduce anything further about their reasonings, let alone the peculiar manner in which they conducted themselves. In truthfulness, I never had much interaction with these groups aside from one occasion, which is telling enough of their dubious nature and intentions.

There was only one instance that sticks clearly in my mind, with the rest just blurring into a series of vague recollections. It was in the middle of the night and I was awoken by the screams of a panicked man. Such callous screams are in any case distinguishable let alone when silence is the status quo. I lay there still in horror as the sound of his voice began some distance away before becoming closer and closer at a rapid rate. His screams were affected turbulently by his desperate and intermittent gasps for breath in between. I got up from my bed and proceeded to the window in a crouched stance. I could see next to nothing out of it, but I could just about make out the man run from the bottom of the street, of which I could only see a short distance down. He reached my house, paused, looked around frantically and proceeded toward the vicinity of my abode. I had no idea what made him select my house as there were plenty of others to choose from that he had already passed by this point. The man jogged lethargically and clumsily up my short path, hyperventilating and crying profusely. He banged loudly on my front door when he arrived at it, so much so that it jolted me to my core. I withdrew from my knelt position and sat curled up in the corner of my room, heart rushing, and pondering over what to do. The most prudent and perhaps deranged fact about this was that my main concern was why he chose my house amongst all others. By extension of logical thought, perchance there was some extrinsic sign, albeit not one obvious to me, that my house was still being lived in. If this was evident even to someone in a hurry, who else had it been visible to all of this time? It was a sinister proposition and not one I had the calmness to properly address. As my thoughts continued to race, the man did not cease his caterwauling. There could be no mistake made about it that he was being pursued by someone who did not wish to be.

'Help me, *please*, help me!' He yelped followed by some more hysterical crying. 'Open the door please, please... If there is anyone in there open the door. They are going to kill me, on God I swear it. Let me in, I will do anything that you ask of me! I will bow to your feet, I will hold you until you burst, anything you ask, anything you desire!' He finished. I remained poised by my bedroom window and could only pray that the door was strong enough to keep him out, which was not something I could be assured of.

I was frozen to the spot upon which I had retreated to, so struck by fear and shock that I could not have moved in that moment even if I wished to. Not much else happened or could be heard for a few minutes, aside from the man's increasingly faint whelps. Soon after, I resisted the impediment to my movement, which had gradually subsided, and looked through the crack in the window once more. I could see some bright torches being shone in the distance. It was clear that they were handheld based on the erratic and probing nature of their movement. They were shining the spotlight from the centre of the street where they originated and towards the houses on either side in almost clockwork fashion. It was evident they were looking for someone or something as the movements were so quick. It was also apparent they had not found whatever they were searching for in the dark of the night on account of their impatience and franticness. The lights continued to get closer and closer to my end of the street, as did the sounds of heavy footsteps and muttering that grew in intensity.

'Oh fuck, they are here. They are here! To hell with you if you are in there, do you hear me, strange man in the house? to hell with you, to hell with he who saves himself! I hope you can bare my death on your conscience and your rotten soul, this will not be forgotten, not by me or my maker... You will be *cursed* for this, of this should you have no doubt!' The man cried as he continued to thump harder and harder still on my door, his insulting comments seemingly a masquerade to disguise his terror. Soon after, his strength appeared to dwindle as the thumps transitioned into faint and ill-inspired knocks. 'Oh God, why, why.' He began to weep further still although it appeared his desperation had waned. His tone shifted from one which was being directed at another to one which was directed at oneself. He sounded like a man who knew he was about to die. Soon after, one of the lights that was being cast around pierced through the crack in my window. I scuttled down behind the frame with my back against the wall immediately. I could see the remnants of light as they shone onto the far wall of my bedroom before being turned away again. It was only a matter of seconds after this that the light ceased to coruscate anywhere at all.

'I have visual on the target, grab him.' A commanding voice eventually asserted in the distance. There was no intonation of pitch, tone or emotion in his cold expression. I found the courage to peek over the window sill once more and onto the street. I could see a group of militants gather at the bottom of the entrance to my house. They looked exactly like those that I had seen wandering before. The torches no longer moved from side to side but rather all beamed directly onto my front doorstep.

'NO!' The nomad screamed. I watched as one of the torches proceeded up my walkway, the spotlight which shone on the house got larger as its source approached. Eventually, this light disappeared. I heard a scuffle, followed by what sounded like the man being grabbed by the feet and pulled down my path back toward the street. I could hear what sounded like his nails and the palms of his hands scratch and slap against the levelled paving slabs as he was hauled across them on his way to the bottom. Once he had been dragged back to the street, all the militants and holders of the torches circled around him in a procedural manner and shined their lights down on his helpless face. None of them did so much as flinch during this entire time. It was the first opportunity I had to see vaguely what the man looked like - he was bald and scruffily dressed with a thick white beard. The nomad was wearing some kind of braided overcoat that was dirty and dejected with a scarf wrapped tightly around his neck. He was gaunt and pale. It was hard to tell anything else. He put his left hand up toward the closest light, turned his face away towards the ground apologetically, closed his eyes and in earnest, pleaded;

'Please, don't do it, I have a...'

'Terminate him,' the same commanding voice said over the top. A thunderously loud series of bangs rang out along with several stark muzzle flashes as four or five of the mercenaries shot him at once. The smoke from the rifles began to cloud soon after the bright interjections of light and I could hear the sound of shell casings clatter onto the street. The bullets ripped through his frail body and his head instantaneously exploded into a red mist, as did most of the upper part of his torso. The lower third of his body slumped inanimately onto the floor and fluttered violently whilst they continued to riddle it with bullets. I recoiled due to the noise, which was undoubtedly the loudest thing I had heard in years. When I looked back up, I just managed to catch a glimpse of his mangled body that was sprawled out in the dirt alongside and a growing pool of blood below it. Soon, the torches moved away from him and continued back down the street. The rising smoke could still be seen as it climbed higher and higher before dissipating.

Like the many other people who had wandered up the street before him, I often think back to the man, who he was, and why he was killed. He could well have been a bandit or an outlaw who was caught stealing or killing. This I doubt due to his somewhat humane aura and genuine desperation. Moreover, his frailty was suggestive of the fact he was genuinely disaffected, and the sincerity in his voice was one which is very difficult to fake. If he had done wrong, he did a convincing act of averring how guilty he was for his sins. This presumption is, however, based on very little else and is likely tainted by the sympathy that I had felt for him as I watched him die. Perhaps he had grown tired or desperate, like many people before him, and wandered into the streets in search of food or a better way of living.

There is also the chance that he had not done anything wrong at all, and was killed anyway. Perhaps he was murdered out of mere dislike for vagrants or some other form of untenable prejudice. I didn't and never had any way of knowing for sure, and the burden of being incapable of finding out anything grew insidiously ever since. However, if I had to place a bet on what caused the man's undoing, I would choose one of the last two possibilities. The only way I could have found out more is if I had opened the door as he had so desperately pleaded with me to do so, and how he cursed me acrimoniously for failing. The only solace I could take from this is that I never did make my presence known and he may therefore have assumed that no one heard or ignored his cries. The issue is that, when you know so little, the question is raised as to whether it is better to know things you rather wouldn't rather than not know anything at all... I did not sleep well that night.

In the morning, I built up the courage to look out of the same window to see if his body was still there but to my surprise, it was not. It was obvious that someone had been killed in that spot but in replacement of his corpse was a line of faded blood where it appeared that someone or something had dragged his body. The thick and large pool of blood where he had originally died also looked as if it had been tampered with; like a toddler had curiously dipped their hand in a pool of paint or a wild animal rolled around in it. Where it was or what took is also something that I will never know. What a world to live in where not only can you not die in peace but neither can you be laid to rest in it.

During the following years, the presence of these groups of mercenaries seemed to become more and more sparse. It is hard to know what is powerful enough to wipe a group of well-armed soldiers out of existence in dystopia, but at the same time, it was difficult to find food and water, let alone body armour and other military-grade hardware. Likewise, I supposed that there was only a limited amount of bullets in the world that can be fired and a limited amount of things to kill. In all likelihood, nothing probably wiped them out at all.

In my conjecture, I reckon that they just ceased to exist. Perhaps some of the members got too tired or just could no longer be bothered. Maybe they could not go on executing people in good faith, or in its absence, no longer deemed doing so rewarding enough. I cannot imagine what they resulted in following their leave. If these people did have families it seems unlikely they would not have begun conducting themselves in such a way in the first place. It was clear they had already been venturing outside for a long time so it also seems improbable that they would have then decided to reticently follow the rules and took abode in a shelter somewhere. Perhaps they did the honourable thing and wandered until the end of the earth, or, having accepted their wrongdoing and turpitude, found a hole big enough that they could crawl into and die.

The fact that someone was so easily murdered simply for stepping outside (or so I sought to presume in that case) promotes the seriousness of the situation in the new world and the depravity of the human condition which seems to surface its ugly head regardless of the environment. This is evidenced concretely by the way things now were; whereby in a ravished wasteland, violence and hostility are still rife despite the obviously enhanced levels of generalised suffering and the apparent need to help one another. Nothing good seemed to remain outside and as one of the final people left, I never even considered wandering outside to be an option for many of the reasons listed. The fact that in the ensuing years, such groups became less prevalent for whatever reason, seemed to be a positive thing when assessed holistically. Even though it enhanced my own wicked loneliness, there was an initial and assured restoration of peace when the militants no longer wandered, and even more so when the wanderers also ceased to because my guilt was able to ever so slightly subside. In the end, the gross irony of it was that the virus, which was cited as the initial reason for keeping us indoors and eventually our extinction, seemed to be the least dangerous thing out there.

* * *

Unlike the other people who foolishly sought to wander the streets, I spent the previous years trapped inside my own home. What is more, when I use the term 'trapped inside my home', I do so in the most absolute and literal sense - with the exception of my garden (which is by rights an extension of my home) I have never left, not even by a matter of inches nor for a single second. My existence has been, as one can no doubt envisage, conservative, frugal, and horrendously dull in ways beyond all manner of reasonable comprehension.

It seems only right that I begin by describing the layout of my confinement and as such, I shall. Firstly, I live in a small two-bedroom semi-detached house at the end of what was a residential area in a suburban neighbourhood. There are many other houses in the area, including those on my street, but most apart from my own have now all but collapsed on account of their decrepitude and lack of occupiers willing to uphold their need for maintenance.

My house is a few metres back from the street itself and hence why there are a few steps to get to my house from the pavement. Next to the path which leads up to my front door is a small square of grass, surrounded by a further perimeter of foliage. It has been so long since I last went out of my front door that this greenery is over five feet in height and it is impossible to see anything out of the front bottom floor windows. There is a small gap between the side of my house and what was that of my neighbours. Down this path were two separate entrances into our respective back gardens but this area is not visible from inside my house and I can no longer recall what it looked like. On the other side of my house is the entrance to another short street which has a cul-de-sac at the end and is separated from the extension of my garden by two fences, which sit directly next to one another. One is an old wooden structure and the other consists of mesh wiring. The first has existed for as long as the house has existed, whereas the mesh one was a security addition during the early stages of the old world's dissolution. I did not particularly deem it necessary at this early point for its erection to be imperative, but it was something that became widely promoted and all other houses on my street, including the house mine backs onto, had already made the installation long before me.

As for the garden that is to my house's rear, (which is not visible from any area of the street), I have a reasonably sized rectangular space. It amounts to, as an estimate, six or seven metres in length and around four metres wide. The entire perimeter of this garden is sealed by the fencing early mentioned. The right-hand side of the fencing, as viewed from the exit to the house's rear, (which runs parallel to the next street) has the addition of a barbed wire wrap. What is more, the mesh fencing itself had an electric current that used to run throughout. I highly doubt it still works and if it does, it probably doesn't have enough voltage to wound even a pigeon, but there never seemed to be a good enough reason to touch it and find out if this was the case. At the back of my garden, the fences signify its end and the beginning of my neighbours, which sits directly opposite, and also has a mesh and wooden setup similar to my own. The only thing between our two back fences is a small two-foot deep and two-foot wide ditch between where the two fences sit.

Although initially not too concerned with the extensive security phenomenon, I began to take it all the more seriously after the murder of the man at my front door, which is when the majority of the additions, including the barbed wire took place. All of the windows in my house are completely boarded by semi-thick wooden beams that I made from various wooden objects around my house, including hand-me-down tables and other such items. The purpose of such things is for protection, and also to ensure none of the animals or otherwise detestable groups roaming the streets may catch a glimpse of me as and when they were wandering around. Part of my daily duties involves ensuring that whatever I do inside my house gives no indication to the outside world that I am indeed still alive. I made the decision very early on that this was a fundamental element of my survival. A lot of this involves crawling around timidly in my home own, so I can move efficiently and quietly. It began to cramp my back at first but I became so used to it that it eventually became less noticeable. I accept that this is inhumane and by extension of this, somewhat embarrassing, but it was a compromise

I was, at the time, willing to take. However, it is something I now find myself doing less and less.

The entirety of my house is dark, extremely dark, true to the very definition of the word in all senses. At nightfall, I almost never used any artificial lighting, namely candles, partly for the aforementioned reason and partly because I do not have many left and therefore I deem their usage a luxury that can only rightfully be indulged in when I can justify it to myself. My only remnant of peace and happiness, of which there is little, is my back garden. I believe this is natural, as whilst it is still technically outside, it is within the realms of my property and unlike the front of my house, there are no consequences for traipsing into it and when wearing my mask, little to no danger either. In the garden, I have a greenhouse where I grow my food and other patches for various vegetables, potatoes and fruits where possible, at the far end of the area in the corner. I receive an ample amount of sunlight during certain hours of the day and also a fair amount of rain, for which I am grateful as such things are affected only by the fortuitousness of my house's position. Such conditions allow me to harvest just enough food to last until the following day. I do not eat well but I eat. It has been a very long time since I ate meat of course as there is no supply of it, and hunting wild animals such as birds or the occasional mammal that have occasionally found themselves in my garden was never something that I took to on the basis that I am in no rightful position. The same lack of supply goes for a large variety of fruits and vegetables which, despite my prolonged efforts, do not grow in the present climate as it is much too cold and the ground is unsuitable.

I have a series of water-collecting devices established around the garden which often provide enough water to maintain a mild level of hydration. When it rains, I have ensured that every last drop of it over my property is captured. I have small, well-like systems planted all around the garden. I also have a system that filters the rainwater which lands on the roof and falls down the guttering. However, water is not always plentiful. During one dry spell, I had not drunk for almost two days. I grew so dehydrated that a delirium came over me. It got to such a dire point that I laid down on the grass in my garden and awaited my certain death until the heavens opened and a shower poured down upon me. I wished for many minutes it would go away and that I could die peacefully, having accepted at that moment that it was my time. Unfortunately, it persisted and I had to return inside as I was no longer just suicidal but also extremely wet.

Most houses in my surrounding vicinity that were unoccupied due to death or vacation, or occupied poorly, were raided by bandits, of which there were many varied groups in the years ensuing the collapse of the old world. Just as with the militants and other wanderers, the prevalence of such groups also grew more sparse as the years went on. However, the main one and indeed the only one that still seemed to survive to this day, which I called the 'crazies' (based on their deranged disposition), is the most infamous amongst my thoughts. This is because they are the most populous and the most barbaric of all the others and in part, these characteristics are most likely what helped them survive for so long. Also, they are the group that outlived all of the others and I do not think this to be mere coincidence.

They collect in packs and wander the streets looking to take anything they need and terrorize anything they want. The crazies became known not so long after the old world's dissolution on account of their barbaric nature, although the specific occurrences that took place and led to such infamy I never heard much of even though I presume they were plentiful. There was word of them whilst the mercenaries were still roaming the streets and there was some contact from the outside world through leaflets that were posted through the doors by brave do-gooders. These flyers consisted of almost inappropriately stylized cartoon images of characters from horror films with bold writing above and below. On them were messages such as 'The *crazies*: do not engage. Stay indoors!' I doubt that many people took these seriously at first and even those who did like myself, still probably preferred receiving them at the time over bills or tax return letters from local councils and similar bodies. I believed that this was still propaganda from the government; that they began to fear that people had surpassed caring enough about the virus and therefore needed a newer and scarier reason to stay imprisoned.

I recall one incident where I heard some of the soldiers outside on patrol talking about the group through their radios as they walked past, which was unusual on account of their typical quietness. It may not have been the exact same group I reference (the crazies) as the names used were not the same but the description of their villainy was noticeably similar. However, it was not until the mercenaries had faded out of existence that they became more prevalent. In fact, the time between the mercenaries disappearing and the rising prominence of the crazies was remarkably short. It is hard to know whether the crazies wiped them out based on sheer power in battle or the extent to which they were willing to go so that they could survive. In the early days, I almost never caught a sighting of them. There was the odd occasion on an evening where it seemed as though something with a slightly hunched back crawled past but it was always difficult to tell. As is the case with the majority of situations I have denoted, it is difficult to witness such things and thus form opinions on the back of them. This is the case as all I have to go on are the things I have seen myself and the resulting ruminations which grow more unreliable by the day. At least this way rumours never took to being passed because there was no communication through which they were able to do so. Still, knowing what was true, such as how dangerous the crazies really were or what they had done, was never something I had any way of rectifying.

Based upon what I know, saw, and was able to deduce, I presume the following took place - At first, the crazies were just raiders and looters of the more typical sorts, looking to make the most of whatever was left by any means necessary. They wandered around, looted empty buildings, robbed or intimidated anyone in their path and were no doubt not strangers to the odd attack either. The people who first took part in these activity were likely to be recidivists and reprobates of the ill-minded sort in the old world anyhow. Therefore, it was particularly convenient for them to adapt to this common way of life in the new world, especially as now it was more accessible and there was less chance of being caught. I presume as such because the manner of their actions could only appeal to such types of people; those without family or friends and without any respect for law, order, and general notions of civilized human behaviour.

However, as the years went by, it seemed they became gradually more and more obscene and animalistic, so much so that it appeared that, for whatever reason, they began to lose their humanity both mentally and physically. Whilst they all once looked and sounded like humans, in the most recent sighting of them I had seen them walking like apes, with their backs hunched and their long arms dangling in front of them. What is more, it also sounded like they made odd grunting noises as they exerted themselves. One of the final leaflets I ever received through my door, which I still have, was a notification of them killing, ripping apart, and devouring an elderly man who had been caught wandering the streets in a bout of dementia. The only thing that they could find of him was body parts that were scattered around. As for how this drastic degradation of their being took place I cannot be sure, it may have been down to sheer desperation and the will to survive at the expense of all else. Perhaps something different was at play.

Surprisingly, in all the time I had spent trapped inside I had never had an altercation with them, and they never sought to bother me whilst I minded my own business and stayed within my own home. Of course, this could just be because they did not know I lived there but it was something that I could not be sure of nonetheless. It seemed that, if they had presumed no one was living in my home, they would have attempted to break in so they could see if anything was worth scavenging. However, they never did. It was almost as if, although highly unlikely based upon their hostile nature and delinquent doings, they too respected the rules when it came to remaining inside. This seems highly unlikely given their incapability, whether deliberate or negligent, to avoid all other laws and rules, even those of the most pure and honest kind. However, unlikely as it seemed and for whatever reason it was, true it still remained.

CHAPTER III - WITHOUT COURAGE

Now I feel satisfied that the context regarding my present situation has been addressed, I can begin to elaborate on the enfolding of my story itself. It's beginning, which I now begin to tell in prose, started at a rather unnoteworthy period of time. My life of daily survival and tedium was persistent but everything grew more and more difficult, both physically and mentally. I could not recall an exact time or date when this took place, rather it just seemed to manifest itself unnoticeably over a certain period. For some reason, although there was very little change in my living circumstances, (indeed they were the same as they had been for the past fifteen years), my health had nonetheless declined at a rapid rate. Before, I could get out of bed and do housework or whatever else to occupy and maintain myself with relative ease. I would read classical literature or play instruments in my spare time, of which I had plenty. When I needed to, I could also harvest crops and rainwater with a sense of normality and almost one of routine. Now, it had become incredibly arduous and as for why I could not be sure, despite being fully aware of its grip over me and the continuous decline of the condition that I was experiencing. This general difficulty of unknown origin intensified so much that I was even struggling to get out of bed in the mornings at all, not necessarily because of physical ailments such as injuries but rather because, in my mind, no motivation of any description presented itself to do so. Sometimes I would lie for what I presumed was days at a time until I was so desperate for a drink I would crawl onto the floor and down the stairs. I became so hungry that I would feel nauseous and dizzy just by turning over in bed. Sometimes I lay there for so long I could feel bed sores forming through my thin and malnourished skin. Although the condition's origin is something that did and continues to evade me, it seemed as though I had reached a point of depression and isolation and guilt so severe and melancholy that I could just no longer fight against it. I contend that there was nothing else that it could have been despite my prolonged deliberation over the matter.

Eventually, I concluded in earnest that I had fallen victim to a disease of the mind; to the sort of depraved and wicked sadness for which there are no causes and no cures. It was the sort of sadness that clings incessantly to one's very being, which starves and tortures its host until there is nothing salvageable left. I did not doubt, even for a second, that I was ill and mortally so. I needed *deus ex machina*, I needed something to come down from the sky and save me - to pull me from my bed or instil a fire within me once more that I so desperately craved on account of now being cold and dull to the very core. I waited for days on end but it was clear that nothing was forthcoming and that I had been left to rot by the powers that be. What is more, every day became more and more hopeless and an easier life (or at least one that was tolerable) seemed further out of reach. Even before, when people were wandering the streets or violent mercenaries were outside, it was of some comfort to know for sure that I was not the last of my kind. I believe that this debilitating loneliness also played its part and had now manifested in a sinister fashion far beyond the normal limits of emotional absorption. It appeared that I had succumbed to neurosis as now, there was nothing - complete and hollow spiritual silence that was victorious over all. The only thing remaining was the voice of this sadness, a quiet yet irreverent voice, that continued to whisper all kinds of horrid things to me during all points of my existence.

Of course, I had reached serious lows in the past but none of which were even slightly comparable in nature; this disease was something new entirely, something that I had not experienced before or at least not to such a horrifying degree. It is difficult to understand why the mind becomes plagued in the way it does and why even though it is capable of recognising such things occurring cognitively, it is unable to offer a resolution nor the will to retaliate. Nothing had happened to give rise to it let alone progress it to such an iniquitous point, and this I cannot emphasise enough because it is the most stark and petrifying feature of the illness. Of course, my life was completely futile as was all else in the world, but this I already knew and nothing regarding my due acceptance of this matter had changed. Therefore, I do not feel I could rightfully allocate any blame to this condition. The disease that plagued me was one that, for all intents and purposes, came from deep inside my very core and it would not vacate nor for it did I have any means of reprieve. I was at a loss with life and it too was at a loss with me. I was slowly dying a sad death and although I knew it, there was nothing I could do other than surrender; I was a victim of my own cruel ambition, I was a victim of my own inner anguish, I was a victim of the tortured embodiment of my soul.

* * *

It was on one of these mornings, that began with me struggling to arise from bed, that the beginning of an extraordinary series of events began. I stared at the ceiling for many hours and concluded (for the final time) that having been in this rut for so long, there was no way out of it. No one was coming to help, and no one cared whether I lived or died. I had survived for a very long time, quite an impressive length of time at that, but in realising that there truly was nothing to live for anymore there was no point in going on. It was hard to know whether this sadness was enhancing my own subconscious thoughts or injecting my mind with new ones of its own. The irony of the situation is that in the old world and in my old life I often felt this way to a lessening degree but little did I know that I knew nothing of having nothing. I thought, having made this decision most certainly, that I would be distraught or shocked or at least a little upset that it had reached this point but instead, I felt very little other than unwavering quietude. I had decided to accept in the absence of any alternative that life was suffering and pain is all.

As a result of these thoughts, I decided to begin a routine that I had done many times before. I entered my upstairs bathroom drearily. Here was the toilet that I used most frequently as I had managed to establish a plumbing system that carried the toilet's contents out into the garden through a self-made hole in the wall. There was a bath and a shower which no longer worked in the far right corner, followed by the toilet and next to it a sink where one first entered, that was covered in layers of limescale and dirt so thick I doubt I could have removed it with a pickaxe. There was also a window in this room which provided the most far-reaching and vivid view of all those in the house. It gave a panoramic view of sorts of my own garden, the one next to it and the street over on the other side.

Firstly, I opened the wooden door in the room to an old boiler cupboard. Inside this were a few odd bits but most importantly, there was a thick piece of jute rope and a small, two-foot high three-legged stool inside. I removed these and positioned the stool carefully below a ceiling tile in the room's centre. In this ceiling tile, where the connection to the light bulb used to be, I had installed a hook attachment which I drove deep into the brick above it with a hammer. Around this wide steel hook was just enough space for the rope to sit comfortably enough without too much strain being placed on the hook itself which would have ripped it from the ceiling.

Having tied the rope to the hook, it extended a few feet from the ceiling and the noose resided at a perfect height for me to place my head through without having to duck or lean awkwardly. The truth is that these accurate parameters did not exist as a matter of luck, rather they existed because I had spent much time establishing the system with accuracy. I had placed the hook in the ceiling and cut and tied the rope many years previously. I did this because, for some odd reason, this ideal and wholly convenient setup for committing suicide gave me a sense of peace for the last few years. Whenever things felt truly hopeless, and this happened on many occasions, I would get everything prepared and then proceed to stand on the stool and put my head through the noose. I would tie it tightly around my neck as if I were looking to commit the act, only to stand still in that position for however long felt necessary. In doing so, there was something created by the sensation of being so close to death that made living seem so much more necessary - it always made me feel as if I had something that I ought to go on living for. At least, I tell myself that this was the case. I also admit that the thought of killing myself was a terrifying one and without the bravery to commit to it, perhaps I stood on the stool hoping that it would break and do the job for me.

Just as I had done many times before, I carefully placed my left foot on the stool. It was an old and decrepit piece of furniture that creaked and wobbled under my weight. I then stepped onto it with my right foot and sustained my balance. The oval-shaped noose dangled nothing but an inch away from my face. I put my head into it and proceeded to tie it around my neck so that it was just tight enough for me to able to carry on breathing, albeit strained. I felt far more impassive on this occasion than I had done on previous ones, whereby at this point the panic and claustrophobia began to kick in, as did the reality of what was about to happen should I continue my course. Although this time was considerably easier it was not quite enough to prevent an impending sense of fear, panic and uncertainty which began to swarm my plagued mind. The thoughts for which I previously did this, of reassurance and opportunity of what there was left to do in this desolate world, were not forthcoming. As such, I felt quite confident that I was about to make the right decision.

I leant ever so slightly forward on the stool and as I did so, an indentation was created below my foot as the aging wood suffered beneath my weight. Once again, dread ensued but it was not overbearing. I focused my weight more centrally as the forward movement was uncomfortable. Using the balls of my heels, I began to shift my weight ever so slightly from left to right, which caused a swaying motion in the stool and I could feel the legs from either side begin to rise from each side of the floor with continued intensity. I leant at one point so far that the stool felt as though it was in equilibrium between falling over and swinging back onto all legs. I stood like this precariously for what felt like a very long second, my clenched palms sweating profusely and my raspy, inhibited breaths growing louder. Just as the stool was about to topple over was when I heard the faintest and most peculiar sound in the background.

I found it rather queer that given the intensity of my situation, I was still able to hear distant noises that were so quiet. The closer I listened, the more I could not be sure exactly where the sound was coming from or what it was. A part of me had hoped it was coming from my garden and was therefore within my control to some degree. I stood there, hanging precariously on the brink of eternal darkness, listening to this sound – it eventually became clearer, it was a sort of vague shrieking sound that eventually grew so loud that my own breath and the desperate creaking of the stool faded. After many seconds, I had become progressively more intrigued. I was desperately eager to continue with my actions, having been through so much and gotten so close to the end, but this sound just would not let me do it. It reminded me of the wails from the wandering families that I never sought to help years before, of the man that died at the hands of my cowardice. Moreover, it reminded me of that sinking sensation in my stomach that followed when I listened to someone plead desperately for help and did nothing. It reminded me of the tortured sleepless nights, the constant ringing of the screams, the guilt so toxic and insidious that it could make me gouge my own eyes out.

'If I was going to kill myself, I could do it at any point. Damn, I have enough time to kill myself a thousand times over. I could kill myself every hour of everyday all day, come back to life and then do it all over again.' My inner monologue rang out. 'Perhaps this is a chance to make amends for earlier wrongdoing, a final chance to do something good in a world so devoid of it, a chance to do the one most noble thing I should have but never did, a chance to save a life.'

It was with this revelation that I hesitantly removed the noose from around my neck. I stood there for a moment further, still on the stool, whilst a gross argument between the two decisions at hand fought within my mind with alarming intensity. I catechized myself for once again being so close but giving up. I stood still on the stool, the noose once again hanging in front of me, listening to this wailing sound as it grew louder and more desperate.

At this point, the stool beneath my feet collapsed entirely without any notice. One of the legs had given way so catastrophically that I was completely thrown off the stool. I ended up being launched from my position and propelled into the bathtub over in the room's corner. By extending my arms instinctually at the final moment I was just able to avoid banging my head ferociously on the steel rim. I lay in an ungainly, scrunched-up pose as I looked back at the stool in disarray. The seat of the stool and two of the legs were situated on the bathroom's far side.

Opposite this was the third leg, which had snapped awkwardly from the rest of it and was surrounded by a ranging size of splinters. The noose continued to dangle with a slight sway. I watched it move in this way until it eventually returned to a still position. I envisaged myself still dangling in the noose, which I certainly would have been had I stood there anytime longer, as it clung to my neck and I dangled helplessly, wrestling with the consequences of my actions, until my throat tightened and everything turned black. It was a strange feeling. However, before I had time to process it, I directed my attention back to this outré noise that continued in the distance. Although I knew very little about it, one thing that was for sure is that it was the only reason I continued to breathe.

After my stupefaction had subsided, I brought myself up into a knelt position and proceeded to peel back a small piece of the wooden board covering the majority of the window so I could peak into my garden. Initially, there was nothing noticeable that I could see but there was no doubt that the noise was coming from this direction and was not that far away. I stood up and rose onto the tips of my toes so that I could see as far as possible. It was here that I identified where the noise was coming from. In the garden directly opposite mine (the one which belonged to my opposing neighbour that I had not seen in much time) there was a small deer-like creature, presumably a doe, trapped within a piece of barbed wiring. As I strained myself to look through my window at an angle most unlike the one I had done before, I was able to see further into my neighbour's grounds on the right-hand side next to the street. I could see a small hole in the wooden enclosing that had formed following the rotting of the wood which ran alongside the barbed wire mesh fencing. I could only presume the doe had proceeded to cram itself through the hole to see what crops it could find in the garden with an initial amount of success, only to get one of its hind legs caught in a barb. I watched helplessly as the doe attempted to pull its leg in an attempt to free herself. In doing so, she sought only to exacerbate her injury and her increasingly weak cries continued.

I continued to watch the doe for a long time, trying to linger over what I should do and what had just happened. Eventually, the doe leant down onto its front on account of its prostration and discomfort.

Its trapped hind leg, still stuck in the barb, extended awkwardly from the rest of her body at an upwards angle. It continued to wail but only faintly and with a great deal less intent and conviction. It was an unusual consideration that two beings in a sparse world, albeit both very different, were both so proximate in time and space and were suffering greatly. However, both I and the doe were completely indifferent to the anguish of the other just moments before. The main difference was that I was now the only one capable of helping. The doe had taken its turn in inadvertently helping me just moments before and now it seemed it was mine. I decided not to think about it anymore and brought myself to my feet. I collected the sharp-edged stool leg from the floor and placed it in my pocket in case it came in use.

Before I could change my mind or convince myself otherwise (and efforts were made to do), I rushed downstairs, through my office and kitchen and approached the backdoor. A new sense of vigour had entered me and the dire fatigue I had been experiencing had dissipated. I put on my gas mask which hung on the rack next to the rear door, like I had done so many times before, opened it and proceeded into my back garden. The first step outside took me onto my patio, which was square but only small. A few steps further led to where the grass began. From this position, I could no longer see the doe beyond the fence but its soft wails were still noticeable. As I shut the back door behind me, the doe's shrieking became more discernible and panicked as it appeared to detect my presence.

I walked over to the bottom of my garden where my barbed wire fence sat right next to the neighbours opposite me. I only took a few steps but immediately realised that reaching the doe at all may propose some difficulty. The fences sat back to back from each other with the aforementioned foot or so gap in-between. It was within this gap that the doe seemed to have crawled through, having found a way in from the adjacent street, but unfortunately, it was further around the side of the neighbour's garden and inaccessible from my own. I turned off my electric fencing unit at the switch. The presence of the doe in my neighbour's garden suggested that there was no electric current running through their gate but it was still a concern.

I had not seen the old man who lived in the house opposite for a very long time. His name was Glenn and he was in his seventies. He walked with a walking stick, wore small rounded glasses and had whispers of white hair protruding from the sides of his head. He was only a short and frail person who lived alone. Nonetheless, he always dressed smartly and clearly took pride in his existence. I had actually never spoken to him before in person. The only interaction we had ever had was a slight raising of glasses to each other when we both were in the garden having a drink at the same time. The last time this happened was about a year after the collapse of the old world. He just seemed to disappear, no sounds, no movements. I knew something had happened when his previously well-catered garden became overgrown and unruly.

'Hello?' I questioned before waiting for a response. I had called out many times before this in years gone by and I am not sure why I felt the need to do it again. Nonetheless, I continued; 'It's me, Glenn, from down the way. I-er, I'm not sure if you're alright over there but erm... Listen, There's a doe trapped in your garden, not sure if you can hear it. It's kicking up a right fuss and I was thinking of giving it a hand. If not, it's just going to keep wailing until it dies and it won't be long before it stinks like hell. If you are over there and see me crawling around in your garden just know it's me. Don't shoot me please, I don't mean any harm, I'm just here to help... Well, the truth is, a bit of a funny story actually, I was just about to hang myself right about now. I had the rope tied and the stool set up and all. It was this doe you see, I could hear it yelping and screaming. I took the noose off for a better listen and the damn thing just bust on me. I don't why, I just... erm,' I retreated into my own thoughts, perfectly aware of the fact I was talking to myself. I gave it a moment or two but as expected, no reply was forthcoming. 'Well, that'll do it then,' I finished to myself.

The practicalities involved in my rescue mission were clearly going to be burdensome and of this, I was becoming increasingly aware. There was no way I could climb over such a high fence, not to mention the barbs spread all over. There were no footholds nor any way to feasibly climb it and even if I reached the top I still had to get back down on the other side. However, I noticed there was a piece of fencing that had begun to peel away from its rooting in the ground. It was only a small and unobtrusive break in the fence's continuity, but it seemed like a good place to start. I began to dig where this fencing was and peeled it back with difficulty. The ground was soft and loose due to it not having rained in a while and it did not take too much effort before a hole began to form. After a while, I had made enough space to scramble beneath it. I climbed in head first and pushed a way through. The fencing kept recoiling back on me as I pushed it and I could feel it scraping my lower back and legs as I pulled myself through. Once I had passed the gate, I had to awkwardly shimmy my body around as I could not fit in the gap lengthways. I managed to find my way up and onto my feet. I was covered in dirt and a short glance backwards at the gap I had just crawled through shocked me as to how I was ever able to get through it in the first place. I could feel drops of blood and sweat begin to seep through the back of my t-shirt but tried to take solace in the fact that I had not been electrocuted.

I began to shimmy sideways in the gap between the fences. It only took a few large steps before I reached the corner of them both. As soon as I began to turn around in the direction of Glenn’s house I knew there was an issue - this gap which ran parallel between the wired fencing and the wooden one which separated the garden from the road was much tighter than the one I had initially entered. Further, there was only a couple inches between my chest and the fence in front of me when my back was pressed against the opposing one. An immediate sense of claustrophobia descended over me and I began to hyperventilate. At the peak of an exhale, my chest firmly pressed against the fence before me. I tried to calm myself but this only sought to make things worse.

'What the fuck are you doing, why are you doing this? Look how easy things were before, you could have been dead by now. You've escaped a mass pandemic, murder, a hanging, and an electrocution and now you're going to die wedged in between a garden fence like a fucking idiot, all for an animal that doesn't care and is probably going to be dead soon anyway' My inner monologue rang out.

It was at some point during this hysteria that I turned my head to look further down the gap in which I was stuck. From here, I could just make out a glimpse of the doe's torso. The situation in which it became to be stuck now appeared clearer - the garden fence which separated the garden from the road had begun to crack and thus a small hole had formed. Not far distant from this, a hole in the inner wired fencing also began to appear. The doe must have seen this hole, had a look through it and decided to wander further, only to be overjoyed when realizing there was another hole which led directly into Glenn's garden. It had managed to squeeze itself through both holes and entered the garden, no doubt finding itself quite the feast hereupon. When exiting, it had surpassed the first hole with its body, only for its hind leg to get stuck at the final moment.

I tried to reinvigorate my motivation for this mission and took another step so I could shimmy further down. The doe let out another wail which was considerably louder than the ones before it and there could be no doubt that it could hear my presence. If it had the capacity to do so, no doubt it too would be wondering what the fuck I was doing. As I took another step, I became even more penned in as the gap continued to close. A multitude of bards from the worn wired fencing protruded into the gap and lacerated my face, chest and arms. The sharp stabbing pains were brief and bearable but consistent enough to worsen the predicament. I looked once more at the doe, it was still some way from my position and I ceased to hypothesize over whether I could make it any further without being suffocated or cut to ribbons. I turned my head to face the way which I had come, only to realize that I had come so far and into a position so tight that it seemed unlikely I would be able to retrace my footsteps. It was the first time I was grateful for my bout of ill health as should I have eaten substantially or even at my usual rate it is unlikely I would have been able to breathe at all. An idea came to me as to how I could make it out of this quandary, but it was most undesirable.

I came to realize during my struggle that if I applied force to the fencing it had enough slack to concave slightly under the pressure, allowing more space until the pressure then ceased. I came to wonder if I would be able to work my way upward by propping myself between the two fences so that I could reach the top of the wooden fence and climb over by shimmying upwards. Of course, this would mean that I would end up on the street, in the outside world, a place which I had not been in so many years it seemed as precarious as a foreign planet. I waited for a moment longer as the cold steel still continued to push into me and my ribs struggled to expand enough for a deep breath. It seemed clear that something must be done. For some reason, the irony hit me that I was so terrified of all the propaganda regarding the outside world that I was more willing to suffocate rather than just taking a chance at it being somewhat better than expected. Sure, I had seen some of the crazies wandering from time to time but is the extremely thin chance of encountering them in the time it takes to untangle a dear worse than a terrible death? My panic and annoyance rapidly manifested into anger and self-deprecation.

'Oh fuck it, you were almost dead a second ago anyway, what does it matter if you end up outside. Would it not be pleasant to experience it just once more? If death is inevitable, what do you have to lose? You can't die here, like this.' A peculiar thing began to happen; my inner monologue continued but instead of a voice I knew well, one which had the sternness of my father's began to take over. He had died over twenty years ago and it was not so often that I thought about him either. Nonetheless, his voice persisted and with it, as did his stoicism and pragmatism that I remembered him for.

'Move boy, goddamn it, what are you waiting for, you are going to die in this damn ditch, *move*!

I ceased to procrastinate any longer. I propped my palms against the wire fencing and pushed against it with all my might. I could feel the cold and sharp steel dig into my fingertips and hand before piercing the skin. The pain became excruciating and I bellowed a scream of both pain and determination. I lifted my backside up further against the obstacle behind me and propped my feet against the fence in front so that I could begin to move upwards by counterbalancing the force. I swiftly made upwards progress, so much so that I was at least two feet above the ground in no time at all. Then, I took another step only for my left foot to slip slightly and my face plummeted forwards as much as it could in the confined space. A barb dug into the bottom of my cheek and ripped through my skin before I withdrew it when it came close to my eye. I screamed in horror. 'What the hell are you yelping for boy, you are wasting your energy, what did I tell you before, stop talking and *move*!' My father's voice continued. I persisted to force my way up the fencing with a laceration or two being made at every other step.

Eventually, although it felt like I had been sliced to pieces, I had gotten so far up the seven feet fence that I could feel my backside being propped against the rim of the fencing's top. I took one more movement upwards which was enough to place my buttocks comfortably on the fence's rim. Just as I made contact with the top of the fixture, I pulled my hand hastily away from the sharp surface disdain and in doing so I ripped out a further piece of my inner palm. I removed such a thick clump of muscle that its thick and stringy texture clung to the barbed wiring as it pulled it away from my hand. I instinctually retracted my hand into my inner belly so that I could comfort it, only to have been so distracted from the pain that I forgot exactly how precarious my seated position was. By recoiling so harshly, I had knocked myself completely off balance, so much so that I remember keeling over and plummeting to the ground head first, still clutching my hand with the other and my knees bent at a right angle as I fell.

'Well, fuck', I had just enough time to think before I hit the ground and everything turned black.

* * *

I came back to consciousness a while later. When I was able to keep my eyes open and sustain an element of comprehensiveness a horrid and immediate sense of panic instilled within me. 'How long had I been here?' The first thing I noticed when I lifted my head from the ground was that it had become dusk. Only a tiny slither of sun was visible over the horizon and the sky had turned to a dark navy colour whereas it was broad daylight when I had been in the garden earlier. I had no idea how much time had passed but it was clear that it must have been several hours at least.

'What am I doing? Have I gone completely mad?' I screamed at myself aloud. 'What if a bandit had found me or worse, one of the crazies? How did they not – I was laid right here the entire time. They could have come along and devoured me on this very spot. It would have been the easiest meal they ever had, what the fuck was I thinking, what am I doing here?'

I lifted myself to my feet and even the sensation of tarmac on my hands felt bizarre. The insistent delirium coupled with the awareness of once again being outside was extremely disorientating. It felt like I was in a remarkably cogent lucid dream. As I lifted myself up, a pain shot through my right hand and it was only after inspection I recalled the damage that I had earlier done to it. It was covered in blood, so much so that it was difficult to ascertain exactly where the injury originated or how bad it was. I put my hands to my face and repositioned the gas mask which had become slanted and affixed improperly after the impact.

Then, I recalled my entire purpose for being here; the doe. 'I bet it's been lying here this entire time, well, of course it has! Surely it will have bled to death by now, it's been hours. All of this fumbling around and fucking myself up for nothing. I can't even climb a fence without almost dying. I am pathetic, I am useless. All of this for nothing...'

Regardless of my conclusion, I wandered sluggishly over to the hole in the fence where the doe was protruding out. It was only a few steps away from where it had gotten stuck and should it have been any closer, it may well have been able to lick my face. To my surprise, its head and neck were entirely laid out on the street. Still dazed and unbalanced, I approached it slowly. I proceeded to kneel down before I put my hand cautiously on its head. I stroked its soft fur gently. 'I'm sorry, I let you down, you saved me and I couldn't save you. Failing is all I seem able of doing and I doubt that you will be the last to suffer from it.'

After a couple of strokes, the eyes of the dear suddenly opened. It looked directly at me and began to convulse and shake in hysteria. It wailed and screamed louder than it ever had done before. I was so startled that I fell from my knelt position onto my back. I glared at it in shock and it returned my look. I rushed towards it and continued to pat its head and eventually, it seemed to calm. I fed my arm through the gap in which its head was stuck and I was just about able to reach its hindlimb which was snagged on the fence beyond it. I had to bend down in such an inconvenient position that my face was almost touching the top of the doe's head. I removed my arm for a second so that I could make space to take a look at the situation that its leg was in. Its hindlimb just above its hoof had been snagged nastily on one of the barbs, so much so that a long string of muscle and cartilage had been ripped out of it, no doubt as the doe continued to struggle after its initial entrapment. I removed my head once more, recomposed myself and stuck my hand back through the gap.

'I'm here to help, be quiet, stay still.' I said reassuringly, knowing that it was not about to be quiet or still. I grabbed its leg as firmly as I could and pulled it upwards. The muscle and cartilage that had been snagged almost stuck to the wiring as I pulled the rest of her leg upwards. The animal yelped once more and shook violently. It flailed and writhed as much as its position would afford. However, I had already done as much damage as possible at this point. Therefore, I reached back in again and yanked its leg upwards with all my might. In a second, its limb was freed with a final tug and the doe's head starkly shot upwards. I stepped backwards in shock as the doe had the realization that it was finally able to move once more. It shimmied aggressively from side to side in the hole until it was able to pull its entire body out onto the street. Thereon, it stood up liberatingly and began to limp around on the spot. Its leg was clearly injured but to my amazement, it seemed to move relatively unhindered.

After a short circular walk, it looked at me, albeit for a short moment, but it did so in a way so gratuitous and sincere that it was remarkable. It was a stare which insinuated the presence of sentience and cognitive depth far beyond that which I thought an animal of such sort capable of. A surge of achievement and relaxation came over me and I began to feel as though all my tribulations had become worthwhile. After affording me its look of gratitude, the doe proceeded to limp off towards the end of the street, which was some sixty feet or so away. The lack of light made it difficult to watch it very long and it soon became a shadowy outline in the distance. I saw its silhouette for a moment only as it paused at the junction. It manoeuvred to face the left turn and ran down it out until it disappeared from view. It was around this triumphant time, just before I began to rejoice at my success, that I began to hear voices.

'L-look, there, there, it's a deer, a real dear. Did you not, did you not see it run? I told you I could hear something, I told ya!' I could vaguely hear a disfigured voice in the distance utter. It spoke in such a disturbed and fragmentary manner it sounded as if it had been chewing glass. Not long after this voice spoke, I could just make out a new series of shadows gather at the junction where the doe had just fled. However, they arose promptly from the right-hand side, as if they were about chase after it but quickly aborted.

It was difficult to make out exactly what was casting such bizarre delineations. The dark profiles resembled that of humans, with arms and legs and heads, but it was as if they were distorted most unusually. The delineations leant over and their necks were being held awkwardly at a downward angle as if they were hunchback. Their shoulders looked as if they were trying to surround the neck and their backs looked oddly short. It seemed most of them stood on their legs but in a scrunched-up way, so much so that their arms draped in front of them and they used their hands to prop themselves up and move them forwards as if they were deformed four-legged beings. However, there was one figure at the back, indeed the last one to make an appearance, who stood much taller and more convincingly. This creature did not hold itself like the rest, it stood in a towering fashion with its shoulder back and head held high like a human being with appraisable posture. Even though its shadowy profile was all I could see, I was able to make out that this was a ginormous being, perhaps six-and-a-half feet tall with broad shoulders. I stood there inanimately, observing the group with confusion. I did not move at all, and it was only after a little while that things had become clearer; I believe that my concussion and a more generalized sense of confusion and disorientation had prevented me from reaching a conclusion that was otherwise easily attainable - this was not a group of apes nor of humans, it was the crazies.

Having seen the doe flee, the group must have begun to pursue, only to stop at the end of the street. The three or four at the front bounced around giddily on the spot whilst the taller one stood still at the back and surveyed its surroundings. It looked as if the disciples were awaiting permission to carry on their pursuit and even with all their imprudent discussions, they still ceased to act. I didn't want to believe it, but it seemed the only sensible conclusion that I could reach through my jumbled thoughts, and it was that the only reason that a group of crazies would stop pursuing a live animal is if they detected one larger. It would not have been very difficult to do so as one stood defeatedly before them - me.

'Meat, deer... deer meet', One of the warped voices said but in a slightly deeper tone to the one who first spoke. The voice of this crazie was even more obscure and mongrel-like.

'No, no, it is a doe, much smaller – less meat. Wait, it is injured, 'tis injured, smell it – I can smell it. It is wounded, I can smell the open wound.' another replied in a jumbled fashion. The pronunciation of certain words was so peculiar it was like they had formed their own dialect.

'The rest of the meat will be good meat, good meat!' The original voice said, finishing with a cackle of excitement.

'Let us get it, get it now! Why do we wait here, why? It is getting away from us.'

'Be quiet!' A new and commanding voice bellowed fiercely, shutting up all the others who cowered in its audible presence. Its ordinance echoed down the street and appeared to carry itself far beyond. Its voice was deep and powerful, but perhaps more noticeable was that it was clear and well-enunciated. The second this command was made the hunchback shadows ceased all animation and leant over still. 'Forget about the doe you small-minded fools. If you took a second to compose yourself you would have realized by now that there is something else out there. Something larger, something breathing heavily and bleeding. If only you could see, it is stood still and it is watching us.' The voice continued.

The rest of the crazies appeared to cast guideless glances at each other as if they were interested in what they were being told but did not have the initiative to follow their master's lead. I could just about make out the faint sound of aggressive sniffing before the tall figure became more fronting. It had turned almost ninety degrees and was now facing me. It raised its arm slowly without bending it and appeared to point directly at me. A momentary silence elapsed before the others also turned in my direction. 'There,' its voice said. It was a calculated comment, as were all its other mannerisms, and it spoke in such a way that a clear sense of satisfaction presented itself.

Having also seen me and realized what their master was looking at, the crazies' animations returned once more and they hopped enthusiastically up and down on the spot. This time, they jumped with much more spring and in a circle around one another, like schoolchildren do when playing skipping rope in a yard.

'Human! Human meat!' A crazie said.

'Human, we haven't had a human in long, so long... Have we? Have we? I forgot how it tastes, forgot me has!'

'It smells good, lively, fresh!'

'Wrong... It smells tired and scared,' the commanding voice reinstated itself and right it was; I was petrified, glued to the very spot in which I stood. I watched as they all turned to face me and began walking in my direction. The tall being led and the rest of the crazies followed closely behind it. They wandered slowly towards me for what seemed like an eternity. I began to come to terms with impending death.

'Just brilliant, well done, you fucking idiot. You narrowly avoided getting suffocated and now you're about to get ripped apart. You couldn't have just stayed on that stool and waited like a real man, could you? This could all be over now. Oh no, you just had to be the hero, didn't you? You just had to go and rescue a stupid little animal, and for what? This is why you never bothered before, this is why you stayed inside all this time. You never cared about that doe, you just wanted an excuse, like you always have done. This is all this was about, it's all it has ever been about. This is why you have never been outside before or saved anyone, it's because you're terrified. You're just a spineless coward. You aren't a man, you're just a weak and pathetic little child... Look at the size of that thing, look how many of them there are. What are you going to do against them? Get on your hands and knees and weep and pray. piss yourself maybe? They're going to pull you limb from limb, they're going to devour you and you know what, you fucking deserve it,' my inner monologue said. I almost thought for a moment that my father's voice would also reappear and offer practical advice but it didn't. A solitary tear began to roll down the bottom of my eyelid before resting in the glass of my mask's eye socket.

The crazies came closer still, but they were still far away

enough that the darkness engulfed them and I couldn't make out any distinguishable feature. As they were about thirty to forty feet away, they stopped in their tracks, seemingly in the way one does when shock overwhelms them.

'The mask, cyclops, look! The human's mask. All broken up it 'tis, they can't do that, they can't do that!' A crazie said sounding distressed. The tall being, who I presume was the one called the Cyclops, looked at the crazie to his right who had just spoken. However, this time, the Cyclops appeared to listen attentively, seemingly as if it were giving the statement credibility.

'I don't see anything, nothin' at all! it's human meat for sure! We haven't had human meat in a long time. Don't listen to him, don't listen to any of that gibber, none of it!'

'Yeah, it'll be fine, it'll be good, we can still eat. It has been so long.' Another voice contested. A sense of unease worked its way down my spine as they continued to assess the culinary quality of my body.

'Shut up, *fool*!' The other crazie protested before turning its attention back to the tall creature. 'Cyclops look, its mask is broken! You must see it, as do I! How can it be out here, its mask is broken! You know it cyclops, you know it! It can't be out here, it can't!'

As I watched on and listened to their conversation, I had become so dissociated on account of the paralyzing fear that it did not register they were talking about me. It felt like I was having an out-of-body experience and looking down on the events as if it were some other poor fool that this was happening to.

'What are they talking about my mask, the mongrel fucking freaks. What are they waiting for?' I thought.

'You are right', the cyclops bellowed, interrupting a tense period of silence and confusion. 'The human's mask is indeed broken. It is breathing the air, like us. I have not seen this before...' The formerly confident creature said with a tone of uncertainty.

Things began to set in and I was able to focus more clearly. They were evidently talking about my mask and whatever it is they thought they could see had stopped them from attacking me. I picked my wounded hand up lethargically from my side and felt around on my mask. I was hesitant from doing so as I just wanted them to end it and to end it quickly but the curiosity was overbearing. It did not take long to realise that they were right. The plastic filter extension at the front of the mask had been smashed, so much so that numerous pieces of plastic had fallen from it. There was a hole so large I could fit my entire index finger through the outer surface of my mask and touch my lip.

'How is that possible? It must have broken in the fall, it was fine when I picked it up earlier... But I have been out here for hours, I have been breathing air this whole time.' I looked down at my body to assess it although I can't be sure what I thought I was going to find. 'There's nothing, there is nothing wrong with me. How can this be? It doesn't make sense.'

I looked back up at them and they reciprocated. The dubiety from both parties was abundant. I grabbed the bottom of the mask and pulled it off my face before discarding it on the floor. It was a sensation ill of adequate comparators. For the first time in years, I could feel the cold breeze brush against my face and through my hair. I took a deep breath in and it was invigorating and fresh. It felt like my lungs had just inhaled liquid nitrogen. I wasn't sure if it was going to be the last breath I ever took but it didn't seem like I was to live for very long anyway. I reopened my eyes and stared back at the crazies, who had recoiled slightly after watching me remove my mask. I stood there expecting to collapse at any moment, but nothing happened. As such, it appeared that an impasse had been reached.

At this moment, the most bizarre occurrence took place; the sky at this point was almost black. The sun had since gone in and there was nothing else in the sky except for the stars, which were bleak on this occasion. A stark, white light began to emanate in the distance. It was only slight at first and seemed to originate out of view on the other side of the horizon. Very soon, it grew at an enormous rate and began to consume more and more of the sky, mercilessly drowning the darkness as it powered on. For a second I was able to catch a glimpse of the crazies as the light was so powerful it seemed as though it was about to light up the entire earth. Its origin eventually became clearer, it looked as though it was a gigantic shooting star or fireball of some bizarre kind. It shot up from over the horizon and came into view. It cascaded a light so pure and blinding that it felt as though it was going to consume the earth in an instant. I saw its trajectory from right to left before I was no longer able to look at it and was forced to shield my face. I created a small gap in my fingers so I could try and catch a further glimpse at this phenomenon. It was a small concentrated ball of light, jagged around the edges but otherwise hard to distinguish. It was moving at a speed that was so surely unprecedented by anything that this world, old or new, had ever seen. It had flown past the far side of the earth, begun to surpass the horizon, and shot up into the middle of the dark night sky before me in a matter of seconds. It swallowed everything and anything as it went. As I was just about able to remove my hand from my face to get a better look, the star appeared to run out of momentum and it started to cover less and less distance. It seemed to have finished its journey and just as it almost ceased to move any further, exploded. Its small, relatively concentrated source shattered into what seemed like a myriad of matter and covered a vast amount of the sky. It was so luminous, so fierce and powerful, I collapsed to the floor in shock, curled up into a ball and covered my face with both my hands. Incredibly, even with my eyes closed and sealed by my hands, all I could still see was a sear of whiteness that was so unbearable I let out an uncontrollable scream. I could hear the crazies in the background also shrieking in complete disarray.

As I lay there, I almost thought for a moment that I had already died and gone to the afterlife. I wholeheartedly believed that this fireball, that this shooting star or asteroid or whatever it was, had engulfed planet Earth and everything it contained within it with its divine light as if it were painting everything with purity. It was as if it were trying to eradicate the world and start it all over again.

I remained there clenched into a ball, waiting to see what would happen next. I envisaged opening my eyes and being in some luscious green field where it would be warm and comforting. Where the sky was blue and the sun kissed my skin and the views around were vivid and far-reaching. Where all animals roamed freely and there were no bad smells nor sights, where the only sound was that of water trickling gently and the breeze as it brushed past the leaves in the trees. A place where there was no danger or hostility, where there was no pain or suffering of any kind. I thought about getting up off the floor, only to come to the realization that I had travelled past my life as a mortal and had reached the next stop on my pilgrimage to eternal salvation. I thought about the utter relief, the emancipation of being freed from all the confines of this world and my existence.

When I opened my eyes once more, I was not in utopia as I had imagined. I was still lying on the same floor that I had been left on. I looked up to the sky to see the remnants of the exploding star. There were streaks of white light which were tumbling through the sky in a variety of directions, leaving streaks of colour behind them as they drifted downwards. The whole scene like an oil canvas painting, only one which was on a scale too great to imagine. I watched in awe for several minutes as the light continued to fall. The crazies must have fled earlier as they were now nowhere to be seen. It was just me alone, seemingly the last person on earth, watching the night sky explode. It was not before long that the light began to fade and the darkness returned.

CHAPTER IV - LIVE HIDDEN

In the winter of 2016, back in the old world, I used to live in a small town where I worked and lived alone. This was perhaps the most recent and sustained period of my life prior to the collapse of the world and although it was on a different side of the country from the one I am now in, my life was not so much dissimilar to how it now is. For some reason, whenever I think of how my life used to be it is always during this period that I reference, despite not that much-taking place and that I had lived in many different places and had done many different things during my life.

The town I stayed in was pretty quiet and uneventful and it was even less glamorous than the most profound critic would endeavour to visualise. However, it was only about five miles from the nearest city so there was always the option of travelling there even though I never exercised it. City life was always most peculiar to me. I never understood why people worked much longer hours and paid well over the odds to live in much worse conditions just because the place they were living in was so much busier and more attractive on the postcards. Sure, there were more bars, restaurants and shops, but there was also more crime and poverty and you had to pay for the privilege. This desire to live in a city was so unusual to me but nonetheless, I could not help but live relatively close to one just in case I fancied seeing what it was all about. I went one time and one time only on a work night out. It was so busy everywhere that we spent most of the time outside or inside queueing just to buy a drink which cost me about two hours of my life. Halfway through, I lost the people I was with and had to walk to find the nearest bus, during which time I was scared for my life at least three times. When I got off the bus, I was nowhere near my house and got home around four in the morning, piss-wet-through and close to bankrupt.

In the town where I resultingly spent most of my time, the buildings were devoid of anything that made them idiosyncratic and mainly consisted of blocks of flats, council buildings, and run-down old warehouses that stretched imperceptibly throughout the streets. They all lined up against each other and were painted with the same ugly grey colour which only contributed to the prosaic setting. All the streets looked the same as the next - faded neon lighting in shops and bars, traffic lights that barely worked but still somehow penetrated through the mist, graffiti and rubbish were spread everywhere. Even the pavement markings were faded and the concrete blocks on the footpaths protruded upwards where they had cracked making it a wheelchair user's worst nightmare. The constant dull, murky weather gave the place a very bleak and humdrum backdrop and with it being in such a useless position logistically and economically it appeared all state-given funding for it had been withdrawn long ago. They were probably hoping that the place would get bombed or that everyone would move out if it got bad enough. There were no places of interest, landmarks, or culturally significant areas, making it a place that no one would ever want to come to willing unless they were a drifter or a fugitive. Most people who lived there were born there and just never found the desire to leave. The ironic thing was that those people who fell into this category were blissfully unaware that this was the case and in their ignorance, never actually seemed to mind at all. In fact, the locals (who were not too hard to miss) were some of the happiest people I ever met. They acted genuinely as if their little microcosm was in fact the entirety of the world itself and that all of its happening were so grand that they felt compelled to talk of it in the sort of way one does when they think the world is about to end. I am not entirely sure how I ended up there myself - I had a job offer at the time that seemed somewhat lucrative but the actual nature of the area it was in ceased to be mentioned in any of the adverts. I never researched it prior, I just took it on the spot and for this, I cannot really blame anyone else. At the end of the day, I have always been on my own so I never really gave a shit about such things. I do not mean to sound overly negative, it was not the worse place in the world, it was just hard to know exactly how far away it was from being in the top one-hundred list.

I lived directly above a small corner shop because at the time when I moved, I did not have much money and it was the only place I could afford on account of being relatively impoverished. In hindsight, I wish that I had actually checked the housing market before agreeing to take a job there. It is a pretty depressing concept to struggle to afford an apartment in a place you do not even remotely like and have to pay for it by doing a job you hate. The only real positive part was that it was a close enough walk from my office and fortunately, I did not have to walk directly through the shop to get upstairs, but rather a gated and narrow side alleyway that was only separated by a thin bricked wall. There was broken glass on the floor and it was severely lacking in light, making it an ideal place to mug someone, or so I thought. The end of the alley was a dead end and the only things in it other than the entrance to my house were industrial bins at the end and a few worn fire escapes hanging precariously above. I could not envisage a situation dire enough whereby someone would risk wandering onto their frail structure – a fire certainly would not suffice.

It was not the alleyway per se or the apartment's location on the main street that bothered me all that much. These two things only came with the usual hindrances that I had become accustomed to having spent a lifetime living in such places. The main issue I had with my abode was the corner shop where my living room window sat directly above. I found it hard to imagine that a small independent business, which I had no predisposition to dislike, could cause me such a world of inconvenience, so much so it is hard to know where to start.

Firstly, all manner of noise, and not nearly that of the relaxing kind, radiated from the shop at all manner of hours, so much so it was hard to decipher exactly what was being sold let alone when its opening hours were. The trivial items most commonly sold in corner establishments seem, by their trifling nature, to not warrant arguments about their exchange, let alone violent outbursts, of which there were multiple a week. For clarity's sake, I do not mean the occasionally over-enthusiastic debate about a product's price or other alcohol-induced and incoherent protests, but rather what sounded like the trojan war was about to begin again. One night there would be laughter, the next shouting and the one after blood-curdling screams. The first two I can tolerate to some degree and occasionally even sleep through, the latter I found to be taking the piss. The issue was that if it was the shopkeeper who was responsible for these screams, which I assumed it was based simply on the fact that he was the common denominator. then it would have been ill-advised to go and take the issue up with him. After all, I was the polar opposite of a confrontational person. Actually, I had never been in a fight in my entire life and I never fancied myself in a situation whereby one arose. Therefore, I found it to be a bad idea to go and confront a person who was making the locals scream on a nightly basis.

One morning, I saw that the entire human-sized window panel had been smashed and on the shards was human blood. I do not mean the window panel had been put through but rather the entire thing had been smashed after what looked like a robust person had been thrown through it. Although, I did also note that the shopkeeper himself looked completely unharmed and was indeed back open for business the next day despite the large breeze. This seemed to be quite a coincidence. I was never sure whether it was a random street brawl that he had nothing to do with or if he was the commander of the chaos. A police officer turned up once asking if I had seen or heard anything after a similar incident; someone was seriously hurt in an altercation he had told me. Of course, I said that I hadn't, even though I had heard the start of a raucous only to pass it off as usual and go back to sleep. I think the police too were glad I said that because they made no secret of the fact that they didn't give a shit and would much prefer to pretend to worry about something else. I felt pretty delinquent about it afterwards however because the argument sounded like it was between a young (and naïve) teenager and the shopkeeper. It eventually turned into more of a muffling noise after I shut my window, only to be awoken later on by a fight that sounded violent enough to fall into the category of not my problem. I guess that I believed in the expression that only a fool can solve the world's problems and as for this one, I am sure there are plenty others out there more worthy of wanting to solve. This is what I told myself at least and they never did find out who was responsible for putting something or someone through the window. The shopkeeper just boarded it up for as long as he could get away with before the council came along and told him he had to replace the panel.

Nevertheless, I wandered in a few times to buy cigarettes and beer purely due to its convenient location but found it to be a somewhat uncomfortable experience. As one first entered from the street, there were four or five aisles. Most consisted of out-of-date chocolate or bread. I suppose this was never where the money came from but rather a way of keeping up appearances. On the far left-hand side of the shop was where the cooler was kept and in which was all the alcohol and soft drinks. I never really looked around much more as the place was gloomy and devoid of life. My issue with the establishment was not the patrons themselves but rather the shopkeeper, who caused the majority of issues, and he only sought to exacerbate the internal quarrel that I had with him and his manner of conducting business. Whatever his incentives were, he certainly wasn't going to be winning any prizes for conversationalist of the year. I always entered by greeting him with the occasional hello or how are you, both of which were never met with a response. In fact, one could go in, look around, walk up to the till and buy something and then walk out again and they would not hear a word from him. I could only presume that he was an introvert, and as anyone can imagine, two introverts in a room together never tend to be much fun for anyone, least of all the introverts themselves. I assumed this was the case for little to no reason - it was either that, he didn't speak much English or was a budding psychopath. Any of these options were feasible and I suppose the first was easier to work with and that is probably why I chose it.

I think the part I found most irritating about buying anything from his shop is that he always gave me a sinister under-stare, suggesting that my general disposition demanded an assurance that I did not intend on robbing the place or worse still, eating him, which was ironic because if either of us were going to eat someone I had seriously doubted that anyone would bet on me. As I previously mentioned, I had never been one for confrontation and I was assured that a man who belonged to the micro-underworld of violent, well-connected and ill-tempered corner shop owners would be able to deduce this from my general frailty and worn corporate attire. Anyhow, this was a rather uncustomary and cynical position to adopt by any shop-keeping standard, especially given the fact that he had nothing in his shop worth the hassle of stealing and even more so that I lived in the small crevice between his shop and the next shithole. By all means, he had no reason to suspect that I was capable or intended to cause him the slightest inconvenience in any way, shape or form. Logical thought dictates that any attempt at theft, which I presume was his primary concern as I had never been mistaken for a thug, would have ended in the world's most underwhelming chase from his doorstep to mine, or an extremely awkward side-eye every time I walked past the shop in future to go home. I am unsure which would have been worse, but both would likely have resulted in the eventual puncturing of a vital organ or me being the next candidate to test out the sturdiness of his new double-glazing. I still to this day contend that he was a man of the most peculiar kind, and maybe that is why I still remember him.

In my flat above the corner shop, one entered by going in through the side door situated in the alleyway and then proceeding up a narrow set of stairs. At the top of these stairs, my door was on the right-hand side. Adjacent to my door was a landing with a small rectangular window that looked into the dump behind it and from the ceiling hung a naked lightbulb from a piece of fray wire that flickered in the darkness. From here, there was another staircase that led to two higher floors where other people presumably lived. On the floor directly above me lived an old woman which I had never had an encounter with that was not unpleasant on account of mutual impatience and hatred of anyone and everyone. I was convinced that she became so bored and intolerant of literally everything that I was her first port of call to seek issues when she felt like it. I can only assume that the top floor was empty because I had never seen a light on in any of the rooms nor had I seen or heard anyone venturing up there. I suppose there was either a dead body up there that no one had to come to check on or there was no one desperate enough to live in such a sombre and wretched place.

I had three rooms in total, a kitchen when one first entered that was open plan and lead into the living room. The living room only had enough space for a two-person settee and a tv which sat uncomfortably close to it on the far wall. In between the sofa and the tv, however, was a large window that looked out on the street and could be opened from the top. Beyond the living room was my bedroom, which was so small I could almost touch both sides with outstretched arms. My old single bed was as tiny as it was flat and deflated. Next to the bed, taking up the remaining horizontal space, was a lamp on a bedside table that no longer worked. I also had an antiquated oak wardrobe opposite this that was leaning in decrepitude over to one side and was just large enough to make it difficult to walk past without tripping over. There was very little furniture in the living room or the bedroom aside from the odd piece of recycled or stolen junk that I had picked up in times gone by. The walls of the living area were painted with a dark opal green colour. It was one which I am sure when it was fresher and lighter seemed quite appealing and almost welcoming. Now it looked miserable and tattered. The wallpaper and utilities in the kitchen were all old and worn. The oven possessed dirt too deeply tethered to clean and the kettle and microwave were not so far away from joining it. The rest of the items and cooking paraphernalia were things that I had acquired over the years from various car boot sales and distant relatives who had passed away or given me out of sympathy for my dejected life. The kitchen floor consisted of old ceramic tiles that had begun to peel away from their position or crack under the pressure they had been exposed to over time. The only real saving grace in the kitchen was a small rectangular window over at the far wall, despite the fact that all I could see out of it was the next alleyway along where people hauled their bins somewhat humorously along the cobbled path. However, the sun did rise over a block of flats in the distance and gave my dying room a little bit of well-needed light.

My corporate job which funded this indulgent lifestyle was as repetitive and depressing as a job could hope to be. I did not do it because I wanted to or because I was passionate about it because I had dreamt of doing it growing up as a child, I did it because I had to. I think what made it so difficult was the fact that I, unlike most of my colleagues and indeed most people that I had met, struggled to accept the idea that this was my existence until I retired or died. I always felt it cruel that we taught children of the old world that they should aim for the stars by being astronauts or rockstars knowing full well that the vast majority of them would end up laying bricks or sitting behind a computer whilst wondering what the fuck happened. Like most, my work was not glamorous nor was it satisfying, but it was relatively easy and kept me somewhat occupied. I worked the standard nine-to-five. I left my house at eight in the morning and for the most part, got home at six in the evening. Most nights after work, which I almost always spent alone, I would return to my flat and cook or clean or do whatever was asked to be done. Perhaps one might think this would be relatively little when you lived alone but it never seemed to end up that way. However, on most of these nights when cooking seemed too trivial to do on one's own, I would do what any lonely existentialist with a tendency to feel sorry for themself did. This was of course to go to the local bar and drink lager and smoke cigarettes until they closed or kicked me out, often whichever came first.

During the first few months I did this all seemed fine. I used to go to work begrudgingly but still managed to get home and maintain my abode before cooking some food and relaxing. I often went to the pub and often drank at home but the sinister part was how this exponentially grew into an addiction with me completely unaware that this was actually taking place. It started with a glass of wine with tea which eventually turned into a bottle which then grew into a case of lager and a few shorts to match. What made it worse is that this is what I did when I was struggling for money, for which I nearly always was, and could not afford to go out. When I could go out, this is exactly what I did and I never actually managed to save any money or go on holiday or invest as everyone kept telling me to and proudly boasting about their own success. Before I knew it, I was drinking every night and the hungover mornings were so distasteful that the only thing that kept me going was the thought of drinking again that evening. The odd headache in the morning that was cured with some painkillers was the norm, to begin with. Towards the end, I was beginning to wake up on the kitchen floor laying in a dried patch of my own sick. Aside from my work colleagues, I never did conversate with anyone during the day and never actually had anyone to tell me that I was a loser apart from my own conscience which too gave up after a long enough period.

It was hard to pinpoint the exact cause of my depression as it manifested itself during this time, perhaps because there was not a single one that it could be wholly allocated. Moreover, it had always boggled my mind to think of how exactly a person with such a stable life could so easily fall into a bottomless pit that is almost impossible to escape. Granted, my life was not exciting nor was it fulfilling but it was not dreadful by any historical (or contemporary) comparison and I do not believe any part of me thought it was. In fact, I actually did make concerted efforts to appreciate the luxuries that I was afforded, namely a relatively warm bed, a plate full of food, and even the sunshine when it occasionally shone through my window. In the same breath, I did not wake up in a mood so foul I catechized my existence, nor did I feel this way in the evening before I went to sleep. Of course, I was lonely and this played its part in it but I do not think it was this factor alone that led to me reaching the place I ended up. I did not have a great time living my life during every passing day but neither did I spend every day hating everything. I think that it was due to the consistency that I wallowed in an impartial state of emptiness and detachment during my passage through time that perhaps led to this decline. Perhaps this is because I never did anything that actually stimulated my mind, perhaps it is down to something else. I think the only way I can describe such a sensation if one really forced me to in the most simplistic sense, is that I was just so completely and utterly fucking bored. Every day just felt like the same and I eventually decided that I was not feeling this way for the sake of it but rather because it was completely true. The same walk to work, the same job, the same people and the same evening routine. Nothing I ever did nor witnessed, save only for the odd random event that reminded me of the world's chaotic way, felt exciting in any sense and this monotonous plight seemed to continue forever with little exception. Even the weekends began to fall into this category, the Friday night was great as was the Saturday but it flew by in the blink of an eye and I had nothing to show for it after its conclusion which only made the contempt I possessed for my own life even greater. Everything just bored me and I think that in the end, this may have been all. However, when I say I was bored, I do not mean that I did not have anything to do physically or mentally to provide temporary stimulation. Rather, I mean bored in a much more deep-rooted sense, as if it were my very soul or the philosophical fibres of my being that were enervated of the same tedious affliction I was subjecting it to. It felt as though my own apathy, albeit only superficial to begin with and nothing more, had morphed into an infirmity so cancerous that it had affected my very being.

The extent of my progressively worsening alcoholism and mental state was best highlighted in the workplace. This is because I was so unimportant, so unnoticeable amongst the drone next to me here that my severe dehydration, shaky hands and pounding head passed by unnoticed for the most part. What is more, even those who did notice only did so in order to pass a poorly executed joke before moving on with the rest of their day. It was so blatantly obvious that no one gave a shit that it was hard to take it offensively. People are very keen, whether it be intentional or negligent, to ignore the presence of suffering even when they see it beginning to afflict someone else, unless and until a situation arises whereby how they react becomes an extrinsic reflection of themselves. There would often be times when I just stare at a spot and drift off into another realm for an hour at a time. On other occasions, I held back tears or clenched my fists in the hope that whatever this feeling was would go away and it very rarely did. Despite all of this, no one ever said anything, not even one single word that would indicate even the smallest, most unredeemable amount of empathy. In truth, I did not really care that much after I had turned to alcohol most nights; it was almost amusing to be drinking a coffee first thing in the morning, nodding an unenthusiastic hello to the blurry two-headed people that walked passed as the room span. When things really began to spiral, I used to put a shot of vodka or whiskey into my coffee when no one was looking and towards the end I didn't even bother to check. It was sometime around this point when I found it favourable that my anguish went disregarded as there is a peculiar freedom in feeling such a way. This is the case because when you care about almost nothing including your own life and health, everything else becomes trivial, so much so that you cease to care about such things that would otherwise bother you unnecessarily. I began to take perturbed pleasure in seeing how far I could push things before people actually felt obliged to say something and I always amazed myself at exactly how far this was. Sometimes, my colleagues were so blatantly devoid of emotion and thought it felt as though I was in a computer game and living in a simulation. The interactions with the people around me felt more like scripted dialogue options so truistic it was laughable rather than an exchange between real beings that were thinking and feeling. The main contradiction to this point is that if someone was playing as me to avoid the boredom in their only reality then their existence must have been truly unrelieved. The number of times I would hear one say 'another day another dollar', 'it's nearly the weekend', or 'how about this weather, aye?' despite there being nothing about the weather became so great I was convinced someone higher up was doing it to mock me. The unnerving thing about dissociation is that when begin to experience it you access another frequency of thought that is very hard to abandon once you have grown accustomed to it. You begin to feel like an outsider watching everything around you through a thick, soundproof glass window and any reminder that you are indeed involved in the present, such as someone talking to you, is extremely shocking.

The more I think about it, the more I begin to feel sure that at some point, someone must have noticed that I was still drunk or bordering insanity, but they either felt it amusing enough to let it carry on or did not care enough to pass a comment. It was hard to tell whether it was me personally that they did not care for or that it wasn't me personally and rather they just did not care about anything outside their remit at all. I think the most likely option is that they did care somewhat just not enough to go out of their way and be implicated or even slightly bothered by statements and questions and so forth. For this, I cannot really blame them. However, part of the debilitating decline into madness is watching everyone around you being exposed to exactly the same thing and not only not being in the same psyche but instead seeming relatively happy. I used to just watch everyone walking around me smiling and laughing, blissfully happy and unaware of the things I was thinking just a metre away. 'How the fuck are they pulling this off?' I asked myself several times a day. If it was a fifty-fifty split between my madness and their contentedness I think I could have lived with it but this was not the case - I was completely in my own category of mental decadence. I came to the conclusion that there are, fundamentally, only two types of people in this world; those who do and those who think. As for myself; I was an outcast, a lost cause, a wanderer amongst stationary men.

Even more paradoxical was that despite all of this I still not only kept my job but actually had limited to no interactions (including disciplinary ones) with any of my bosses. Oddly, keeping everyone else happy was pretty easily done. All that it seemed to take in order to appease my superiors was pretending to type on a keyboard or answer the phone even if it didn't ring. It did not seem to matter that little to no work of merit was actually being done, only to pretend it indeed was because no one checked. After a few months of employment, it became easy to forget exactly what it was I was doing that even made the company money or made it worth me still being employed. I presume the most likely answer is that no one could be bothered to sack me, or that I had not done anything quite incompetent or grossly negligent enough to warrant it. The solution to doing well at work seemed to be the same as being a functioning member of society as after all, both are all about appearances and pretending to be and do something you aren't. As long as the outward appearance is superficially satisfying to those who do not desire to look any further, all of the substance below it becomes irrelevant. The ones who care about the substance and go prodding around are so few and far between it is pointless giving them any mind.

I spent most of the time in the office, when I was there, scrolling through email threads so monotonous my eyes wanted to bleed, struggling to find why I was even tagged in them in the first place. Buzzwords like 'motivation' and 'hard work' often got thrown around but no one actually contextualised them or elaborated on what they meant by it, they just seemed to say it because they heard someone else say it and thought it sounded important or made them sound important. Other times, I would find other random people who had been tagged in the background, and send them a passive-aggressive email regarding a topic that I had just made up and ignore the response. On other occasions, I would sit in video meetings which seemed to be about nothing other than the previous video meeting and the next upcoming one, without any substantive matter that was to be covered in these meetings ever actually being discussed. Sometimes I would just ignore emails and phone calls for as long as I could, which could be days at a time, to see if anyone actually cared whether or not I replied, and they very rarely did. On other occasions, I would just get out of bed at ten in the morning and see if anyone even noticed that I wasn't there. For quite a while, they didn't. I mean, I am sure people noticed that I was not at my desk but they probably just assumed I had called in sick or was off and no one actually endeavoured to verify it. I would wake up at ten, check my phone to nothing, think 'fuck it' and go back to sleep. By the time I had stopped fretting about whether or not they were going to call me the day was already over. They probably hoped that I had died and they could have just sent some flowers somewhere as this would have been easier than spending the mornings wondering if I was going to shoot the place up or even worse, having to file a gross misconduct charge so they could sack me. I think it is fair to say that redundancy would have been out of the question. I eventually got a phone call from my manager who asked what I was playing at, only to later to found out that the one day he did this was when our site was being inspected by some high-ranking executive. My other daily tasks involved seeing how many coffees I could drink in a day without collapsing, how many times I could say good morning to the same person without them looking at me like a psychopath, or how long I could sit on a toilet seat before my arse effectively died. Workplace drama was the pinnacle of my existence. One time, a man who was allergic ate a birthday cake with nuts in it. He went into anaphylactic shock, had a seizure on the floor and almost died. One of my colleagues was fired for making a remark, on a video call which he thought he had muted himself on, which collated the dying man's appearance to a frog who had eaten dynamite. I never knew many people who had actually been fired, but I imagine a lot of those who have been are lacking a story as funny as that one. I suppose my point is, however, that it was possible to be a little less than eternally miserable (even if only momentarily) in the old world if one drained every drop of pleasure from the old dirty rag of time. In succeeding to do so on occasion, I believe it was the only thing that kept me going.

* * *

One instance, when my drinking had truly spiralled out of control, I resorted to all manner of disturbed ways to feel more alive. When you become so emotionally insensitive and dull to every sense of mental input, it seemed logical that the only way I could instil a sense of liveliness was to inflict physical pain. A person's thoughts have the power to be as cruel and callous as the day is long and sometimes, in places of such turpitude beyond that of what a reasonable man knows, he is forced to go to extremes to remind himself of what it means to be alive. On this occasion, I had booked a day off work so I could begin drinking as soon as I awoke. It only took a few hours at it to become inebriated. Having convinced myself of this big idea, I decided to follow through with it and I sat down at the small table in the kitchen area which was only big enough to accommodate for one, or two if you sat awkwardly close to one another. The sun was still high in the sky and I could hear as families with small children wandered past happily beneath the sun. I had to laugh at the dichotomy our two situations presented because I was drunk as all hell and about to do the devil's work. Before me on the table was a set of appliances that I had recovered and set out with precision. I did this earlier in the morning before I had gotten drunk so I had a few further hours to debate over whether or not it was a good idea. I was very grateful that a Jehovah's Witness or police officer had not turned up at the door and spotted it because I would have severely traumatised someone or been sectioned before I had time to react. There was some thin plastic tubing, old but unused bandages, an open and half drank bottle of bourbon, and finally, a meat cleaver. I had cleaned it vigorously and doused it with strong liquor prior to putting it on the table, of course.

I took a seat reluctantly, took another sip of my drink and placed my hand palm down on the old tabletop. I immediately felt a sense of fear come over me as my palms began to sweat. I tried to shake it off but no efforts were successful. I spread each of my fingers so there was a few-inch gap between each of them. As they sat there, ignorant of what was next to happen, I consulted myself over which I believed I needed the least. In hindsight, it was not a conclusion that should have been too difficult to reach but nonetheless, I gave it some thought. Most would probably say the pinky finger, but this one is already small enough, or so I thought. I was not convinced I would have had the accuracy to cut it off in one clean motion. I started thinking that the third finger would be a better choice since it looked very unlikely a ring would ever be upon it and it was pretty useless other than that.

'The damn thing can't even move anyhow unless the ones next to it are', I said to myself assertively before laughing aloud, fully aware of the objectively certified levels of lunacy I had submitted to. However, I was quickly drawn back into my internal debate where I considered how there was something ghastly about the thought of missing the middle finger, especially as it is the longest one and that one would be most recognisable when missing. The thumb was out of the question of course, as it is far too useful, not to mention how ridiculous and useless my hand would have been without it. 'Well, ring finger it is' I said to myself with a sense of resolution, as I curled my pinky finger into my palm so that it was not caught up in the forthcoming.

I heaved the cleaver far above my head, much more so than necessary to create a satisfactory amount of force. I was certainly being dramatic, which made me think that I was indeed doing it as a cry for help even though this was an idea I found distasteful and rejected. What is more, it would have been hard to make a cry for help as the only person who could possibly have heard it would have been the shopkeeper. The cleaver was so far past the back of my head and elevated so much that I probably could have put the table through and maybe even the floorboards had I wanted to. The position I was holding it in was one so uncomfortable that the cleaver began to feel heavy and my arm strained after a matter of seconds. I thought about lowering it but I was not an expert on forceful amputation and had no means to assess whether or not my bearings were accurate. However, if the position was not high enough, I wouldn't have cut it cleanly enough and that surely would be worse. I remained there for a moment, thinking about what I was going to do and why I wanted to do it. It was not lost on me how depraved my actions were but I just could not manage to talk myself out of it no matter how hard I tried.

'Who gives a shit? No one cares anyway, who is going to say anything? No one pays attention to you, no one is bothered. You could lob your entire head off and no one would care in a day or two apart from the cleaners. The people at work would probably joke about it in a group chat if you gave it long enough. You've come this far, don't bottle it...' My inner monologue continued on.

As I held it there, my arm began to grow dull and ache, the wooden handle in my hand becoming harder to grip with every passing second as the sweat of my palms soaked the material. What felt like a solitary bead of sweat dripped down my forehead, across my eyebrow down onto the floor. As I remained in this position, time seemed to move slowly, and I could not hear much noise outside. With a dramatic deep scream, I brought the cleaver down fiercely upon where I believed my ring finger to be. I closed my eyes much before the metal could make contact with the surface and it was possible that the blade could have landed anywhere in the table's vicinity. I felt the dull thud vibrate the tabletop, so much so that I am sure two of the legs furthest from me rose from the floor. The bottle and other random items were lifted from the top of the table and some even fell onto the floor. The blade sank deep into the surface, so much so the tip of it had penetrated the wood entirely and was sticking out beneath the table too. I was quite lucky that I had not thrown it down any harder or I may have also lost a leg. I could not be completely sure where the blade had landed in the ensuing seconds and everything felt like a traumatic blur. I tried to tug at the blade but it would not move. I pulled harder and harder still and yet nothing happened. I considered opening my eyes but the terror and confusion within would not allow it. Eventually, I pushed my chair back to stand up so I could get more leverage and as I did so, my entire body and hand came with it, despite the fact I was initially anticipating resistance. I almost stumbled back due to the force with which I stood. Only after this did I remember my reasoning for doing it in the first place and I proceeded to assess my hand. Sure enough, both my pinky finger and ring finger were gone. The pinky finger was missing only by the final two segments in a rather neat cut and I recalled that I forgot to withdraw it as earlier planned. From the ring finger protruded a thick piece of bone that stuck out, surrounded by jagged bits of muscle. On the nubs upon which they now were, thick blood began to spew down my hand and up my arm. I leant over to see the remnants of my finger still on the table, just behind where the blade had landed.

At this point, I felt a dull, aching sensation which began in my upper chest and sank down into my abdomen. It was sort of panicky dread that you get in the ensuing seconds after you almost crash your car or gravely injure yourself. It was such a powerful feeling that I collapsed back into the chair. I looked at my fingerless hand once more and then it began – a sharp, excruciating pain started to brush my missing finger's ends. At first, it felt as though someone was poking the ends, should they have been there, with hot needles. It then began to proceed down my fingers and into my hand. It was a horrid and intense burning sensation which felt as though boiling water was working its way through the veins. From here, it shot up my arm in an instant. It was a terrifying, all-consuming barrage of pain. I flinched so hard when it began that I collapsed from the chair and onto the floor, wrenching in agony. I thought that if I moved my arm it would help compensate for the pain but it did not. It was like burning candle wax was driving its way up through my body, coursing through every fibre that was capable of feeling pain and just when I could take no more, it started all over again. As I span on the floor, using my feet to do so, I remember screaming harder than I ever had done. I bellowed so hard I felt sure that my throat was going to implode and silence me for good. The sound of which did not feel like it was created in my vocal cords but rather from much deeper within. I screamed so fiercely that I threw up all over myself. I thought this might also stop the pain, but it didn't seem to. I cried and begged for it to stop until I could not see anything through the tears and my face was covered in snot. No matter how hard I pleaded with the powers that be, nothing worked. It went on for several more agonising minutes until I simply began to laugh aloud for reasons I still am unsure of. I laughed, cried, and then shouted some more before eventually passing out.

Soon after I awoke, covered in blood and vomit, laid on the floor beside the table. The bourbon had been knocked onto the floor and after a few seconds of a light trickling as the rest of my alcohol worked its way onto the floor, silence returned. I saw that my hand had gone pale and felt numb. A pool of blood had begun to grow where the nubs had been suspended as I lay there. The tip of the blade stuck out from beneath the wood which I could now see from the ground. On it, thick drops of blood slowly ran alongside the metal before reaching the end and dripping rhythmically onto the floor.

Only one person actually came to knock on my door in the ensuing minutes - it was the elderly woman who lived a floor above. I only knew this because I could hear her light and distant footsteps making their way down the stairs that went upwards. She was the sort of person who felt like she owned the place for no apparent reason other than a heightened ego and a tendency towards being intrusive that she seemed to have developed long ago. Clearly, her own life was so miserable and unfulfilling she had nothing else to do other than pry into other people's business but it was hard to berate her because she certainly got more than she bargained for on this occasion. She banged so hard that I awoke from my position on the floor that I had once again yielded to as I drifted in and out of consciousness. I wanted so badly to go back to sleep that I got up and hastily made my way to the door in a bid to get rid of her as quickly as possible. I nearly collapsed several times on my way and had to use all manner of props just to keep myself suspended. I accidentally caught a glimpse of myself in a body-sized mirror by the door before I opened it. I was pastier than a piece of fresh paper, I had sick covering my top from the cut around my neck down past my belt buckle, and a steady stream of blood continued to gush from where a finger used to be and a trickle of it had worked its way up my arm as I had been lying. I opened the door slowly until it was fully open, and she looked at me with a look of sheer disdain and horror. I did not say anything nor accommodate her presence, I just stared blankly in her direction. She cast her probing look slowly from my feet all the way up to my eye line and then back again several times. The absolute dread on her face suggested that she had just watched me do something as barbaric as eating a toddler before her.

'Just keep it down,' she croaked before turning and disappearing back down the corridor.

CHAPTER V - BETWEEN FRIENDS ALL IS COMMON

The following period of months was unnoteworthy and my life continued on at the same tedious rate. All the days were completed in a perfunctory manner and as such it hard to be able to distinguish one from the other due to their repetitiveness. Albeit, lots of things happened, it was just a case of every happening being so similar to the time it happened before that it was impossible to recall it actually happening. However, something unusually memorable took place on one monotonous night, a couple of weeks after the finger situation (which is something I look back upon in shame). I had been at work that day just as usual. A few people noticed that I was missing a finger, but only one or two actually asked about it, the rest just stared at me like I was a madman and should they have verbalised such a suggestion, it would have been hard to disagree. For those who did ask and showed concern somewhat akin to the genuine kind, I made a story about how it got torn off by a motorbike timing belt that I was working on at home. I have no idea if that is actually something that is capable of happening from an engineering perspective, it just sounded believable enough in my head. Ironically enough, I have never even rode a motorbike nor have I ever owned one and I am pretty sure the people who I told this lie to probably knew this as well.

My bosses also certainly noticed that I was missing a finger, but none of them said anything. What they did begin to comment on, however, was the late mornings that began to get noticed and I was promptly placed on my final written warning so I made as much effort as possible to get myself out of bed and make it in on time, although there many days where I debated just not bothering and getting sacked before proceeding to waste away in bed and being transferred to a world where I was better suited. If there ever was a situation in which I would be able to sustain my own life without money I would have quit in a heartbeat but as this is not the case, I continued to plod unwillingly through my tedious life. I thought about looking for something else or moving away so I could find something else, but I was so dejected and unmotivated to simply be alive that anything which required any effort never got any.

Nonetheless, I did remember the beginning of this day in particular because of how cold it was. It was much colder than usual at this time of year and it took a great deal of commitment to pull my duvet from me and wander amongst the freezing rooms of my apartment to get ready. Other than this, the day was typical in almost every sense, dull as all hell but only with the added excitement of almost slipping over half a dozen times on my way there and way back. I wore an old scarf that was ragged and the only pair of gloves I owned which had the finger ends cut off them. My old brown and braided suit coat was so old that you could see the fibres extending from it in disarray and it was only its pattern that made the old stains and marks less visible. I was quite surprised that no one had offered to give me any change on my journey there and back to work but I suppose they would have just been happy that I left them alone. Having eaten a microwave meal on my own, in the cold and in the dark due to an unpaid bill which led to my supply getting cut off, it seemed there was only one thing to do, which was to drink. However, the day had been one which was slightly worse than most so I felt like treating myself to the comfort of drinking around others. The best part about going out to drink was that there was always the opportunity for something interesting happening even though it hardly ever did. The difference was that when I drank at home it was certain that nothing of the sort would take place with the exception of losing another finger.

Just like the morning and afternoon, it was a frigid winter evening and it had been snowing throughout most of the day, which did not taper off as it became darker but only seemed to get more intense. I immediately knew what this meant and it only excited me more with the prospect of going to the pub. It meant that more people than usual, due to the impassibility of the roads, would go to the drifters' bar that I often began frequenting after being thrown out of or beginning to dislike the others. Most of the other bars which I had been to several times were nothing special and I could not have cared less that I was not allowed in the majority of them again. When things become boring the weaker sorts of people look for things to do or people to take it on. The ones who do this most of all, in my experience, are barmaids and bouncers, so much so that I began to wonder if it was a term of employment. I was never removed from any place for sinister reasons, just for falling asleep or being annoyed when getting cut off unnecessarily. I never abused anyone and I never fought anyone or broke anything, which seemed to me to be the only logical thing that you could get removed for. I presume the staff in there thought I was a loner or that they just did not care enough about the business' profitability to tolerate my strange disposition and the extension of my aura into the room. Regardless, it mattered not at all to me because they were shitholes and their absence from my evenings was a blessing. Fortunately, the drifters' bar in question was not quite like this. It was very laid back, so much so it seemed like no one actually cared about what happened in there like the rules of the universe had forgotten to apply themselves to the confines of its four walls. Although this may, in part, seem like a security concern, it undoubtedly also made for a better night of entertainment for those who did not care about such things. No one was judging you for how much or how little you drank, no one was trying to fight you or debate you about some ill-advised political opinion. No one cared that you were on your own nor that you were a loser because in most cases, so were they. For this, I actually found myself most grateful because there is no failing of character as depraved as a lack of self-acceptance. All manner of strange people could just wander through the doors and be welcomed without prejudice. It was a completely hopeless place that never pretended to be anything more. One thing about this bar which made it unique, perhaps to some degree on account of its hopelessness, was that it had character. The people who walked through its door were those who had been to many places and were en route somewhere else, which is exactly the opposite of how I had lived my own life and thus could not help but be endeared by them. I don't necessarily mean that they had achieved anything or were interesting individuals but rather had seen enough to make them slightly less dull than most. Fortunately, its occupants came from far enough away that sometimes they were somebody, as most people tried or thought themselves to be, but as is usually the case, they were nobody at all.

Its location also aided itself greatly. This was because it was visible from the main bypass which took one from the start of the town, all the way through it on the western quarter and out the other side. In fact, people could drive along this main road, look briefly out the window at the miserable town that was my or someone else's entire life, then forget all about it and keep driving past on the way to a better place. Something about this was both hilarious and depressing. The importance of this bar's location was that all manner of travellers could easily stop for a drink if they so desired, all they had to do was pull in from the aforementioned main road.

On this night, it took me much less time than usual to decide I was indeed going to the bar. Normally I would ponder over it and catechize myself for once again falling ill to the temptation before proceeding to go anyway. On this occasion, this was not the case. I left my apartment through the side alley and it was before I had even turned to close the door behind me that I felt an intense chill on my cheeks. I thought about locking the door behind me but there was nothing in my apartment worth locking in and if someone did decide to burgle me, at least I would have been able to negotiate a day off work. It was still snowing at this point, but not the sort of pretty snow you want to show your boding children as it falls graciously from the sky. Rather, it was the more rainy, sludgy type that is completely inconvenient and very little fun. As I walked past the corner shop, I pulled my hat down further and wrapped my scarf around my face before gesturing in the shop entrance's direction as if I was going to do something unpredictable, just for a little thrill. It was always worth keeping him guessing just to ensure that he thought I was enough of a miscreant that he would be enticed to leave me be. However, it did not seem to work, the shopkeeper didn't even flinch but rather stared at me in disapproval like one does to a mischievous child when pretending to throw eggs at one's car. I suppose there were much more dangerous people than me on his mind, or rather something much more dangerous indeed. I didn't care any which way so I shrugged my shoulders and carried on.

The bar was a few streets away, so the cold was not much of an issue, or so I tried to convince myself. An occasional yet powerful gust of wind blew fiercely through the street and lasted just long enough to warrant wrapping my coat tighter around my person. Litter ruffled as it blew across the streets and a couple of loud voices could be heard emanating in the distance. Fortunately, I only had to walk in a straight line past a few poorly lit intersections before getting to the far side of the carriageway opposite where the bar resided. There were not many cars out on account of the weather and I walked across most of the crossings whether the lights were green or not. The town looked very similar to how it always was, murky and dull with an added mist. There were a few dim lamps on in different venues and the poorly lit streetlights tried desperately to make themselves known through the precipitation to little avail. It was already dark at this point and there were not many people out on the street aside from the occasional elderly person lugging a shopping cart who must surely have been lost. There was a group of hooded youths sitting on bikes not too far away from the shop. They were the sort of indiscriminate group which made it tricky to determine between harmless children or thugs about to mug you at knifepoint. They wore long, puffy clothes and balaclavas that covered their faces which made it difficult to ascertain whether they were thirteen or thirty. Although I never actually got mugged, I was almost disappointed that this was the case, perhaps because I was such an awful candidate for someone to choose and the irony appealed to me in a deprecative sense. The reason for this is, as I presume when you mug someone, you want the person you mug to have something that is worth mugging and be a character who possesses enough care about their lives to let you take it. As chance would have it, I had neither of these things.

I eventually arrived at the narrow footpath one could take to get over to the other side of the carriageway, where the bar was situated. There were two dual carriageways next to each other which went in opposite directions. The tricky part is that there was a grass island in the middle of the two meaning that one had to cross a carriageway twice. I must confess, crossing twice over two lanes of high-speed cars at night was pretty daunting. It seemed unusual to me that a council who, I assume at one point cared about its citizens, would put a watering hole only a stone's throw away from a dual carriageway that was both poorly lit and signposted. Perhaps they presumed that no one who lived in the town would go there out of their way to walk there and would instead opt for one of the more trendy places in the town's inner vicinity. Nonetheless, the fun part was always when trying to cross it on the way back.

When I arrived at the bar I opened the large, old-fashioned revolving door, entered and took off my hat and scarf. The bar was well-sized but had an unusual square shape, making it particularly easy to view every area of the pub and giving very little privacy for its patrons. The long bar was over at the far right-hand side and stretched across the majority of the wall. The barkeeper stood behind the bar for obvious reasons. Behind it were large open-plan windows, albeit dirty and stained, that you could see the bypass out of and the blurred lights of cars as they drove on in either direction. On the left of the bar were a series of booths that outstretched from the wall, and in the middle was a series of small circular wooden tables and chairs that had long surpassed their heyday. When I got there, there was only one young couple with a small child at one of the middle tables who I assumed were stopping off whilst en route to a destination much more desirable. Over in one of the booths in the far corner was a man sitting alone wearing a flat cap who appeared to be doing a good job of minding his own business. There was no one else in the place.

I approached the barkeeper and ordered myself a drink. He was a youngish man I had not seen before and it was only when looking at him that I began to wonder how he ended up here. He was dressed smartly in a white shirt and a black bow tie although he looked tired and despondent. The man sported unusual goatee facial hair that made him look both old and peculiar. Nonetheless, his hands were smooth and clean. He did not say anything to me at the time that I was sitting there but rather tended to wipe the bar and put bottles away, both of which were tasks which looked as though they had already been done to an acceptable degree.

* * *

I had probably sat there for around an hour or so and had about four drinks before a tall and somewhat approachable-looking man wearing a suit that fitted well but lacked care and attention entered the bar somewhat noisily by swinging open the front door. The door looked heavy but wasn't, which always made it easy to identify if someone opening it had done so before. He removed his coat in a rush and promptly came and sat next to me. It was odd that he chose to do this because there were more than enough seats he could have occupied that were far away from anyone else. It was an unwritten rule in such places that you never assume someone wants to speak to you because most of the time you would be right. It seemed that this was a memo that no one had given him. His tie was still around his neck and below his shirt collar but it hung loosely and the top two buttons of his shirt had been undone. He had dark hair that was thinning at the sides but this was not overly noticeable. He had a thick, messy beard that looked like it had once been groomed. His eyes were dark and bloodshot, his skin was dry and wrinkled beyond his years. He sat on the stool next to me with a sigh of difficulty and the barkeeper came toward him;

'Scotch, neat' the man said.

'Yes sir' the barkeeper replied before pouring the drink and putting the glass down before him. The man picked it up and chugged it in one rushed yet uncompromising swig. He took the strong liquor with such composure that it was clear he was no stranger to it. After finishing it, he pointed at the glass and the barkeeper filled it up again. As we sat next to each other facing forwards for many minutes a sense of tension seemed to arise on account of their being two people in close proximity, seemingly both with lots to say, who actually were saying nothing. He eventually turned to face me.

'Mind if I have a cigarette?' He addressed me tentatively, noticing I had a pack rather obviously on display in front of me. Usually, I would have told anyone in this hellish place to fuck off should I have felt the desire to. However, there was something endearing about the way he presented himself - not the usual lonely alcoholic loser looking for a punch-up, but certainly not too far a stretch from one. I could not help but want to know more about him and it seemed that as far as the night's entertainment was concerned, he was the headline act.

'Sure', I said whilst sliding the packet with the lighter on top over to him. The lighter slid off the packet's surface and he made a somewhat panicked attempt to redeem it as if it was actively trying to escape him. His hands were shaky and he sat in a somewhat anxious position. One leg rested on the stool's lower frame, the other extended below and his heel was propped up off the floor by his toes. He shook his leg rather rapidly as if being still made him uncomfortable. He nodded with a sense of impatient gratitude, took one and lit it. His first drag was particularly heavy and a scornful look came across his face as if he had forgotten what a cigarette tasted like. He blew it out and coughed furtively. I could tell that something insidious was on his mind – a heavy, overbearing thought that he was trying to kill via the only methods known to the simplicity of men. I kept thinking of something to say but I was pretty sure that it would not be long before he would start the conversation. Soon, he looked at me once more and addressed me solemnly.

'What happened to your finger?' He asked, clearly noticing I was missing one and a bit as I lifted my hand to take a drag of my cigarette. I detected that the addressing of this visual cue was indicative of the conversation's ensuing desultory although I hoped that I was wrong.

'Oh, funny story actually. I was toying around with my motorbike the other day in the garage - just attending to some minor maintenance work. The engine was running and I got it trapped in the timing belt, tore the damn thing clean off.' The strange man looked at me and for the first time in all the times I told the story I could sense immediately he knew I was lying, perhaps because I was so bored of telling it that I no longer had the enthusiasm to do so convincingly, perhaps because he wasn't an idiot, or perhaps because he was accustomed to being lied to. Nonetheless, he engaged with my charade in a somewhat charming manner, as if he knew I was hiding something but also knew enough to not prod too much further.

'Damn... That is one hell of a thing. Did it hurt?'

'Not really, to be honest, didn't even feel it at first. By the time I had even realised what had happened, I was already pretty drunk. I don't really remember it being painful, it just looked pretty weird.' He laughed at my response, seemingly humoured by my facetious attitude.

'You were trying to fix your bike drunk?' He asked further. I looked at him but didn't respond. The man flicked his cigarette ash into an ashtray rather dramatically as if he were prompting a conversational switch.

'Why do you ride those death machines anyway?'

'What do you mean, why?'

'I mean they are dangerous, aren't they? What is wrong with just using a car? When do you feel like getting on it? When it's warm out?'

'Oh, not very often - just when I feel like dying.' I finished, quite sure my dark and self-deprecating comments would scare him off. However, he laughed before he focused his vision on a distant point and drifted off into his thoughts.

'Long day?' I enquired further, unable to withhold any longer. The man seemed to be in an even worse state than I was and I could not pass up the chance to make myself feel better at his expense, especially when I had already no doubt done the same for him. The man looked at me with intensity, as if he had been waiting for someone to ask but was also shocked that someone actually had.

'Don't you ever wonder, what is going on with all this?' His voice echoed around the gloomy pub and sounded a lot louder than he apparently intended, so much so the barkeeper looked up from his newspaper as if he had just done something untoward.

'With motorbikes?'

'No.'

'With drinking?'

'No, with all of it,' he said, signalling vaguely to the room around him as if that were a satisfactory reference for the existential angst he was hinting at.

'Would I be here if I could answer that?' I replied, attempting to make a joke but his facial expression did not change.

'I am never normally one to get into a rut like this, if I may refer to it as so, but today one of the most enervative sorts has come over me and I can't shift it no matter how hard I try. I just can't stop thinking, what is the point in it all? And by all, I do literally mean all - all of life itself. I know it is such a cliche - this I do not avoid and yet true it still is. Oh Lord above, is this what I have been reduced to?' The man paused. 'Some strange thoughts have really took a hold of me today, I feel useless, like I do not matter to no one, no how, despite no one suggesting this to be true. But what is stranger, these thoughts seem to have too infected my anatomy, my physical being; it feels like even the walls would crumble if I touched 'em, like nothing is real, like everything is spinning round and round in circles and I couldn't pin anything down if I wanted to, like everything is closing in on me. My hands are shaking no end and I can't stop 'em, my heart is beating out my damn chest. I feel dizzy, my head is pounding. I just don't know what the hell to do. I come here to take my mind off it, but I look over at you, and I just got this strange old feeling for a second there, that I am not the only one - looking at you, I do not feel so mad after all. I hate to be so forward but I have to ask you, friend, do you have any idea, even if it be one just slight or vague, of the things about which I speak?'

'So what if I did?' I hist cynically as his probing nature began to bother me. He looked at me vacantly before standing up with his glass and moving closer to the stool next to me.

'Please friend, I am not here looking to jest or offend; I am sincerely searching for some assistance tonight, I - I just don't know where to find it. It ain't at the bottom of the glass, that is for sure, I seen enough of 'em now to know. But you... I feel as though I have seen you before even though I know I haven't.' He stared at me with a level of innocence, like a puppy or a stray toddler, only a lot more sincere and desperate. The growing dilation of his pupils and the whimpering of his lip were indicative of a lost man, searching the wrong places for answers he did not want to find. Seemingly on the verge of tears, he came in close to me, put his hand softly on my shoulder and pleaded 'What is happening to me?' Truth be told, I did empathize with the man, who was evidently not familiar with such dissociative feelings.

'In times when I am consumed with the unwanted extensions of my own thoughts, particularly of the kind you seem to be alluding to, I try to envisage myself traipsing past their boundaries and looking at the thing from a detached perspective as if I am above or beyond it and as such, it cannot hinder me in the way it tries to. That might help - to think of life in such generalised terms so that you are no longer a consideration given its scale, rather than doing as you are, by viewing things in relation to yourself within it whereby you become fundamental.'

'You mean, to consider things relating to the meaning of life itself, as opposed to the meaning of my life in an attempt to fulfil a desire to contribute to its greater purpose?'

'Perhaps, if that helps. You can't leave your mind but at least you can pretend to. Do not let such thoughts belittle you, command them, remind them that you are much more than they can possibly imagine and that you are not limited by their efforts to diminish.' The man look confused but as if he were trying to work through it.

'Well, what would you say the meaning is if you do not mind engaging me on the matter?'

'Alas, that is not a very easy question to answer, and I certainly am not an authority on the subject. However, since you ask so sincerely, I suppose, true to the scientific manner, it is to survive and reproduce...' I said after considering his question with due attention. His eyes widened and he leant back with a heightened sense of vigour as if my distraction was proving ample.

'Like rabbits?' He asked assumingly, waiting for me to finish my thought. He appeared unaware of the unusual nature that his question posed and I began to wonder how drunk or sane he was.

'I'm sorry?'

'Oh, don't give me all that simplistic, ill-thought and hopelessly scientific nonsense. I have heard it many, many times before and quite frankly, would be happy if I never heard it again! It is an axiom of the most mundane kind, of which a man as astute as you should look to avoid as it only seeks to dilute your intelligence on the matter. (To survive and reproduce) that's what rabbits, birds, or animals in the wider regard do as their purpose is limited to it. I'm talking about humans, about the likes of me and you, what do we do?'

'Well, what makes us any different?'

'Because we have a conscience, right? We think about lots of things, and not just about where the next meal is coming from. We think about things above and beyond us, this must give us a higher meaning that we must pursue, it is within our nature to want to do so.'

'I guess that is where I disagree with you friend,' I replied attentively. He looked at me in an intrigued fashion. I noticed that since our debate had started his leg had stopped shaking as much. 'I agree, we have a conscience, such a fact is not disputable, but I certainly don't think that makes a difference to our nature. Those are concepts which are, for all their varied implications, deeply disengaged from one another in every sense. We are just like animals, well, we are animals – like a rabbit or a bird. We respirate, we eat, we procreate. We have similar organs, occupy a habitat, and most importantly we are all alive. I agree our conscience gives us superiority in terms of what we are capable of, but the fact we are able to consider anything other than our basic need for survival does not make a difference to the fact that, in the end, it is all we have to do.'

'Please do continue' The man responded.

'Well, if you shall insist... I agree the human development of consciousness is most remarkable and indeed separates us from all other species which live and breathe, but as is its uniqueness, its burden is our own. The fact we have surpassed the difficulty that it is to survive and have, therefore, developed further deliberations regarding the meaning of our existence is wholeheartedly irrelevant. The truth is (as I see it), from all that I have witnessed and know, that we do not have one, and the fact we are capable of debating whether or not we do adds nothing to the actuality that we simply don't. We live by the same means as an animal or a bird, that is by eating and sleeping and surviving and at its core, it is a primal matter. The fact we can think beyond this does not alter the fact that we do not need to and in doing so, it aids us very little, if at all.

We are not biologically different to a lot of animals in many ways...

We make our energy through whatever means necessary in order to survive, and in doing so seek to pass this gift on to others. If we fail in doing so, the end of our species is guaranteed. A rabbit or bird debates nothing over its higher, philosophical meaning, not due to deliberate ignorance but because it simply knows nothing of this concept and for that, we cannot attribute blame or assume a sanctimonious position. Surely, I agree with your insinuation, would a bird have so easily surpassed its need to survive and if it were both luxurious and cursed enough to consider things further than this, it too might have similar stipulations. In fact, I am assured it would. Perhaps it would share a drink with us right now because only with the affordance and burden of conscience comes the weight of its vexatious nature. How else would you evaluate a man's inclination to fall mentally ill or their inexplicable addiction to vices of the most tumultuous kind? Maybe you would disagree, but consider this; do you ever see a rabbit doing such things to deliberately avoid the thoughts in its mind? To physically harm itself with toxins because the heaviness of its very existence warrants it to do so? Perchance you could suggest that it would if it had the means to do so, but I would find such a proposal lacking substance. For example, did you ever see a bird, as free as the sky above it, commit suicide by driving itself to the ground, despite its clear physical ability to survive another day? I thoroughly believe our affordances are our downfall friend, and so surely will be the death of us all, both in the physical sense and all others. The world for us, for those who think, is not an easy place and no extent of creative or well-intentioned thought changes this matter. It is amongst the wildest, deepest depths of these pitiless ideas that have led us both to be here, in this hopeless, utterly meaningless place, right at this very moment.'

'Well, allow me to contest; I have seen a bird once jump off a building, didn't spread its wings or anything, just plummeted straight to the ground. Furthermore, I hit a deer once in my car. But you should have seen the look on its face as I came hurdling towards it, there was something in its eyes - a look of solemn regret, almost. It didn't want to be here anymore, I am telling you for a fact. I know it sounds mad and all, but I know what I saw. Who are we to decide what other beings are thinking about? Sure, it seems highly unlikely, maybe even impossible they have advanced thoughts similar to ours, but where do you draw the line? The expanse of thought is a spectrum of grey, not one of black and white.'

'I do not know where one should draw the line because I don't think a line anywhere would be appropriate. There is no way to categorise thought nor anything of such subjective complexity. Things as they occur just are and our need to understand them and allocate them somehow is just a result of our inability to deal with the truth...

Maybe you are right to some extent. I do not doubt what you saw, only your extensions of it. I also don't doubt that sometimes animals do end their own lives, but what is pertinent to my position is why they do it. For example, wolves, amongst other animals that roam in groups, have been known to leave their pack when they are gravely ill and find a place in solitude to die. Sometimes birds may get a broken wing and be incapable of travelling or hunting. Dogs turn away food when their time is near. This may well seem like suicide or efforts for it, but they are doing such things for physical reasons and within this fact, I would make an important distinction that coincides with my ultimate point. They are aware that they are at their end and as such are, quite nobly so, accepting that it is the fate of their natural being to eventually expire and even with their lack of care for extrinsic concepts, they are still capable of this self-awareness. Consequently, the point on which I would differentiate is that animals are not doing this because their mind is burdened, because their thoughts are plagued, or because they are at a loss with existential matters, such as the ones which have brought us to be having this very conversation. Would a wolf leave its pack if it was in all good health and of benefit to its companions? Have you ever given a young pup food only for them to refuse it without any physical ailments? I would propose that you haven't, for I certainly have not.' I finished.

'So, would we be better off going back to being animals that don't think about such things? That certainly seems to be the way your submission is progressing by extension of its narrative.'

'Not necessarily, there are affordances to being sentient and they are abundantly clear. What is more, in an absence of hope other promising things are often found. To accept that there is no reason for it all, no further meaning, and to conclude that it is all just randomized chaos can be liberating. It is not fun all of the time, of course, I would not be sitting here if it was. But we can try to make things easier for ourselves by ceasing our desire for control and simply letting go. I must say, this is me at my optimistic best. A conscience can be little other than a burden the vast majority of the time, you being an unfortunate example of this as you sat upon that very stool. Letting go seems like an easy solution but it is something that must be worked at, and even if you are successful in doing so, a lot of things get lost in the process.'

'I like you, friend', the man said as if he had considered the implications of what I had just proposed in an insulting instance. 'However, I do not feel as though you adequately answered my question. Also, your position, as provocative and shrewd as it is, seems to neglect other things. You suggest a conscience is not wholly negative but still contend that it is a – a burden as I believe you put it, was that correct?'

'Yes, I believe that was the term that I used.'

'Well, instead of emphasising the hinderances, why not directly focus on the positives that such a phenomenon has to offer? I mean, how often do you see a bird or a rabbit go to the moon, or build a skyscraper? What about the theory of relativity and the ancient pyramids? Are these not achievements that extend, in some capacity, from the existence of a conscience? I agree that there are negatives which are present but is the ability to think entirely burdensome, or is that a side effect of what is otherwise a unique phenomenon for which our race benefits at large?'

The man's response threw me off guard somewhat. It is unusual to engage in a discourse with someone who thinks enough about such matters enough to have an intellectual debate with them. He appeared stern in his view, but I do not think he was attempting to be an adversary for adversity's sake, rather it seemed as though he too was trying to encourage introspection on my own behalf. He did not express any gratitude at the fact I was attempting to help alleviate some of his angst by conversing but somehow I still felt as though he was thankful. I took some time to consider his proposition duly, which made me feel quite guilty at the negativity it appeared he was construing from my point.

'Well, perhaps it isn't, friend. I do often find myself getting caught up in the hopelessness of my own views so it is beneficial for someone to make suggestions for the contrary. I agree that our achievements are remarkable and singular to us, especially those which you name which are certainly a result of intellectual capacity. However, you must assess both sides of this postulation.'

'And what would you consider to be on the opposing side?'

'Well, for all the perks of our principles and comprehension, it cannot honestly be said that they are enough to prevent compunction. For example, what about the Holocaust? About wars, atomic bombs, and all-out destruction? What about murder and rape and corruption? I agree that it provides us with the capability to be innovative but it seems, from my perspective, that we still remain better equipped to destroy than we are to create. Sure, a lion may rip a deer apart, but it does so to eat - it does it because it must. It is not motivated by race, money, political aspirations or sadomasochism. This is because only those who think could act to appease such motivations. In fact, to those who cannot think in the sense we are discussing, these motivations cease to exist and as such, in my humble opinion, a species is all the better for it on the balance of the whole. True it is, a man (unlike all else) could build a marvellous structure as tall as the sky may be, however, the man intelligent and ambitious enough to do so, as I propose, is also the one most equipped to jump off it.'

'It is an interesting point, and one which I concede to in principle. It is a hard balance to enforce and an even harder one to measure. However, I still like to think, perhaps if only for my own sanity even if I know it to be false, that we are more good than we are anything else.'

'Well, I cannot fault you for that, nor would I want to. If I could surpass my own cynical complexion in order to wholeheartedly view things in the same way then no doubt I would.' The man stared off into the distance for a second as if something had just drawn his attention before continuing once more.

He paused as if he were going to ask something, stopped, and then proceeded. 'Do you think you could ever kill yourself?' He looked instantaneously apologetic and a loss of composure enfolded him, 'Gosh, I am infinitely sorry, I do not quite know what came over me...'

'Do not apologise, it is not something I refrain from commenting on... People treat the subject of suicide with such contempt, they avoid the conversation like it is the plague or a vile taboo. This is a monumental shame because it is very easy to do and it is never far away. By avoiding it we are giving it more power over us and only seek to enhance its allure. Therefore, to answer your question, it hasn't quite gotten to that point yet, thankfully, but in truth, I think everyone is capable should their situation be hopeless enough. What is more, I do not fear death because in it I know nothing of me shall remain. Rather, I try to embrace it and in doing so it takes a great deal of pressure away from how I try to live my life and my failings when they come. The way I see it, it is the whole being alive bit which is the odd part in our story; the most unusual, the most daunting and the most temporary period. The rest of it, that being death or whatever you believe comes before and after, is the part that goes on for eternity and is no doubt much more common by comparison to all else. So, I guess my attitude is that if it will all be over soon (which I do not doubt), what is the need to rush? I can always suffer here a short while longer.'

'I see, and if I could probe just a little more, how do you manage to carry yourself with such a mindset and interpretation of such principles?'

'With difficulty and I make no secret of it. However, to live is to endure and I try to accept my minute position in the world with as little hostility as I can. It is not easy, but I cannot change the way I think and I certainly cannot change the world.'

'I appreciate that I have asked a lot of questions that I have no right in asking, and am quite amazed at how candidly and graciously you have responded. I suppose I just felt the need to ask such things of someone else because I can no longer bear the weight of carrying such thoughts to myself and myself alone. In having the desire to do this, I could not have wished to have met a better person, so I thank you, friend, the world needs a little more of you. Finally, I sincerely hope that I did not offend you.'

'You did not offend me, but if this is a concern, then feel free to get me a drink, at which point your mind can be settled.' He smiled, signalled the bartender over and got two of the same which he slid over to me across the bar.

'Well, to being, not thinking' he said gratuitously whilst holding his glass out for me to salute. I gladly obliged.

From this point forward, we shared another drink, and then another, and it was not long before he unravelled to me his entire story whilst we were the only ones left in the bar and darkness had consumed all outside it. The man's name was Frank. Frank was not travelling through the town on business as it seemed he may have been initially, having ended up in a drifters' bar. In fact, he had already finished work earlier that day and had been home to his wife, Dolores, and his young daughter Hera. He and his wife had gotten into what one can only describe as an explosive argument before he had walked out and was now on his way to his parent's house to stay for the night. He spoke of doing this in quite a nonchalant manner which indicated it was not the first this had happened. I found it somewhat disappointing that his earlier expressions were not so much coming from a place of philosophical malaise but rather driven by catharsis. I believe this was the case because the emotional situation he had been placed in due to the present state of his family life was not something I could relate to as well and as such, felt all the more lonely. I suppose that I had selfishly wished that he was an esoteric loner as well.

Nonetheless, it was difficult to blame him for his motivations and I could not help but empathise with his situation. It had, in part, made me feel quite glad in being the recluse that I was, based purely on the difficulty the situation was presenting him with and how much of an outwardly apparent toll it was taking upon his being. I took some satisfaction in this, albeit perturbed, as somehow I tried to use it as justification for having lived my life in the way I had. This was the case up until I saw his eyes light up with the kind of intensity that I only ever saw when one spoke about their child.

Frank was a surveyance lawyer from the outer suburbs of the nearest big city. He had done this job his entire life since he had left school and it seemed that he had reached the point where he felt it was too late for change despite craving one. Regardless, he did well for himself by all means even if he never quite fell amongst the corporate bigwigs that wore flash suits, drove expensive cars and felt important about themselves. He appeared to me to be an intelligent man but perhaps lacked the requisite ambition to really drive himself to achieve his potential which, based upon a brief inventory, would have been quite remarkable. I think this is something that is quite common as often men need a given framework and stability in all aspects of their lives to really go beyond what is expected of them. It is often the case that men are only treated favourably under the condition that they impart something on another and such a burden is a heavy one for many. As far as career ambitions go, I suppose I was not one in a position to comment but I doubt he would have disagreed with me on this matter because he seemed like an honest man who made no mistakes over who he was. He was an educated and bright individual and I found him to be endearing in every sense. I trusted it to be the beginning of a long-lasting and affectionate friendship.

Unfortunately for Frank, his wife, who he had been married to for a couple of years, was an alcoholic and not the kind that falls asleep at seven o'clock but rather the type who screams and throws inanimate objects. Based on what he told me, he was never fully convinced about marrying her but after the surprise announcement that she was pregnant, he thought it the right thing to do. A chivalrous act but also, in his case and in others that I had heard of, a foolish one. It sounded like it was the sort of relationship that feels like love to begin with during the phase when you are impressionable and do not actually know the other that well but quickly falls apart when you begin to. After all, Frank was certainly a character who was not short of opinions and it did not sound like Dolores was either. The bust-up that had taken place that evening was the first of many and Frank phrased it as to suggest they were getting worse with every occurrence. One thing that I was pretty sure of, despite it being an inference and not something Frank said, was that it was Hera who was holding their relationship together. When he spoke of her, he sat upright like he was proud, and his entire aura shifted into one of passion and hope that shot its way through every fibre of his being. His hands began to move animatedly and he laughed and smiled as he spoke of the things she had done and said. I did not doubt that he loved her in a way far beyond that which I had ever dared to love anything.

CHAPTER VI - PANDORA

I met Frank's wife and daughter only once. After hearing the word of me from Frank, the distant, wandering friend he saw once in a blue moon, she invited me around for a family meal they were having during a period of reconciliation, about a year after I first met Frank in the bar. I had not seen him for a while at this point and was not particularly up to date with how he and his wife were getting along. The things he had told me previously would suggest the best course of action would be for them to never set foot in the same room again. I suppose the only other factor affecting this was Hera. However, she would not be present all of the time. I often sought to give people and situations the benefit of the doubt as when one looks upon the world too cynically then cynicism becomes all one sees. If one partakes in a positive outlook from the outset, disappointment is the worst outcome and no matter the frequency of it, it never feels quite as lingering as it does to be cynical.

As soon as I received my invite I was concerned about the general nature of the event. The things that I heard about her were not at all good. What is more, I had known Frank a long time prior to this and nothing had been mentioned about me meeting his wife or her having a desire to meet me, now it was being framed as though she was the initiator of the event. This was most bizarre as Frank tended to keep his family life separate from all else for whatever reason. Of course, there was a likelihood that her invite was indeed a gesture of goodwill and there was nothing more to the matter. Perhaps everything else that the affair could or could not be was an extension of my inherently incredulous nature. I truly wanted to believe this, but what is within me simply would not allow it. It seemed like she was doing so to prove something to Frank, and I was merely an accessory to this perfunctory ploy. I did however recall a comment Frank earlier made in a letter about how she had changed for the better and even managed to give up the drink but I was not sure if this persisted in being the case. Perhaps she wanted to play happy families, to play the devoted, loving housewife who welcomes and cares for guests, even when these guests are invited merely on the merit of the husband's recommendations. I supposed it was not at all unusual for people to do this, but I felt as though I knew her all too well, and people's general nature even better still. For the most part, people are wholly self-serving and only do not serve themselves or pretend not to when they are scheming in a grander way for their own benefit. Genuine acts of selflessness are hard to come by and genuinely selfless people are even harder still.

* * *

I arrived at the end of their street around six that night and it was already turning dark. They lived in a less identifiable area outside of the suburbs. It was not quite far out or occupied enough to be classed as a town and certainly not far enough out to be classed as a village. I had driven past a decrepit park, a small shop, and a dimly lit railway station after entering their local area and this was about all I saw that could in any way be considered slightly noteworthy. I had not seen anyone at all around on the streets; I suppose this could be due to the weather or the poor lighting but it seemed eerie nonetheless.

Frank had told me that they did not have their own drive so I parked in a more seclusive spot further down the road. I reluctantly stepped out of my car and into the frore. It was cold when I set off an hour prior to this but the temperature dropped at an astonishing rate. The wind blew so bitterly that my fingers and earlobes chilled in a matter of seconds. A light maroon colour that earlier sat high in the sky had faded and a much darker hue of thick navy had stolen its place. A gang of clouds had begun to circle above as the night quickly approached.

The street Frank lived on was a strange sort of slope, situated on a lower level to the nearest road at its far side. It was a remote location and most of the houses sat far apart from one another. Opposite the houses was a steep embankment that eventually levelled out and allowed for a small yet dense area of tall trees and foliage. It was so dark on this side of the road that one could not even make out any outlines of anything else that could have been hiding beyond. There were no street lamps nor paving on this far side, only on the side where the road was, making for an oddly sharp contrast.

A light snow drifted delicately down onto the street. The flakes were occasionally illuminated by sharp flickers of the street lamps before falling onto the floor to be forgotten. It had been raining earlier that day and instead of the snow settling as a sightly blanket of white, it gathered in large black and brown sludges in the dirt, where it had been driven over or stepped in grudgingly. The air was particularly gelid and intrusive even when the wind ceased to blow. What was more noticeable, however, was the silence. Every so often a car driving past could be heard in the distance but only gently so, as if it were trying to be soft on the surrounding ears. There was no chatter, no sounds of TVs or other signs of life except those of my own. In fact, the only other noise I could hear at all was the wet crunch below my feet as I sank into the mounds of semi-frozen dirt with increasing difficulty. I thought it odd in these moments that Frank chose to live in such an area - that is assuming he had a choice at all. The area just seemed so remote and distant from the rest of the world when in reality it was not at all. It seemed like nothing here was happening. In hindsight, it was easy for me to say such a thing given the town I lived in, but I still contend with a strong feeling of unease and displeasure in the time it took me to walk from the car to his house. Moreover, Hera was at such a young age and it seemed there was very little here for a child to do other than wander into the microcosmic forest or tempt fate with oncoming traffic and whilst I did see a park, I certainly did not see a school or any surroundings features that would suggest the presence of one was apt. Maybe Frank was trying to protect her, to shelter her, but I was never sure this was actually the noble parenting strategy it seemed to be. At some point or other, a child becomes an adult and has to step out into the world and the less they know of it the harder things can become. Of course, certain considerations are not for the mind of a child and there is no benefit to exposing one to it, but shelter can only be seen as favourable by the subject when they know what they are being sheltered from.

When I arrived at the address he gave me, I looked at the house from the street for a moment. It was not particularly grand and by no means impressive but given their recent familial situation it was an achievement nonetheless. The house was a small and narrow semi-detached hidden far away from the street. It was the last house on the corner and had I not coincidentally stopped at the right point I may well have walked straight past it. It was hard to see it clearly in the faint light. A sizeable holly bush covered up most of the house from view when standing on the street and I had to approach closer to see better. The house did not look old but neither did it look new. The orange of fresh brick appeared to have been washed away and with it remained only a greyish-looking colour. There was the front door and a large window pane next to it, above were two further windows situated parallel to one another. All of the windows had their curtains drawn. A tattered drain pipe ran up one side of the house and looked due for replacement, as did the ceiling tiles that housed a thick layer of moss even I could see in the darkness. A pair of blackbirds rested somewhat inanimately on the corner of the roof. There was a walkway which led from the street to the front door and contained a few unevenly placed steps which elevated the house from the street. On the right of the walkway was a small ten-square-foot patch of grass that had been well-groomed. Likewise, the plants that lay in a bed beside the path also appeared well tended to. In the middle of the grass was a small tricycle which looked almost brand new. I could tell that it had been well taken care of and cleaned beyond the expectation of a child's toy. Once I had reached the front door I waited for a second. A sense of apprehensiveness and fear began to brew within me but it was hard to understand why. I suppose I was scared that this envisagement of a happy family was soon to be shattered. I shook my head in denial and catechized myself for being unduly pessimistic, took a deep breath and straightened my back.

I could hear music and laughter coming from inside. After I had knocked Frank answered the door and greeted me with a familiarly warming smile that was no doubt genuine but beneath it appeared a sense of hesitation and angst. He presented the same bloodshot and tired eyes that I had noticed when we first met long ago but his hair had been pomaded back and his beard was trimmed neatly. Nonetheless, his ageing was somewhat apparent. His forehead appeared to have acquired a new wrinkle or two. He was wearing a white polo shirt which was ironed with precision and tucked in, greatly enhancing my fear that I had come underprepared for the situation. It was by far the tidiest and most presentable that I had seen him looking.

'My God, here he is!' Frank opened with. 'It's good to see you friend, I have been most excited for this evening.' He signalled me inside with open arms. 'Come in, please do come in, it's freezing out there.' Despite Frank's efforts, I could not help but notice that his home was not much warmer than it was outside. I removed my shoes and proceeded to hang my coat up on the rack but before I could do so Frank took it from me and did it himself.

'They are both excited to meet you, so excited. I am so glad we have got the chance to finally do this. It has been a long time friend, much too long. I do hope you refrain from deeming the time spent apart as representative of a friendship's vigour because this could not be further from the truth. I have kept you in my thoughts, and you look exactly as I imagine. Just one thing, if I may...' Frank gently pulled me by my shoulders into a small crevice in the hallway before checking over his shoulder and continuing in earnest. 'Before we go in, I just wanted to say... It's just a minor thing, but...'

At this moment, light footsteps could be heard and a blonde woman dressed smartly entered into the dark hallway where me and Frank were awkwardly crammed. We both adjusted our posture to refute any indication of tension or seriousness but it was hard to tell if we did this effectively. The woman presented herself in the hallway and looked at us eagerly. She was wearing an apron on top of formal business wear. Moreover, she wore a considerable amount of makeup and her hair was held up in a tight bun. She had on earrings and glasses and looked rather firm. Her skin seemed tired and worn. Other than this she looked youthful. She came over in a hurry and wrapped her arms around my neck before giving me a surprisingly tight hug as if we were long-lost friends. Eventually, she withdrew before turning to Frank.

‘What on earth are you doing hedged into that dark corner, Frank?' She addressed him in a light tone but an underlying sense of conviction seemed to protrude. She turned me and recomposed herself. 'You must be Frank’s friend, it is so delightful to meet you. He talks about you a tremendous deal and has done for some time. I am very grateful that you were able to take us up on our offer, it is not so often we have guests over. Gosh, what a wonderful evening this is destined to be!’

'It is a pleasure to be here, Ma'am, and I certainly appreciate your hospitality. Truth be told, I am not the easiest person to make arrangements with and even lesser so of the social kind. Therefore, I apologise duly if you feel that there has been any delay on my part.' Frank looked at her as if he was waiting impatiently for a response. No one said anything else and his wife hoisted us from the dimly lit hallway and dragged us quickly through the living room. There were no lights on in this area and it was difficult to make out the way in which things were set.

'Sorry about the state of the carpet, Hera had been painting in here earlier' Dolores said. Before I had time to look around properly I had already been quickly escorted out of the room on the other side, which was a mixture of a dining room and a kitchen.

In this room was a small, rectangular dining room table which was next to the wall on the far right. On top of it was a velvet cloth which covered the table’s surface but where the fabric draped over the sides the legs were still visible. They looked worn and shabby, and by extension of this, I presumed the rest of it would also look the same. In the middle of the table was a tall and lit candle surrounded by a plastic wreath. The dining table had already been set with impressive precision and attention. The cutlery sat in a parallel fashion alongside the mats. Seasoning pots were in the middle of the table as were other condiments.

Opposite the table on the left-hand side was the kitchen worktop where most of the cupboards and kitchen appliances were situated. There were bowls and knives and chopping boards spread around the various sides. It was only when I took my seat at the table I could tell that it was pushed up towards the opposing wall and was slightly too large to fit comfortably into where it was positioned. Behind the table was a door which led into the back garden but I could not see anything out of it,

Sat at one side of the table, nearest the wall, was a young girl with long black hair draped in front of her face. Her small figure was accentuated by the backdrop of the tall seat she was sitting in. Most of her body and her face were covered by her thick hair. She looked directly down into her lap as if she was playing with something in her hands. She did not pay any attention to me or either of her parents as we entered the room frantically, not even to check who had just been brought into the room. After a few seconds, she eventually lifted her head slightly and looked at me through the slim parting in her hair before returning to her original position.

After a few moments of silence, Frank walked round to the table where the girl was, put his hands on his knees, leant over and whispered something in her ear. However, I could still make out some of what he was saying.

'Hera, This here is one of Daddy's good friends from a long time ago. I know you can be shy, but I assure you that he is a good man, and he is very eager to meet you and your mother. Had this not been the case, I would not have come and most likely would not have been invited. Please be kind and say hello to him as he has not been to see me in a while. Therefore, we must make sure that he feels welcome, just as you would hope to feel welcome were you to go to someone else's home under the same conditions. As you know my dear, it is not very often we have guests, and I am not sure when the next will be that I will see him... No doubt he will leave me hanging for a very long time.' Frank looked at me and smiled before continuing.

'Therefore, it is very important to me that we just enjoy tonight whilst we are all healthy and present. Can you do that for me dear, please?' Hera lifted her head some more and gave me an agitated look. She appeared shocked and almost offended at the idea of having someone else in her home. Her eyes were a vivid green colour, she had a small button nose and freckles which were abundantly evident. Her entire disposition - the secluded posture, small frame, and quiet nature radiated naivety and innocence.

'Hello,' She said with a soft, quiet voice, although there could be no doubt that it was forced. Frank smiled at me. I rested my elbows on the table and leaned in a little bit further endearingly before addressing her.

'Hello, Hera. I am very pleased to meet you, your dad has told me much about you. Please do not feel worried about being shy, as a matter of fact, I am also a shy person, so I know that it is not easy to meet new people. It is very generous of you to have me inside your home.' She paused for a moment as Frank returned to his feet and walked to the back of the kitchen where his wife was. He wrapped his arms around her waist affectionately as if to see what she was doing but she subtly brushed him off her being. Hera looked at me once more but this time with more warmth and conviction.

'If you and Daddy are really good friends, why do you not see each other much?' She inquired quietly, although it was hard to tell whether she was asking me or just thinking aloud. I noticed Frank and his wife both stop what they were doing before turning around to look at me, seemingly in shock at Hera's initiative and newly-found confidence.

'Well, that is a good question and for the most part, you are right - friends should see each other often. However, when you get a little bit older you begin to realise that a lot of the time, life gets in the way of what you want to do. You see, I live quite far away now. Your dad used to live near me and when he did, we would see each other much more frequently, and...' I responded with enthusiasm before being interrupted.

'I don't think that Daddy wanted to move here, I don't know why he would, it's boring.' A palpable sense of tension filled the small room, and I could hear the drop of cutlery coming from the other side of the kitchen area. I turned to look at Frank and his wife, who was scrutinising him with an intimidating glare. After a second or two, Frank rushed over.

'Now now sweetheart, I certainly did want to move here, why would you say that to our friend? Me and Mummy both wanted to move here so we could start our new life together, isn't that right darling?' Frank directed to his wife as she was facing the opposing wall with little animation. After a moment, she turned to face the table and as she did so, I noticed that Hera abandoned her confident and curious nature that she had just displayed and returned to staring down at the floor.

'Yes, that is right dear,' Dolores interjected dismissively after seemingly recomposing herself. Eventually, she continued; 'Anyway, enough of that, the starter is ready.' Dolores said as she turned around with a set of plates containing a small portion of calamari and approached the table. 'Sit down then, honey' she said to Frank with a wide smile. She placed the plates on the table, removed her apron and then sat down directly opposite me. As Frank also went to pull his chair out to sit down on it, she grabbed her empty wine glass that had been set out at the table, raised it in his direction and smiled at him; 'Would you mind, honey?' Frank looked at her inanimately for a little bit longer than what I would have deemed customary, before proceeding to get a bottle of red wine out of the cupboard. He poured himself a glass, then filled Dolores to about half of where he had poured his own. He then proceeded to fill mine up. 'So tell me, how much older does Frank look since the last time you met?' She said to me satirically after a long pause.

'Perhaps a few' I replied with jest. Frank looked at me and smiled uneasily. Something was wrong, I just knew it even though I could not put a finger on why. A subliminal feeling somewhere in the gut region protruded and I tried with all my might to suppress it. I looked around at everyone, smiled and then proceeded to start eating.

* * *

Little else was said for a while, we ate the food, (which did in fact exceed my expectations), in large periods of silence, which were interjected with what seemed like genuine and insightful conversation that was stimulating enough as to not be overly generic. Frank seemed to relax as the evening progressed and I noticed him slowly reclaim his older, ardent self. Dolores was chatty enough although she was clinical with her words. Still, I appreciated her efforts. As for Hera, she had barely touched the food on her plate and continued for the most part to stare downwards into her lap. A few more minutes passed, and for whatever reason it became quite obvious to me that Dolores had already drank her glass of wine, whereas me and Frank had barely had a sip. Nothing about it was mentioned, although eventually, Frank did fill it up for her reluctantly.

Eventually, I felt enticed to break another stretch of silence;

'If you don't mind me asking Hera, what is that you're playing with in your hands? Whatever it is, it looks like good fun, I might have to get myself one.' Hera lifted her head once more and looked towards me, the enthusiasm and playfulness she showed before seemed to have returned, albeit in a meagre dose. With a wry smile, she lifted her hands so that they were next to her face. She turned her wrists around slowly before extending her fingers to reveal empty palms like a magician showcasing the big reveal.

'I'm not playing with anything!'

'I see, you weren't actually playing with anything at all. Very clever. Were you just imagining?'

'Yes! That's it, imagining. Sometimes I just like to imagine.'

'When reality falters, imagination can be the best gift of all.' I said with a smile before her face relaxed and her thoughts appeared to abscond her. 'None of Daddy's friends ever come here, what made you?'

'Well, I haven't seen your dad in a very long time. we were quite good friends him and I. Nothing made me come, I came because I wanted to. If I can be honest, which I think I can, given how smart of a girl you seem, I feel a constant sense of guilt at the distance between our friendship. Unfortunately, this is often the nature of life and there is not much that can be done about it. What is more, I've never met your mother before either so I believe we all thought it would be an appropriate time to make acquaintances. Don't you think so?'

'I certainly think so,' Frank adjourned. Dolores rose from her chair and began collecting our plates and putting them in the sink without saying anything. She made a series of nondescript facial expressions that seemed odd, almost as if they were involuntary. After some time, she brought over another dish - a homemade lasagna. I looked at it with anticipation and after she saw my reaction, poured another glass of wine, before continuing with a satisfied look on her face:

'I hope you are enjoying the food, it has been a while since I cooked properly but I must confess, I do sincerely enjoy it. It often feels like the idea of it is unappealing in the forthcoming, perhaps due to the effort or the planning, but once you begin you realise that you do indeed enjoy the act itself and even more so when you get to eat the result, especially amongst company. The strange thing that I contest with is that the next day you find it unappealing once again and it is hard to know why, when just the day before you once again reaffirmed that you did enjoy it... Do you cook?' Dolores asked me before taking another sip of wine. Her tone was warm and inviting, but her inanity coupled with over-enthused mannerisms infused an underlying sense of scepticism, as if she was entertaining some kind of cryptic euphemism.

'The food is delicious, I am very grateful for it and delightful as it is for you to cook and find pleasure in its act, I can assure you I am taking more satisfaction in being the consumer. To answer your question, I don't cook much, no. It is unfortunate because I like to eat well and truly appreciate good food, it just so often seems the case that when I get home at night and it is dark and the next day is so rapidly approaching, I naturally find other ways to fill my time. Food, or more broadly any of the things most people consider necessities, never appear to be something I indulge in. Of course, I do not mean that I do not eat, I just rarely find myself preparing palatable meals to such an extent as if it were a priority.'

'And what do you prioritise?' She responded quickly, seemingly offended at what I had answered despite the grand levels of benevolence I was striving for.

'It is delicious dear, thank you very much.' Frank interrupted. 'So, anyway, tell me, friend, are you still working at that soul-sucking office of yours, that place which you wholeheartedly despise and make no secret of?' He giggled mischievously.

'As much as I would love to come here and tell you otherwise, I must confess that this is indeed the case. I have wanted to leave many times, as you know, and many times I still do want to pursue something more fulfilling. I suppose, I just can't find the motivation to change something I have grown complacent in despite a deeper, more subliminal part of me desiring so.'

'Nothing kills a man like a lack of ambition as he is not a man without one... There must be something preferable. There is so much out there that you know nothing of, you even said that to me yourself some time ago. Maybe a move away would suit you - a new place, a new start, it might be just the reset that are you needing. You always talk about abandoning it, about running free... You are an intellectual and a restless spirit so it may serve you well to do such a thing. What is stopping you other than your own parameters?' Dolores looked at him disapprovingly although Frank seemed genuinely interested and joyous at the prospect he was vicariously indulging in.

'Now now honey, maybe he likes it where he lives and doing as he does. Most people do not hop around from one place to another with no intention, you know? It is very common, in fact, quite sensible and rationale to stay in a place where you have developed a foundation. It is, in my opinion, bizarre, almost inhuman, to desire something different every day. Routine is not the enemy that people think it is and we should be encouraging of it and its affordances and thankful that we are able to experience it at all.'

'Well, I think I like that I know it if that makes any sense at all. I don't think it is the place per se that I am fond of, just the comfort of knowing where things are and how things are going to go. I must confess, by even stating such thoughts aloud I find my own attitude distasteful. The reason being I always envisaged that to be trapped in one place for eternity would be my own idea of hell; and yet here I am living it, completely of my own accord and entirely devoid of any reasonable excuse. I do agree, Dolores, that it is sensible to stay in one location, but for me personally, that is more of a socio-economic ideal; the benefit is for employment and housing and relationships, predominantly. I do not wish to imply I think there is anything wrong with setting up somewhere. It is just that... Well, I cannot help but feel as though I would love to just vacate to some distant seclude with no plan or recourse, just for the thrill of it - just to satisfy a part of myself that I am not overly familiar with yet know that it has not been satisfied in some time, if at all ever.'

'I do know what you mean friend, I do not think you are the only one.' Frank replied. Dolores looked at him again only this time her sense of annoyance grew. She gripped the stem of her wine glass firmly and took another sip before turning slowly to face me;

'Well, life is not supposed to be filled with excitement, it is supposed to be disciplined and balanced. You may dream of such things in bed at night but to get up and go to work and provide is the reality, I think it best not to confuse the two, at least not in practical application. Life in the modern age demands this, if we want to live in a society with buildings and roads and healthcare and governments then we must contribute to it in whatever way we can. If we had none of these things we may be free, but we would have no directive - we would be like animals in the wild all over again. Life is supposed to be stable. Let's say you did fly away to some random paradise, as you put it, then what? Where do you live? How do you make a living? Who do you go to when you need to speak to someone? Who do you call if you became ill or had an accident? Even if, after some time in a certain place you were to answer some of these questions, if you moved once more you would be forced to start all over again. It sounds to me that these suggestions are, if anything, ill-conceived and childishly idyllic.' The room went silent.

'Dolores' Frank hissed whilst trying to maintain an element of softness to little avail.

'Well, I certainly did not mean to offend you, Dolores, if that is the case then I apologise profusely. Your point is, of course, valid. I dispute nothing of it. Rather, I recognise that there are numerous practical difficulties involved in the sort of ideas I am discussing. I am certainly not trying to advocate their permissibility, just entertaining the thought as a last resort. Surely, if I did not agree with you to any extent, I would have already tried it, I may be in some distant corner of the world right now, running wild along some beach or in a hut somewhere. Alas, it is because of the realistic stipulations that you have rightly mentioned which keep me here in this usual form of life that we have grown accustomed to. I do not mean to pass assumptions on whether this should or should not be the case (as I am certainly not a proprietor of the way in which one should live), just to make the observation, for my own sanity if nothing else. I respect our advancements as a species and also the comforts that society affords and I too respect the notion of routine for the balance it undoubtedly instills. I suppose the desires I speak of, speculatively of course, I do not apply to the reality of life as we know it because I accept it is unbefitting. Of course, my basic needs are satisfied and for this I am grateful, I suppose the desire for something more arises from deeper within myself, there is a part of me that has these wild ideas and it never seems to settle. I wish things were not this way, surely I would be happier and more content if they were not, but unfortunately, they are and I try to make no mistakes about it. Moreover, if I had followed through with my radicalism, I would not be able to enjoy such a hospitable evening as a benefactor of your hospitality.' Dolores looked at me, paused, and then smiled.

'You have not offended me dear, of course not. I respect a man who stands up for what he believes in as after all, they have a duty to. What is more, Frank had informed me prior to your arrival that you were not one to avoid conversations of a more philosophical and deep-routed nature. I always endeavour to expand my way of thinking, so please do not think yourself outspoken, nor attempt to diminish any sense of your dialogue on account of myself.' Things returned to silence for a few more moments. Frank began glancing short panicked looks across each person at the table.

'Could I come with you?' Hera inquired through the hair which covered her face. We all looked at her confusedly. She lifted her head and looked at me specifically as if to refute any confusion over who she was addressing.

'Come with me where sweetheart?'

'When you fly away.'

Things went silent like they were before, but somehow it was even more deafening this time around, as if the room itself had been enclosed by it. I rattled my brain profusely to find an appropriate response but none was forthcoming. Frank had paused with his fork only a few centimetres away from his face as bits of food fell from the cutlery, his stare fixated on Dolores who pushed her tongue to the side of her closed mouth which extended through her cheek. Soon, she reached rather clumsily over the table to pick up the bottle of wine. She had to stretch so far that her lower abdomen collided with the table and shook the contents on top of it. It seemed Frank had positioned it in such a place deliberately. As she sat back down, she opened the bottle and poured it into her glass. She did so in a rushed manner, so much so that the wine spiralled up the side of the stationary glass and droplets of it landed on the table. Frank gave her a subtle yet scornful look which she did not seem to pay attention to. Hera continued to look down at her plate and appeared unfazed. It seems she had abandoned all hope that I was going to answer her question and instead, seemed fearful and overwrought.

Dolores took another sip of wine before sitting further back in her chair in the sort of arrogant way one does when realising they have the upper hand in a negotiation. After a while, she continued.

'Frank tells me you are single, is this true?' She said rather abruptly, seemingly in ignorance of the rather sensitive topic she was trying to engage with me. Everything that she said to me seemed to be in the form of a probing question, nothing seemed to be asked for purposes of entertaining conversation or genuine interest and such a sensation grew exponentially. Frank looked at me with a sense of concern, his face was crotchety and wrinkled.

'It surprises me very little that he seeks to embarrass me in such a way. Nonetheless, the fact remains that this is indeed true. I have been on my own for quite some time now.' She smiled at me whilst looking down and sardonically smirking as if she was resisting the temptation to laugh at one of her own thoughts.

'May I ask why, a man as charming and fervent as yourself? It must be lonely, coming back from work to a dark, cold apartment. Surely this is the best part of the day for anyone, coming back to your partner's warm embrace and the life that you have built together. I just can't really imagine what that must feel like.' Frank opened his mouth as if he was looking for a way to intervene but I carried on regardless.

'It is a question I ask myself daily, and as many scripted and banal answers as I have to tell you or anyone that asks, I will be forthright as you have shown me such hospitality. The truth is, I am not completely sure. I suppose I never felt the incentive, or perhaps more accurately the need. I have found relationships to be based, in some capacity or another, on dependency. I have never felt the compulsion to seek someone who I might rely on in this way nor do I desire to be held responsible to such a standard myself. Further, I rarely seek companionship or reassurance. Rather, I value the fact that I can be self-sufficient. Sure, there are some days my loneliness becomes consuming, but when it does I distract myself by going to the pub or doing something that takes my mind from it. I do not need a significant other in order to do this even though this appears to be the general mandate from which deviance is impermissible. Fortunately, my apartment is not at all cold and dark as you suggest - just because someone is available does not mean they are a neanderthal. However, if on any given occasion I would warrant my abode to be both freezing and unlit, it is a decision that I could dictate autonomously.'

'Nonsense' she replied semi-playfully. Hera looked up from her plate for the first time that I had noticed. 'It is the greatest gift in life to have a family, to have children. It is our purpose and it is natural. Everyone, or so I believe, wants to have someone in their life who speaks to their soul and loves them when they need it, which all of us at some point do. I am assured that you are a very unique man of unorthodox consistency but not even you could surpass this. It is ingrained within us to ache for fellowship, even if platonic. Perhaps you may disagree, this I would grant you, but to not have any reasoning for it? That I struggle with.'

'Now now, why don't we let the man finish his dinner in peace? He didn't come here to be interrogated about the rationale behind his personal choices', Frank intervened. His impatience became rapidly apparent and his tone grew rash.

'I was not interrogating him' She snapped with scorn.

'It is perfectly okay Frank, I don't mind at all... Maybe you are right' I began with a fraudulent smile. 'Family is the greatest gift of all, unfortunately, the truth is that a life of family is not one I have been akin to. I won't go into detail but what I will confess is that this is, as a matter of fact, the first time I have eaten a meal in association with any other in a very long time. As such, I suppose I have become accustomed to being alone. My life is not enthralling but it can be satisfactory enough. I do not see myself with anyone at this point in time. It is not so much about having reasoning, more so a lack of it.'

'Well, it isn't all it's cracked up to be' She said. I looked briefly up at Frank who stared at her in disbelief. Hera continued eating obliviously.

'Relationships require work, don't they honey?' Frank said reassuringly. His reaction of affection, whether genuine or false, was as convincing as it was surprising.

'Tell me, what do you think is the hardest part about a relationship? As a single man who does not seem to believe in them, maybe your impartialness can help give some insight. Where do you think the problems normally lie, if you were to assume?' She said, directing it towards me with sinister intensity. I began to feel uncomfortable. She took another gulp of wine, put the glass back down, refilled it and took another sip. Frank discarded his upright position at the table and retreated to the back of his chair where he flung his head back and stared at the ceiling, seemingly defeated.

'That certainly isn't for me to say, all problems are, to some degree, idiosyncratic. It wouldn't be my place to comment. I do not think that a man or woman is, as the status quo, more liable than the other, if this is what you are insinuating.' I finished with a wide smile which, after its conclusion, felt more sarcastic than intended. Truthfully, the effects of her hospitality were wearing off and I began to grow impatient. She returned the smile before pointing towards my glass of wine with her eyes. I clenched my left fist beneath the table and felt my nails dig into the palm of my hands. I kept doing this until the pain distracted me from the annoyance of knowing where the night was headed. It is hard to know for sure but I believe I was red in the face. Nonetheless, she let her look linger before continuing.

'You have hardly touched your drink.'

'I was not under the impression that tonight was a night for drinking.' She looked at me fiercely and paused as she was halfway through wiping her mouth with a napkin.

'And what exactly do you mean by this?'

I dropped the cutlery from my hand and it clanged on the plate.

'*Enough*!' Frank exclaimed, slamming his fist on the dining room table. The weak furniture absorbed the force poorly and a slight jingling of cutlery rang out as it lifted ever so slightly into the air before falling back down. This was the first time I saw Hera lift her head from her meal and look at her father. She was shaking with fear. She looked at me for reassurance but I cannot be sure the look I returned gave it to her. It was easy to relate to her fear and even easier to forget that I was in much less of a position to feel it. She placed her hand on the table, spread her fingers, and began to play five-finger fillet with a blunt butter knife. Tears began to pour through her now-closed eyes. She tilted her head back distractedly and increased the pace as if she was an expert.

'Oh *now* look, she is doing that tomfoolery again!' Frank protested with a lenient hand gesture as if he were not in a position to do anything about it.

'Now now darling, why don't we let your guest finish? He is his own man and it is abundantly clear that his thoughts are indeed his own. He doesn't need you to fight his battle for him.' Frank sat still as he seemingly tried to manage his rage.

'Why don't you be the remarkable and intellectual man that you claim to be, and tell me what you *really* think.' Dolores directed at me.

'Are you *mad*?' I yelled, leaning over the table and pulling the knife from Hera's hand, utterly dumbfounded at such behaviour that did not appear to have been addressed nor construed as such by any other. She burst into a loud cry.

'Is it really so much to ask, that just for one night, we could have a guest round and enjoy a pleasant evening as a family? IS IT? He has not claimed once to be a remarkable man, rather all he has done is respond to your scrutiny with admirable patience and grace. To hell with you and what this does to you.' Frank stood up from the table eagerly, picked up the bottle of wine, walked over to the sink and signalled as if he were about to pour it down the drain. As he did so, Dolores also rose to her feet, pushing the chair back so fiercely it fell over.

'You wouldn't dare' she hissed, pointing at him with a crooked finger. Her once smooth-looking skin creased with wrinkles of rage and depravity.

'Truth be told, I have been biting my tongue for some time now, which is something I have developed quite the talent for, having spent most of my life in the clutches of detestable people. It was never my intention to speak my mind, but rather to enjoy a pleasant evening with a dear friend. However, since it has become nothing other than blatantly apparent that such an evening is impossible in your grotesque presence,

I will tell you what I think and I will tell it true. I think you are a reckless, out-of-control drunk, so narcissistic you seem to believe the world revolves around you and your own shameful levels of self-pity and delusion. It appears that not even on the most fortuitous of occasions you are capable of hiding your inner being from view and all it takes is a well-mannered disagreement (which appears to be something you are unaccustomed to) to provoke it. I could forgive it some, perhaps even empathise, if it was not for your complete lack of hesitation to display this level of turpitude in front of your own daughter who, for the record, looks terrified of your every move. She couldn't sink any lower in that chair if you carved a hole in it.'

Once I finished my unsavoury monologue, I spent a moment in shock at the words which just left my own mouth, seemingly out of my control. I could feel myself blush as my warm blood clung to the surface of my skin. Frank's jaw could not have been wider if it had been pried.

She ran back over to the table and picked up a steak knife. She held it so that the blade was facing downwards as if she was planning on using it in a stabbing motion. Dolores scowled at me fiercely, her bloodshot red eyes bulging out of her head and her once tidy bun now had hair draping out of it across her face. Frank had pinned himself against the countertops over in the corner of the kitchen. Maybe he genuinely thought that she was going to go through with her proposal and the reality of his wife killing his friend before him materialized in his mind. I was less sure of this actually transpiring and what is more pertinent (should I have been wrong), I didn't care.

'How dare you speak of me like that in my own home, you know nothing of me; nothing of me at all! How dare you... You unwedded vagrant; you sanctimonious, disparaging coward! That is what you are - you are not an intellectual or a philosopher, you are pathetic and you are an outcast, you will rot in your own solitude... How *dare* you! I should slit your throat.' Her hands and arms shook with palpable hatred as if her being compromised of sheer abhorrence.

'Well, what are you waiting for? After all, I have work in the morning.' Dolores continued to shake and shake until it was overbearing, she dropped the knife to the floor and leaned over onto the table with her palms resting upon it. She panted heavily and looked as if she were about to implode. I couldn't make out if she was preparing to attack me or begin to cry. Before I could react, she rose quickly to an upright position, bent over the table, and threw her empty glass of wine towards me. I dodged it at the very last second before the glass went hurtling into the wall behind me and smashed. Small splashes of crimson red that sat in the glasses' bottom cascaded over the cream wallpaper. As the realization of what had just happened began to sink in, I looked to Frank, who returned my gaze with one of unparalleled horror - his skin pale, his eyes white.

She looked at me with a callous stare. However, the unusual part is that she did not look merely offended. Rather, she looked challenged and engaged. It was as if she was, to some wicked extent, enjoying the night's rapid decline from pleasant to a verbal bloodbath. Hera pushed her plate away before bursting into tears once more and fleeing from the table. Frank and his wife were so engrossed with one another that neither of them seemed to notice. She continued running away from the table, through the living room next door and up the stairs that I had entered when I first got here.

'Dolores!' Frank screamed at a volume higher than I knew he was capable. 'How could you! Apologise this instant.' Dolores approached Frank where he was standing by the sink and situated herself only a matter of inches from his face. At this point, I also arose from my seat as it seemed like a situation in which sitting was inappropriate. I began to back away slowly from the room and the last thing I caught sight of in the kitchen was a solitary tear that rolled down Frank's face. Before I knew it, I was in the living room. I turned around and began to walk towards the door without thinking my actions through. In the other room, I could hear the argument continuing although it grew muffled.

'You think I should apologise? After what he said to *me*! Did you not hear him, what he called me? You should apologise for letting a loose-tongued reprobate into my home!' Dolores said.

'Oh I heard what he called you, I heard every word, and not a single one of them was mistaken. I agreed profusely with the utterance of every syllable. In fact, having him confirm it assures me that it is not I who is the issue... It is *you.*' Frank responded. The argument continued in the distance as I walked towards the door. As I entered the hallway and went to put my coat on, I could just make out Hera's small figure sitting on the top of the staircase with her hands over her ears. She was rocking subtly back and forth whilst whispering the same thing to herself over and over. I looked at the door, then back to the stairs. A large part of me was telling me that I must leave immediately. After all, I almost spent the rest of the evening picking shards of glass out of my eyeballs. However, another part of me, the more sympathetic part, found it impossible to flee when looking at that poor little girl terrified in her own home, shivering in fear and neglect. Her distinctive and almost routine reactions insinuated that it was not the first time she had fled upstairs in distress.

I grabbed the banister with one hand and began to cautiously walk up the stairs. I did so slowly as to not surprise her and had reached the second half of the staircase before she saw me. Hera lifted her head from her hands and looked at me with a cold stare, she stood up and ran further into another room. Without thinking into the matter any further I followed her into a room which I eventually realised was her bedroom. It was an extremely small, box-shaped room with a bed in the far corner next to a window. The landing light was on and I stood half in the hallway and half into her room. When she noticed that I was standing there she turned away from me sharply and faced towards the wall, which could not have been more than a few inches away from her face.

'I'm sorry to have followed you into your private space but it felt like the right thing for me to do. This is because I would like to apologise for speaking of your mother in such a manner, especially in your presence, and in your own home. It was completely out of character from myself and it certainly was not my intention to do so. It is very rare I have lost my temper in such a way and I still find it hard to believe that those words had come over me. I showed a lack of control which is most detestable. I completely understand should you not wish to hear it but I hope you can forgive me. There is much of the world you are yet to know, a lot of it is unpleasant and a lot of it is not worth knowing. However, one of the better things is that adults, in the heat of the moment, can get angry with one another and say things they do not wholeheartedly mean.

Unfortunately, the truth of the matter is that life is not easy, and simply enduring it can put a lot of stress on a person. When people experience this stress together, sometimes they take it out on one other even when it is not necessarily their fault, nor when the other can do anything to help it. It can be difficult for parents to deal with such matters, and even harder still to keep their children from this truth.'

'The things they say sound true when they say them.' Hera responded with a stark amount of maturity and intuition.

'They certainly do, you are right. I am both impressed and shocked that you are aware that this is the case. Sometimes there is some truth to what people say, this I know. But not everything is true, and not everything that is true needs to be said.'

'So was it true, what you said?'

'Well, in my mind, some of it is, yes. This is based on lots of things I have heard about your mother, and also partly on the manner in which she conducted herself this evening, which I contend was inappropriate and hostile. What is more, I would be lying if I said she did not probe me into disclosing private matters that I do not wish to be evident. A lot of it is also anger that I feel on behalf of your father and on behalf of you. However, truth is not a simple thing. Moreover, just because I or someone else thinks something need not mean it is true. Truth is its own entity and often, we bestow too much power upon ourselves to treat it how we wish when really, it exists independently outside of our conception of it. What matters is that soon you will be old enough to decide for yourself what is true and what is not. Once you have done so, then you can react to it in any way you see fit. Until this time, can you promise me you will take no notice of the comments I made earlier?' She turned around to face me.

'Do you really want to just go away?' At this point, it had occurred to me that we were operating on different wavelengths. I was trying to help her feel better about her situation and its difficulties but at this moment I realised it was futile. She had already given up, she was no longer looking for a solution to her predicament. The only thing that she was looking for was an escape. It was a feeling I knew all too well, the only distinction being that I was the creator of my own suffering and she was imprisoned by someone else's. I moved further into the room and sat on a child-sized plastic chair that was in a corner.

'Sometimes I do yes, but things are not so simple. Your mother was right about some things and one of those was this. As much as I would like to, there are many things to think about and many things that make it difficult or ultimately undesirable given everything it would entail.'

'Can you take me with you when you go?' She looked at me as if she were begging, her wide eyes beginning to become watery.

'Oh Hera, I could never do that. Your father loves you, I could never take you away from him. It may not seem like it at times, but I solemnly swear to you that this is the case and it is something I say honestly, with conviction. He loves you more than anyone could or would love anything, never forget this, I implore you. I know you are young, and it seems like running away is an easy solution, but disappearing in such a way is facile. True problems are deeply ingrained within us. Therefore, we cannot escape them through physical means. I know that this is not the answer you want to hear, and I hope you know that it is not the one I want to give you. Unfortunately, this is just how it is and there is nothing I can do to change that, no matter how much I wish I could. We have to try and accept our place in the world - it is the only way we can pursue peace. Things will get easier, I promise. Maybe not today or tomorrow but eventually.'

She looked at me for a moment before turning back around to face the wall. I believed that she understood me, albeit in her own naïve way, and the fact that she did no doubt may her situation feel more entrapping. She did not wipe any of the tears from her face as they continued to drift down it. I listened for a moment as she sniffled quietly to herself. After a while, this noise stopped and a light snoring took its place. I stayed still in the small chair for some time before my back began to ache. I rose from it as quietly as I could, shut the door behind me as I left the room and returned back out onto the landing after closing her door, I could hear the fight continuing downstairs as the muffled shouts eventually drifted back in to focus.

'Oh, because aren't you just the father of the fucking year. If I took her away from here, she wouldn't even ask about you! You would never see her again.'

'You will never take my daughter from me, you vicious cunt!' I heard Frank retort with malice.

I took my coat from the railing and walked straight out the door and into the cold. I am very sure that they were so caught up in their own loathing that neither Frank nor his wife realised that I had left. I wandered back down the well-groomed walkway and back into the darkness of the street. It had stopped snowing as it was earlier and instead, it slowly began to rain. I stood still at the bottom of the street for some time. Every now and then a faint shout could be heard emanating softly. The rain soon began to get stronger and with it, the cries from the house drifted into insignificance. The birds that were earlier on the house's rooftop had since flown away.

CHAPTER VII - AN UNSPEAKABLE GAIN

Back in the present world, I lay there for quite some time (which passed most slowly) after that shot of light had saved me from what would no doubt have been a gruesome death indeed. I felt relieved to still be alive yet confused at how I was. I must confess that breathing fresh outdoor air whilst watching the dark night sky being lit by a mysterious otherworldly entity was the most enthralling thing that I had witnessed in years. There were no longer any remnants of what had happened in the sky above me and the night's darkness had returned once more in its entirety, seemingly prompting me to get up and do something. I arose from my position and having felt unsure about what to do next, looked over to the mask that I had earlier discarded.

'All this time and I never needed it, all of these hours and days of months and it was futile.' I took another deep breath, as deep as I could muster, just on the off chance that I was wrong and it was just a matter of consumption quantity before I finally keeled over. Still, nothing happened and rather than feeling satisfied or relieved, a sense of anxiety and overwhelming confusion assumed a tight grasp over me.

It is hard, perhaps almost impossible, to accurately delineate how bizarre it is to spend years locked inside small confines, only to have the entire world revealed to you and be readily accessible in such a short, stark period, punctuated by horror and shock and some kind of ethereal occurrence, each of which alone would have been enough to unsettle. What is more, I had probably spent more than a thousand hours, picturing and dreaming and drawing what the world now looked like. And yet, all of this time, there was nothing stopping me from going out and experiencing all of it. Alas, I was so convicted and loyal in my compliance, so utterly convinced on behalf of uncorroborated means that I almost killed myself before even endeavouring to go outside once more. My annoyance grew as my mind bickered with itself despite my internal efforts of protest - the need to retain my sanity by rejecting any notions of responsibility battled with a voice of moral superiority that would not allow such to happen in good conscience;

'Why should you be punished for not knowing something you could not reasonably be expected to? There was nothing to insinuate that you should have left sooner nor was anything presented which would suggest it possible. Even if this was not the case, what would leaving have achieved? It certainly would not have led to anything productive or meaningful. Indeed, the most likely thing it would have led to was a sooner death, this I am sure of on account of the fact it almost just happened without any time to spare. And anyhow, how was I supposed to know I was being lied to on such a scale, how could I have presumed such gargantuan deceit to have taken place without resolve? Why would I gamble with my own life that such was not the case, what sane man would do such a thing and what end would he be searching for? It is a preposterous proposition that I should have known the outside was indeed available... Farcical, that is what it most certainly is.' One of the voices in my head said.

'Why don't you take some responsibility for what has come of you? How dare you contend that this was anyone else's fault other than your own. You know that your imprisonment was entirely unjustified and wholly self-inflicted, you damn well know it! How could you have been so blindly indoctrinated, how could the thought have burrowed so deep in your mind, that leaving the house was such an impossibility, so much so that you never sought to doubt it, not even for a minute second? Damn you, you absolute moron, you fool, you have betrayed the one and only thing that is yours... Your own mind; you have betrayed the one thing that makes you whole and in doing so, you have suffered, (and rightfully so). You are your own imprisoner and your own torturer. You are the governor of your own downfall, you are the commander of your pain, and you are the captain of the wreckage. Accept these facts, I implore you!' I catechized myself belligerently.

Such a battle of wits continued but the only thing I remain sure of following that realisation was that I wished it did not happen at all. I wished that I had died without coming across and thus inhabiting such insidious, soul-sucking knowledge. Only if this was the case, would I not have felt this dire sense of wastefulness that continued to drive me mad.

* * *

No matter how much I consulted myself I just could not decide what to do thereon. The one thought that was by far the most persistent was to go and find Frank and Hera, to see what had become of them. There was a highly unlikely chance that they lived close enough, or that I could find them, or that they were still alive. Nonetheless, no other solutions over what to do had surfaced and I gave them plenty of chance to do so. They were, after all, the only people I had even remotely in my life and the only ones left who I cared for.

As for how to find them, at first, I could not be sure no matter how much I probed. Soon, I remembered something - I recalled that I had kept the last letter he had sent me a few years since in one of my cupboard drawers. It had been a while since I last looked over it but I knew for sure it was still there. What is more, a vague yet tenacious thought grew in my mind that suggested something within it hinted at his location.

I wandered back around to the front of my house dazedly without paying attention to any of the streets beyond that I had not previously been able to see, aside from a quick glance to make sure that the crazies were not perching on a corner.

'That can wait,' I told myself. 'Find the letter, there is no more time to waste, if he is still there you must find him now. If he is still alive (I felt a need to doubt it but still, I didn't), there is a chance that he too does not know he is free to wander - that the expanse of the entire world is at our fingertips. We could flee this dreaded place together and go searching for a better place... There must be one out there somewhere in the yonder, there must be! Even if it is just ever so slightly more tolerable.' Such thoughts filled me with passionate vigour that I had not felt in a long time and a sense of haste appropriated my thoughts. I proceeded through the side gate of my house so I could get back into the garden and go through the back door. The front door had been boarded up for years as I never had any reason to use it and I cannot be sure if it even still worked.

Re-entering my house was a strange experience. Despite the space within it being the only one I had known for so long, it now felt so claustrophobic and suffocating, as if it was closing in on me as I stood within it. I had experienced such a drastic change in environment it felt so I was developing a headache just from the shock. I shook it off as I reached the cabinet in my living room and searched through it fiercely, discarding all else on the floor as the drivel it was. Soon, I found it. I recognised Frank's handwriting just from the way that he had written my name on the top of the page.

We had written many letters to one another over the years. In fact, it was our preferred choice of communication as were both quite sentimental about the old-school way of doing things. This was somewhat expected as it was always so reliable and catered for the distance between us. About six months after the incident at the house, he had sent me another letter, although this one was much more jumbled and rushed than was usual. In it, he denoted how he had separated once more from Dolores but this time it sounded like it was for good (at least, Frank made it sound as such). Frank had moved about half an hour away but Dolores was given custody of Hera. He still saw her on weekends and indeed in the week whenever he was able. As open and honest a man as Frank was, I could not help but feel as so though there was always more to the story than he divulged although I do not hold him as personally accountable for this as it is commonplace. There are four sides to every story, or so I always believed; one side, the other side, the truth, and the lie. The first two most usually bore elements of the latter two but never, no matter how reliant its teller may have seemed, were completely distinguishable from them in their own right.

We continued to write to each other after this, even when the world was plunged into chaos, we remained in touch, discussing how we were, what we were doing and what we made of it all. This letter which I had just found was the final one that I had ever received from him. It came just before the mail service disbanded and after such time, there was no way to communicate between houses. It read as follows;

'My Dear Friend,

How are you? I know it has been a while, please forgive me for taking so long to get in touch. I have the most amazing news – amazing. Hera is back with me, I have her. I have no idea what happened to Dolores, so much so I do not know where or how to begin telling the tale - she just up and left. They found Hera wandering around a supermarket about two months ago, frozen to the core and soaked from the rain, trying to find a bottle of water. They only resorted to alarm because she walked out the door without paying for it and someone rang the police. They rang her mother, even I tried to eventually, but nothing. The phone didn't even dial. She just disappeared from the face of the earth, with no message, no letter, and no over-the-top suicide or ploy for attention. I have no idea what happened to her Frank and despite it all, I cannot help but feel a bit concerned. I went back to the old house to get some of Hera's belongings and I could not help but snoop around. Dolores had taken a few things, some clothes and some cash but that was all. Her room looked like nothing out of the ordinary. She did not take any valuables or any food. All that was gone was enough for her person to carry.

What the hell was she thinking just walking out like that? I know what you think of her, and you know what I think of her too but I could not envisage her leaving Hera behind in such a manner. I am concerned, of course, I am, but what am I to do? Hera is my priority now and I must focus my attention on her. She keeps asking about her mother and I just don't know what to tell her. I keep saying that she has just gone on holiday for a while but the girl is clever, much too clever for me. I can tell she knows that something is wrong. Even stranger, whenever I ask about what happened to her mother she acts most peculiar, as if she is avoiding the question. I doubt she knows anything (how could she?) But still, it adds to the unnerving nature of the situation. She still smiles and we have fun together, but there are times that I can tell she has drifted off somewhere. She reminds me of you when you do that, that vacant look becomes in your eyes when you leave the other dullards in the room but never go anywhere. She is a clever girl and a deep thinker, she will do well for herself and I am sure of it, but not having a mother in her life... How does a woman fair in this world when this is the case for her? I am paranoid and my mind will not cease racing, I cannot even sleep anymore for the worry, for the not knowing.

The police came around a few times asking all manner of probing questions, even insinuating at times that I had something to do with her disappearance. As offensive as this was, I suppose I cannot blame them for having their suspicions. I wasn't even in the country when she went missing so there was little reason for them to keep interrogating me. It has died down now however, I have not heard anything in a couple of weeks. I asked them to give me updates should they hear anything but they haven't. Truth be told, it seemed like they didn't even care a wink. They know that she was a drinker and I get the sense that they feel like there are more important matters to attend to than a runaway drunk, presuming she will turn up on a random street somewhere with a cheeseburger in hand or get administered to a hospital as a Jane Doe. I do hope she is okay friend. I know that the goodness in you would join me in thinking so.

I don't have much time to write this, me and Hera are moving. I got enough of my savings together for us to move out of here even though it has cost me all I have. We're moving to the city – 33 Kingfisher Walk, I'm sure it is somewhere near where you mentioned you lived the last time we spoke although I cannot be sure. It might not be a stone's throw away but it is more than doable. We would love nothing more than for you to come by again friend and hopefully, the time will soon come but what with all this virus frenzy I cannot risk it for her sake. What the hell is going on with all that anyhow? One minute they say on the television there is nothing to fret about, the next they are advising us to stay indoors and that city where it all started is up in flames. We were told we should buy gas masks last night by a neighbour. Apparently this horrid virus is even present in the air itself, can you believe that, is it even possible? Just as everything falls into place for me the world goes and gets itself in this big mess. I am concerned and I know you will be too. They keep telling us not to but something is going on behind the scenes, and I can sense it. I can only pray that I am misguided.

Enough about me, how are you friend? I am sorry it has been so long, you know I never intend to keep you out of the loop. I hope you are well and coping with all this chaos as best you can. I do hope you have good news for me, maybe you have even found yourself a woman, Lord knows it would be about damn time. We could be inside for a long, long while friend and some company would not do you any harm no matter what you say. You are a clever man, but clever men know better than to spend all day amongst their thoughts. I do hope to see you again and that it will be soon at that. Better times are coming for us all, they have to be as they can't get much damn worse. When I next see you, it will be time to celebrate and put this horror show behind us. Please take care and don't do anything stupid,

Your friend until our end,

Frank.'

* * *

The address that I was looking for was there, which was a relief. I had gotten to a point where I could not remember exactly whether he had included it in his letter or I had just imagined it. I recalled at the time when he first sent me the letter looking the address up on a map. It was only a main road and a few streets away, about a twenty-minute walk at a brisk pace, if that. The thought of walking so far was a concern but I knew that I had to go and see him. It had been years since I last received that letter and he could be anywhere. I had another chance at life thanks to that doe and I could not let it go to waste like I had done with all else. Besides, what was the alternative? Remain inside the house once more despite knowing full well I am free to wander the earth? I had made up my mind and I knew it, I just needed to compose myself and let my mind settle.

I left through the back door once more and tried to suppress the intruding thoughts before beginning to walk down the first street and corner in the general direction I believed Frank's house to be in. A profuse intrigue came over me at what the area, which was previously filled with busy pedestrians and cars the last time I saw it, now looked like. It was quiet – hauntingly quiet. The buildings were boarded up and the outer brickwork and paint had begun to rot and peel off. Street signs were bent or faded beyond recognition. The tarmac had cracked and dissipated, and small chunks of grass and weeds had begun to seep through the many indentations left in the once-used roads. Old rusted cars with smashed windows and flat tires sat discarded all around.

The overwhelming sensations I had when wandering around were disillusionment and despondency. Everything appeared exactly how I had conceptualized it with almost nothing to the contrary. I do not know what I had anticipated expected from an apocalyptic world but such subconscious feelings still remained. Everything had been forgotten about, and everything felt lonely. It was not a typical living alone type of lonely either, it was one which was crippling and seemingly permanent. I could not envisage anything brave enough to make so much as a sound (other than the crazies) as it seemed such a minor disturbance to this banality would shake the world to its core. The was silence quite unlike one that I had ever witnessed before - the only thing that presented itself was the dull sound my feet made on the pavement or the intermittent gust of wind. Other than this, I could not hear anything at all. It was one of the first times I actually began to miss people, although they were no end of a nuisance to me before. Now, I even missed the people that I used to loathe; the noisy teenagers, the ignorant self-centred types and the vagrants hanging out on the end of corners threatening you or asking for change. It was completely incomprehensible as to exactly where all these people had gone or what had become of them. It was arduous to take in everything that I saw, it felt like a lucid dream to be experiencing the sensation of walking down a public road once more. Everything seemed blurry, like it was not actually tangible or as if what I was experiencing was not actually true.

Eventually, I reached the corner of a road I recognised somewhat but not entirely. I thought that I was going to have much more difficulty in finding it than I did but it seemed I had studied the location more than I had realised and therefore it was ingrained into my mind. As I had been walking, it did not feel as though as was paying much attention to my position or direction but nonetheless, here I was. On the corner, there was a road sign, bent in decrepitude and smothered with dirt. Regardless, I was still able to make out the last half of what it read – 'Fisher Walk'. This must have been the street that Frank was talking about. Whilst looking down it from the corner's edge, it somehow reminded me of the last house he lived in that I had previously visited; the eery quiet, the lack of people, and the overbearing sense of anticipation. I had only had to walk past a couple of houses before I reached number 33. The second 3 had fallen from its original position and hung upside down but it was just enough for me to make it out. I could feel the sweat beads starting to form in the palm of my hands and my heart was beating so loudly I could sense it in the back of my throat.

It was a semi-detached house – tall and narrow. The door sat many yards away from the street itself and there was a small pathway which guided one towards the entrance which was also similar to his previous house. His abode appeared to be, by such standards in which it now existed, in a reasonable state. The garden and outside area were a mess but this was inevitably the case whether the homeowner was alive or dead. However, one thing I did notice was that although one of the windows was boarded there was a large hole gaping through it.

The neighbouring building on the right that Frank's house was attached to was completely trashed. Its main living room window was not merely damaged but completely torn out of the frame as if it had been ransacked. The front door was wide open. Its exterior was covered in faded red graffiti and the long grass had even begun to grow inside the front room. Although Frank's house looked shabby too, it was not nearly as destitute by comparison which interjected a well-needed dose of hopefulness.

I brushed my way through the foliage on the path leading to Frank's house which was so overgrown it made navigation difficult, so much so I had to brush the greenery aside with both hands. The paving slabs were cracked and dislodged and through them, a series of moss patches and weeds began to perforate out. I arrived at the doorway and paused for a second. The fear I was experiencing was now palpable, and I wondered exactly what I was going to say or do having now arrived. It seemed inappropriate to just knock and say hello as I would have done in the old but what was the alternative? Just barge straight in? I reached my hand out as if to knock on the door, replaying in my mind the occurrences of the last time I had visited with angst, and relaying a series of scripted introductions as if to help decide which one was best. Just as I had looked distractedly downwards as my thoughts consumed me, and before my hand could make contact with the tarnished wood, I saw a sight that stopped me.

The door was slightly ajar from the comfort that would have been offered by its complete closure. It was only a small opening and I had at first missed it. On further inspection, I noticed that the door's lock had been entirely broken as if someone had forced their way in from the outside. The locking mechanism on the door frame which was embedded into the wood had been snapped away from it and appeared as if there were no way for it to remain closed due to the extent of the damage. It was impossible to tell how long ago the door had been broken or how it had been broken. If I was guessing, it looked like it had been kicked or pushed in with brute force.

I swallowed deeply as if to contain my emotions before I pushed gently on the door. It only took a small amount of force before it swung open in a slow, intermittent fashion. It creaked incessantly as if the door was shocked it was actually being required to move. The door continued to open all the way until it hit the wall behind it and stopped. Before even taking another step, a rotting stench met me immediately which was so putrid I almost threw up on the spot. I covered my nose and mouth with my hand before entering the lethargic-looking hallway. Obliterated picture frames had fallen from their hooks and onto the floor. Directly on the entrance's right was a smashed mirror and a narrow shelf that was hanging defeatedly from the wall. A hole had formed in the ceiling from where it looked light a light fixture once was. The wallpaper was peeling away and behind it, a black mould-looking substance had crept its way in. The floorboards, for the most part, were no longer affixed to the floor and obtruded out from the position they should have been in as if the wood had grown unshapely.

I also saw a staircase directly in front of me and a doorway on my right just before the stairs began, at the end of the hallway. It was clear that a door once stood here as a series of large marks indicative of force and a series of splinters clung to the empty frame, alongside a large chunk of the remaining door that had withstood whatever had happened. After a few steps further, I could now see into the room beyond. Through it was an open-plan living and dining area. It too was dilapidated but the first thing that caught my eye as I got closer to the doorway was the door, which presumably was the one once in its frame, which was laid jaggedly on the floor alongside shards of it. A few feet further into the room's far side was the motionless leg of a girl who was sprawled out on the floor face upwards. I took another step so that I could see fully into the room. The girl was lying on her back in an awkward and strained position. One foot was bent and outstretched and the other lying beneath her back. Her arms were laid outwards, away from her body. Thick clumps of black and matted hair were covering her face. She was wearing what looked like a thick and braided satin white dress, which was ripped and stained. What is more, it was covered in blood, most of which seemed to have radiated from her genital area. It had long since soaked deeply into the carpet fibres and dried a dark colour. Beside her, ribbons of the white clothing garments that had been torn off circled around her body.

I walked over as slowly as I could. I bent down beside her pale body and rested on my knees. I carefully reached over my right hand, which was shaking violently, to move the hair from the girl's face. The second I walked in I knew deep down who it was but it was only once I had brushed the hair away that I could confirm it was Hera. I knew as soon as I saw her small buttoned nose and freckles. Her vivid green eyes were now vacant and gazed up inanimately towards the ceiling. Amongst them was a distant look of perilous fear that had now been replaced by apathy. Her lips were dried and cracked and her skin looked haggard although her body did not seem to have decomposed much. I had to put both of my hands over my mouth just to stop the screams from escaping. The organs in my upper chest felt as if they had sunk below my knees. My emotions were conflicted between violent rage and fragility. I was not sure if I wanted to pull the house down with my hands or lay in a foetal position and cry until I died of dehydration. I cried and cried and cried and eventually just let myself scream because there did not seem any point in hiding it. I did this for a couple of impossible minutes. I held her face so softly as if I carried the weight of her very soul in my hand. Her cheeks were rigid and cold to the touch. The sounds of her soft voice as it once spoke to me continued replaying in my mind;

'Can I come with you... When you fly away?'

'I'm sorry' I managed to whisper to her in a spluttering manner, tears continuing to pour no matter how hard I tried to restrain them, my voice cracked with agony. I was not sorry for my own doing, and I remained practical enough to know that there was nothing that I could have done. Rather, I was sorry on behalf of all humanity that such a fragile soul was ever to have been placed in this vile, barbaric place. I knew that since she has laid here like an undignified lamb at the slaughter for an unspecified amount of time, no other apologies of such would be forthcoming and she deserved that at the very least. After some time had passed, the emotion began to fade and instead, I felt a powerful numbness and insensitivity. I presume this happened because I knew that this was the worst-case scenario and as such, nothing could surpass its horror. It had occurred to me that I still had to find Frank, but I knew that he would never have left her side and therefore, he probably would not be far away.

I muscled up the courage to rise to my feet and leave her side, shutting her eyelids gently before doing so. There was only one other door in this room that I had not yet been through. It was open and beyond it resided a small and narrow-looking utility room. It was obvious that Frank was not in there. I headed back into the hallway and began to climb the stairs. With every footstep, the wooden boards creaked and moaned with infirmity. I could feel the wood bend in a concaved fashion beneath the souls of my feet and I was quite surprised that the entire staircase did not collapse with every passing step.

At the top of the stairs was a narrow open hallway with a series of doors lined up on the far side. However, there was only one of them that remained slightly open on the landing and all of them were visible from this position. All of the doors, however, including the one that was slightly open were covered in a thick layer of grime and dirt from top to bottom. In between the doors, there were what looked like old holes in the plaster that were about the size of a fist. I was drawn to the door nearest me which was open and approached it apprehensively. I found it ironic that I felt this way because I was sure that there was nothing left for me to see that would justify this emotion.

I only opened the door an inch before I saw it - the corner of a three-legged stool, laid upon its side, with its legs pointed towards me. Beyond this, on the far end of the bathroom, which was the only thing I could fully see through the slight opening, was a sink and above it a smashed mirror, dotted with spots of blood, that was open at an angle. A large shard of jagged glass still clung onto its position within the mirror's frame. In its dirty reflection, I could see the dangling arm of a man that was suspended. I continued to open the door further and that was when I saw Frank there, hanging by the throat on a thin corded ligature which draped down from the ceiling. His back faced me as his front looked outside the bathroom window over in the corner and unto the back fields afar. I immediately knew it was him by the thick black hair on his head and his skinny physique. His pendulous feet, which were pointed downwards, trailed lifelessly just a foot or so from the floor. He did not sway in the slightest. I approached him without hesitation and clasped his body in the hope of suspending him.

'Oh my God Frank, what the hell have you done?' I said panicking, the sharp and concentrated pains of shock once more reeking havoc within my brain. I tried to free the burdensome weight of his body on his throat although I knew that it was already much too late. Whilst holding his lower torso in between my arms, I shimmied my body around so I could look at his face. His neck was bent at such an angle that his head was pointing directly towards the floor. His skin was white and his dark and inflated purple tongue protruded far out of his mouth and rested on his cheek. His eyes, like those of his daughter, were lifeless and dull. Around the site of the ligature, his neck was purple but it was discoloured in such a way that it was almost black. Leading further up towards his chin, thin veins bulged out of his skin. Like Hera, his corpse appeared well maintained and it did not seem that he died more than a few weeks ago.

I eventually surrendered to what had happened and let go of him. I managed to find some small scissors in one of the cabinets and proceeded to hack the cord until it snapped and his body plummeted to the floor. I managed to pry his legs from their stiff position so that he was laid straight on the floor and in a somewhat dignified position. I used my fingertips to close his eyes and as I did so, I heard the high pitch whistling sound that the wind makes when it finds its way through a small crack.

Upon looking upwards, I noticed something over by the window that I had initially missed. There was a piece of paper on the window sill and the corner of it, which was bent sharply upright, was flapping around in the slight breeze that was seeping through the tarnished frame. After approaching it, I saw that a thick ink pen was lying over the middle of the paper and had seemingly been placed there deliberately to act as a weight. The pen, having sat there for what I presume was quite some time, had begun to leak and in doing so I had covered the top half of the page with a dense, black pool. As it continued to leak, it eventually dripped from the paper before tapering off the side of the sill. It then began dripping down the wall where it dried and faded after a foot or two. I removed the pen and picked up the sheet. As I had done earlier, I recognised Frank's writing immediately. I had not even read a single word on the page before I realised what it unmistakably was. Due to the leaking ink, I could only make out the last half of the letter. I desperately tried to scratch and blow on the ink pool in the hope of gnawing it away and being able to read what he had written but it was to no avail. What was left on the page was all that was ever to be on it and it read as follows:

'- So there you go, it is out. I cannot believe I had made it so far by keeping it to myself. Truth be told, the burden of its knowledge has been more than I could bear with and surrendering it is my final relief. I never meant for it to happen and I have regretted it with every passing moment of my existence... What else can I say other than that I am sorry friend? I doubt you will ever read this but I write it in the hope that you are still managing to salvage something from this feral form of life. I never thought it would come to this for me after everything that has happened in the past but the pain has now finally surpassed unbearable. It is hard to come to terms with what is worse, the fact that she is gone or that it is my fault entirely. They rushed into the house and there were several of them. They did not seem or move like humans even though that was how they looked at first glance - but they couldn't have been. They were more like wild, rabid animals. I never stood a chance. I cannot disclose exactly how it happened because I cannot put myself through it again, but if you have been downstairs you probably could figure it out for yourself. If you have found this note, I'm sorry that you had to see all of this friend, and I am sorry that I am such a failure of a companion and more importantly, a man. I want you to know that even in death I do not have any delusions over this matter.

Hell, I would be lying if I had said I haven't felt

sentimental whilst writing this. I still remember that first conversation in the bar. They were damn good times and we didn't even know it. All we did was complain together and little did we know how we never rightfully had anything to complain about. I never told you this because I know how much you pride yourself on your intellect, but you were damn right about near enough of everything you said, not just then but always. I wish I had paid more attention to your words and I hope you forgive me for deviating from them so often.

I have thought about how if we had placed a bet all those years back on who was more likely to kill themselves first, I would have put it all on you (in the nicest way possible). Who would have thought it would be me beating you to the gallows, aye? I suppose you have already topped yourself by now. Even in your depressive state in the old world, it was always a worry, so I would be amazed if you had lasted so long in this one, assuming that something else didn't get to you first. If you had gone through with it, God knows that nothing or no one could blame you. You are a good man; a great man, and the next place will be kind to you for it...

Well, that is all from me. If it is you reading this friend, I want you to know that the pleasure was all mine. If my ex-wife somehow reads this, I want you to know that the pleasure was all yours. If anyone else stumbles upon it, good luck - you'll need it.

P.S. If you see that thing out there, that big ugly one-eyed freak that took her from me, do the world a final favour and send him to hell for me, will you?

I will see him down there.

Frank.'

Nothing else on the letter remained.

CHAPTER VIII - THE PHYSICIAN HIMSELF

I reread the letter quite a few times before leaving the house abruptly. I suppose I should have buried their bodies or spent longer with them but I just could not bear it. The smell, the letter, the coldness of their bodies as they were left there to rot. I stumbled outside in some kind of surrealist trance, vomited and then proceeded to sit down on the curb outside. I tried to stare at a single point on the floor but everything became bleary and disorientating, so much so that I had to look elsewhere in sporadic intervals to stop the sense of impending doom that would not let me go. I was extremely dizzy and nauseous and I could only assume a panic attack was soon to come. I tried to divert myself from these cruel sensations by focusing on what to do next and attempting to forget all else. Only by enforcing such a distraction could I manage to find a way out, or so I believed. The thought of going back home seemed futile to me at this point, as did that of living any longer. I had nothing left. I suppose I never had anything left, but now the reality of it hit me and it hit me hard. There was nothing that I feared at that moment, only the pain of having to endure another day whilst carrying the sordid burdens that had become incumbent upon me. No matter how I tried the urge to burst into tears would not let up. I could not help but yearn that I had just stayed indoors:

'Just had to go and be the fucking hero, didn't you... You just had to be the man; had to go and venture out, had to be a noble crusader, had to go and save the world, now look at you. If you had just stayed on that stool none of this would have happened. Well, I suppose a lot of it would still have happened, but you wouldn't have known it. You would have been none the wiser.' I said to myself.

As I sat there, deep in the complexity of thought, I noticed something before me that was so uncustomary I forgot about all else. On the other side of the street and a few houses down there was a decrepit old public bench residing unobtrusively on the street. It seemed to be made of darkly coloured metal and had rusted so much that it was an outlandish shade of green. It seemed to be an odd position for such a thing to be as this area was not particularly scenic and no obvious reason was presented as to why one would desire to sit here for any length of time. I could not say I had noticed the bench before but now I couldn't help but do so because on it sat a man who had seemingly popped into existence. I was far enough away for what my eyes were seeing to appear deceitful but still, he remained constant no matter how long I looked at him and after a few seconds, I was almost certain that he was real.

Everything about him seemed as if it were transcendental, his disposition, his look, his composure. I struggled to try and ascertain how he had got here or who he was but no answers were forthcoming and my intrigue only grew more formidable. He was seemingly a shortish man, sitting composedly on the seat and taking in his surroundings as if he were admiring them affectionately. He made no physical displays of angst or confusion and instead just sat in a way so nonchalant it was disconcerting. It appeared on the first inventory that he was actually having a pleasant time and just enjoying his environment, as if he had no awareness of the state of the world he was present in and its dangers or just did not care either way.

The man was bald and clean-shaven and had a long beakish sort of nose. His skin looked well cared for although it was pastel white in colour. His hairless head gleamed in the bright sunlight. What was more anomalous is that he was wearing a three-piece suit despite it being a relatively warm day and that no circumstances any longer existed within which one would need to look so presentable. This was not just any suit pulled from a coat hanger either; it clung in a shapely manner to his physique and there could be no doubt that it was a custom-made tailored suit, which looked as if it were brand new as there was not a stain or crease upon it. The suit was entirely black but he wore a white shirt that was pristine and ironed. He also wore a black tie that was in a full Windsor knot and sat attractively beneath his collar that folded eloquently over it. He had on dark leather shoes that were polished exquisitely and every now and then the sun would catch them and send a glimmer dancing towards me as he dangled his leg slightly. The oddity of seeing such a well-dressed and groomed man in this world was enough to raise suspicion per se, so much so that I transitioned between being confident he was real to doubting what I was seeing entirely. A situation in which one would just casually sit outside and enjoy their day had long since surpassed and why he was on this street, alone, and just sat there in such a blasé manner was perplexing.

Just as I began to wonder whether or not he noticed me, which I presumed would be hard not to given the fact I had just thrown up and was indeed the only other person around, he looked in my direction and gave a subtle smirk as if my presence was not in any way shocking to him unlike his was to me. He released his right hand from the intertwined position with his left and tapped on the empty space next to him as if he were inviting me to join him. Confused but enticed, I raised myself from the curb and walked across the street dazedly in his direction. The sun was strong and I could feel it beaming down onto my neck and I began to sweat in anticipation as my anxiety grew in vigour. I had already pre-empted the thought that he would just begin to disappear as I got closer but this did not happen, and rather his features that I had earlier identified just became more prominent and such followed the realisation that he was indeed real.

As I lumbered over, I did not take my stare from him and nearly tripped over by doing so. Nonetheless, he did not look back at me, not even when I walked directly passed him. It was like after signalling over to me he just forgot that I existed. He just continued looking up into the sky in the way one does when consumed by thought or trying obnoxiously to ignore someone. As I got so close I could vividly see his face, I noticed that his eyes were closed and his head was tilted slightly as if he were enjoying the sensation of the sun on his face. I sat next to him cautiously without taking my stare off his person. I glared at him for what seemed like minutes. He had crossed one of his legs tightly over the other and dangled the suspended foot rhythmically. Once more, the fingers on both his hands were intertwined and rested on top of his crotch. Also, I noticed that he made absolutely no noise whatsoever, I could not even hear him breathing. After a while, I began to grow displeased with the man as it seemed he had no purpose other than to goad me and as the shock of first seeing him died down my anxiety returned in full. Just as I began to tense my legs to raise myself from my position, cursing him to myself beneath my breath, he began to speak but continued to look forwards in the same manner.

'That was a terrible thing that you just witnessed.' The man said confidently and clearly, his voice was deep and controlled but also unimposing. There was no tone variation in his words as if he had managed to remove all emotion from them before they left his mouth. He uttered in a very subdued and accurate manner without rushing or hesitating. Between every word was the same gap as the one before it like a pendulum as it oscillates.

'Who are you? What are you doing out here... Have you been following me?' I finally asked as my patience reached the end of its tether. It wasn't quite what I had wanted to ask nor what I meant but I said it nonetheless. For the first time, the man looked directly at me. He had dark brown eyes that maintained a sense of seriousness and allure with his affixed stare. He smiled, then looked forwards once more.

'A truly terrible thing back in that house. We know that you have not had it easy. Unfortunately for you, neither has anyone else and therefore this has had little impact on the judgement of your character. Although, it seems this has just altered and in my estimation sympathy has burgeoned after the regrettable events which you have just witnessed. It cannot be pleasant to see a friend and his daughter's corpses after suffering such terrible expirations. True it is that for all the life forms and beings across the universe that I deal with, human beings certainly do not die well.'

'What kind of twisted charade are you playing at? And what do you mean across the universe? Are you saying that you're some sort of space traveller?' I interrogated aggressively, as the emotions I had experienced in the past hour began to culminate. I was a complete inner wreckage, shaking violently and spluttering as I spoke, conflicted between the need to both laugh and cry. I sunk my head deeply into the palms of my hands, closed my eyes and tried to drift off somewhere else. 'Space traveller? Have you gone mad? This isn't happening, it is all in your mind. You are going mad, you are going mad. He is not real, none of it is real.' I said to myself in a perilously anxious voice, my legs quivering and my dried lips whimpering as I shook my head in paranoid disbelief. I lifted my head up and turned to look at him once more, praying that he had vacated, but he hadn't.

'I know you have questions, you are bound to, as are most. Do not think that you will have seen me before because you won't have and true it is that you will never see me again. In fact, you would do well to ask no questions because they are unlikely to make any information of use to you available...

For contextual purposes, I am obliged to inform you that I am a gatekeeper, officially. But I have done this for quite some time now and my role would perhaps be described more accurately as a keeper of worlds. There are many like me but to you I have been allocated and this is not something which is subjected to discussion. You have come to our attention of late for obvious reasons, and as your life is coming to an end, so too has your time for judgement. There is no need to be alarmed, this is the standard procedure and to it, you are no exception.'

'What does that entail? I mean, are you even real? I have had quite the day as you already seem to be aware and if you aren't, I would much prefer if you could reschedule at a more convenient time.'

'Real is a term that is entirely subjective, contrary to the typical way that it seems your being would interpret the word. In such a sense, I am before you and you can see me and you can hear me so in all manner of ways in which the term can be construed by local design, yes, I am real. If you arrogate the term "real" to mean that I am a human being just like yourself, then this would be another matter. However, as it is one I do not presume you were inquiring about, I will cease to elaborate upon it, for I am here with a specific purpose and my time is valuable.

My occupation and the very nature of my being are not ones that your world is familiar with, so do not concern yourself with trying to comprehend any of these things because it will prove futile. Besides, any confusion could well dilute the importance of what I am here to do. What is critical is that you listen to what I state, because I am only going to do so once and should you forget any of it there will be no one to remind you in the forthcoming. I can assure you that if ever there was a time to pay attention, it is now, because how you interpret and subsequently react to the following words will prove indispensable for a long time to come, both in this world and in all others that are to follow.

The organisation which I represent, albeit the vast majority of their affairs are conducted in another realm and in a state that bares no resemblance to any of which you would be familiar, is concerned with the transition of an individual's energy from one world to the next. Although it may be ostensible that this is a straightforward matter, it is indeed quite the contrary. It is an extremely complicated procedure that demands a scrutinous level of inquiry and due diligence, in order for it to be regulated adequately. It is a tremendously involuted process that involves an exchange of anatomical energy on a grand scale between different bodies and forms, all of which possess varied constitutions across millions of light years in distance. Officials such as myself are commissioned by a higher body which transcends the boundaries of time and space in order to ensure such processes are conducted on a subject in the correct fashion following the event that life has expired, which in our definition, is when the vessel of their soul becomes objectively inanimate on a permanent basis. More specifically, individuals and the incumbent nature of their being must be categorised correctly to ensure their transition is appropriately allocated to a given realm in line with a keeper's finding. We must make sure such determinations are accurate in the first instance to avoid any administrative shortcomings. The arousal of which always presents a risk that, in such cases whereby the risk materialises, may later prove problematic for the organisation I represent and result in my own ruination. Please confirm that you are following, at the very least, the general nature of what I am trying to disclose so that I may continue.'

'I think so'. I responded. The man did not seem to acknowledge what I said as if he already knew what the answer would be.

'All manner of subjects in all realms are surveyed during the course of their lifespan in the given world that they have been presented to. Indeed, the initial allocation of their anatomical being is done naturally and the decision has been taken to leave this as so in the belief it is the most innate way of allowing the natural world to form of its own accord without interruption. Unfortunately, an uncontrollable variable of this is that there can be no way to ensure a being has been placed in a world which is optimal for its biological nature and the given framework of life it is presented to. It is only following the conclusion of their first passageway that we are able to intervene and attempt, with difficulty, to find a more appropriate setting for their energy to conduct itself without becoming a detriment to all else. Often, this can be done with ease. Other times, it is difficult. This is because some forms of energy are damned and in such cases, the exercise of my duty becomes extremely difficult.'

'Can you not just get rid of it as and when it becomes burdensome? Seems like the easiest way to be done with it.' I responded irritably. The man chuckled as if he had played out a scenario in his head where he patronised me but then rejected the actioning of it. I knew as soon as I had asked him that this was some being that possessed an intellectual capacity so vast I only embarrassed myself in attempting to engage.

'If only it were that simple, then perhaps I would not be needed at all. The answer, in the simplest way I can put it, is no. Energy is only capable of being transferred between different states of existence and we must deal with it accordingly. Energy cannot disappear nor can it die. Rather, it undergoes a permanent state of transitioning through various forms. Albeit this is something that we could change, we cease to do so. This is the case because it has been deemed by authorities infinitely higher than myself and my employer that this is one of the most crucial laws of the natural universe that applies to all worlds without exception. By tampering with it, we would be putting space and time itself at risk, not to mention the efforts it would take to administrate such alterations would be beyond infinite. Therefore, we channel its route through the realms without seeking to create or destroy it out of respect for the aforementioned natural laws and in the belief that doing so is contributory to the greater good... Satisfied?' The man finished. I nodded my head.

'As I was saying, beings are monitored for many things, some of which are factors that humans are not accustomed to nor are they applicable to and as such, I will not waste time by trying to explain them, because they will not aid in any manner and may only seek to complicate what is pertinent. The point of my visit is that your time for commissioning has become due. This is the case for all beings so it is not unusual nor are you special. Admittedly, and as I am sure you are aware, there are not many humans left in this world and visits of this nature have become gradually more sparse, meaning that your case has acquired a certain level of attention that is usually uncustomary to beings of your sort. (We are still, of course, bound by a regulation which enforces our impartiality.) Nonetheless, a visit is inevitable as it is to all others and now yours is.

Unfortunately, as I previously touched upon and perhaps without due expansion, the state of the given being in question and that in which life exists with reference to its social and cultural atmosphere is not relevant to our considerations. This is the case because many different forms of life exist in many different worlds that are subject to judgement and as such, it would be impossible to objectively regulate so many variables that are incomparable from one another. I appreciate that this may seem unfair, especially given that you have endured a vastly different climate than most humans who have previously undergone this intervention. However, inequitable as it may seem from your perspective, I can assure you that such is the case for a reason and an astute one at that. Ultimately, it is the inherent nature of the energy within you that we are concerned with and how it seeks to conduct itself within its organism. If I were able to consider the continuity and availability of barbarism in a given world into consideration, with regard to how a human has acted in their time, I most likely would, as my few-hundred years of experience dictates that it is a conducive factor to what we must determine. However, I cannot. If you have any questions regarding the purpose of the visit and its nature, presuming they are relevant, articulate and capable of being answered, now would be the time to ask as I have already spent more time on this preliminary introduction than is customary.'

'I don't.' I replied.

'Good, then I shall begin.' Once he finished, I felt my entire being freeze. I could not move a single muscle nor could I even blink. I was locked in a position staring at this entity before me, entirely incapable of deviation by any means. However, it was not a particularly malicious sensation and as odd as it was, I actually felt quite calm and focused. The man looked forward, also in a completely still manner. It seemed as though he were looking at a screen that was being projected by his eyes and that only he could see. What is more, it too seemed like his being had been frozen and was being controlled remotely by something above. He soon began to speak but this time his voice was much more robotic and scripted.

'This is commissioner number X3964C conducting an assessment in vessel V654, galaxy 63,457, article number M4, otherwise known as planet Earth, the local year is 2038. The subject is a human being, case reference number H456/756/83. I hereby declare that through the application of all goodwill, and pertinent skills relevant, and following the accurate processes as governed by the employer and sworn to by myself, I conduct this assessment in true nature to the regulations dictated to me during the exercise of my duty whilst understanding the reasoning of my assessments and their importance. The subject has been disclosed about the nature of my being and the purpose of my visit and as such, his compliance has been registered. Hereby, the assessment may begin:

In assessing the nature of the subject's being as it has traversed through its existence, it is worth noting that the overall result is one of positivity on account of its general probity, and there is no doubt in my judgement that this being is one worthy of an allocation to a superior realm. I note this finding from the commencement as such a determination negates the requirements to make certain investigative inquiries in which one otherwise would be required should the findings not be of such nature. With this having been stated, the following report will explain its findings in relation to its conclusion.

The energy form is not deemed to be malignant nor hostile via its actions or conduct and this has consistently been the case over a sustained period of time, equating to almost all of its lifespan with a few minor exceptions I do not render of such extent to warrant inclusion. I do however, deem it worth documentation from the offset that there are no findings that warrant a grave case or any which would be consistent with a categorisation of B2 or B4, that being allocation given to those who are either slightly or wholly damned beyond reparation by reasonable means. As such, I shall not disclose the requirements nor any of the matters relevant to a situation whereby a vessel is in contention for such a ruling as this purports to be unnecessary.

Although it is ill-advised and therefore not a conventional manner of my practice, a generalised assessment of conduct is, in this case, appropriate as the vessel has not displayed any signs of iniquitous behaviour that warrants disclosure. By warrants disclosure, I mean something that may wholly or in part be something which would contribute to an alternative finding or be something that the commissioners' board may find relevant in the forthcoming. Such examples that I have excluded would equate to; causing harm to other beings, conducting themselves in a profligating manner, or acting in a way grossly unconducive to its common kind, with reference to part iii) of the Article Codes preliminary guidelines. I also advise, in correlation to the guidelines of the statute, that it is permissible to make approximate judgements due to the fact that life of any form is an extremely complex matter. What is more, it is an oddity, in fact almost completely irregular that an individual vessel devotes itself entirely to one moral code of conduct and conforms to this during its entire lifetime. Therefore, we commissioners do not have the time nor find the necessity to disclose every single one of them. As for such acts that constitute minor, which tends to be the overriding majority, I remind the report and those who bear witness to it that a keeper need not indulge in every act assuming that it is not one which demands inclusion. I utilise the guidance of this section due to its relevance and applicability and confirm that any acts which were abhorrent, reckless or sinister enough in nature would have been included should they have taken place. In their absence, I retain the right to negate their inclusion for the sake of brevity and avoidance of redundancy.

However, I find it apposite to include in my report that much of the subject's presence is suggestive of an inability to be complacent within its being and a finding of spiritual restlessness is one that is, in my judgement, one which is accurate. This finding was reached via an actioning of Article Code part 1)iii)3)a) regarding a keeper's ability to ingress a vessel's thought processes to better understand its general nature for the sake of and only of the benefit of their findings. Namely, an assessment of the subject's mental condition and prolonged substance abuse are ones consistent with mental malfunction to a degree which, in this case, certainly raises a cause for concern. The cause for concern arises not necessarily from the mental state which has arisen but rather its effectuality on the rest of the vessel's state. The evidence which denotes such a finding is on the basis of the vessel's continued mental depravity, which has affected both its thoughts and ability to contribute effectively to the continuation of its life in certain circumstances. I also note, as it would be inappropriate not to, various attempts at suicide, albeit perfunctory in part, and also an act of self-mutilation which have taken place and are, in my estimation, as a result of the aforementioned plague of the mind. I note such acts because pertinent to Article Code part 673)i), a key indicator a commissioner must bear in mind when making an assessment is any conduct or manner of behaviour which can reasonably be conceived as something which may affect its capability to adapt to another foreign vessel.

I too note that although the subject's mental state has caused it both physical and mental harm, it too has provided the instruments necessary to action cogitation on a rather extensive level, something which is a favourable quality and often one which is deficient in beings of this kind. What is more, the subject has utilised its position effectively to consider both philosophical and existential postulations. By doing so, it has managed to supersede the more common self-absorbed trope of its kind and form a more altruistic composition that has boded it well, even if its origin was unbeneficial and as a result of it, it too has suffered a companion of deficit. It is unclear, but in my estimate unlikely, that the subject has utilised these defects intentionally to benefit from its position. Nonetheless, the introspective quality that the subject has displayed also supports a positive finding as the case history is indicative of the fact that individual beings with such qualities prove much more favourable during the transitional period. This is often the case even when such qualities as they present themselves in humans per se do not often lead to productivity during the course of this singular lifespan. What is further, the report must highlight that it is wholly or partially impertinent of how a vessel's mental and physical constitution comprises. This is the case, unless and until, such factors are directly correlative with a situation whereby these factors have materialised to impact other beings of their kind. In line with this, I note that case history is suggestive of the fact that a negative mental constitution in some form is likely to result in the mentioned. However, I do not find this to be the case hereby; rather I find that the vessel's constitution, although hindered, has not led to acts upon others which have had negative or serious consequences, with the exception of those whereby it has brought harm upon itself. However, harm of a self-inflicted nature is not a factor which may contribute to a negative finding due to the generalised connotations of such actions being consensual and without collateral damage. Despite this, I feel it apt to issue an advisory cause for concern during the allocation process for these reasons, as it is my duty to bestow the board with the pertinent information in the allocation process, which such a finding may prove to be.

The subject's navigation through its lifespan has been, in reference to the universalised nature of its kind, wholly uncustomary. It has displayed, on numerous occasions and persistently too, an innate desire to act in a way opposed to what its kind dictates is normal. The status quo is that this leads to undesirable manifestations of the energy form in its vessel but I note that here this has not been the case and for the purposes of clarity, I do not mean a lack of conformity in terms of crime or by being a debauchee of sorts. Specifically, the subject has shown a persistent and stark lack of dedication to work and ambition for anything else. Work, in this being's illustration, is a custom in the given world whereby individuals are required to exact some form of economic benefit in exchange for currency that they use to live by bartering with it for items such as food and water. Whilst in similar cases of beings of this kind, a tendency to accept their way of life is most common and rebellion, even when it does not extend past the thought process, is most atypical. It is most likely, in my appraisal, that this facet is due primarily to a strict socio-economic and cultural environment whereby people are trained to manifest in such ways whereby they can benefit their given society without thinking about any means beyond it. The subject has persistently demonstrated an inner complexion whereby they ridicule such a system and the complacency for which it asks by way of refusing to conform to it and thinking of ways in which it may exist in other conditions. I do, however, note that a deal of this neglect is in part due to the being's intelligence which has encouraged it, often subconsciously and often to the subject's dismay, to wander into deeper existentialist thought not only not required by the society in which it operates but seemingly at its own onus. Although the subject has failed to actualise its potential with regard to the societal norms that are expected from it, I would like to emphasise in the report that this has not been done in a manner which is dire or extensive. What is more, the guidelines are abundant in how they express disinterest in an individual's capability to conform to the idiosyncratic standards imposed by it in a given world. Where a vessel has failed in doing so, it is often the case that this may fall outside the parameters of assessment due to the fact that each condition of a being's life is vastly incomparable and of its own nature, in line with Article Code 42)ii)2)e).

In conclusion, I find the subject to be a positive form, suitable for categorisation in line with this finding. I note in brief that its restlessness and tendency to self-sabotage is something which should be considered when the time for allocation comes but nothing else presents itself, in my opinion, to be a cause for concern and I solemnly swear that this is the case as I see it. In line with the prescribed procedure, I will ask the vessel if they are able to understand, to some degree or another, the connotations of the assessment for which they have just undergone. I shall maintain my recording during the course of this consultation, should any of the questions asked or information given in turn prove to be useful to the board during the witnessing of this assessment.'

As soon as the keeper finished, I felt the control of my body return once more. It was a strange sensation, one unakin to anything that I have previously experienced. All of my bodily and indeed mental control had been surrendered to it during the entire time it spoke and yet, I felt no hindrance as a result. I was heavily focused on the keeper's words, not only because they were of great importance, but also because it felt as though I could not opt otherwise. The odd part was that it was not a case of me trying to move my head but being unable, but rather that I was in such a hypnotic trance that the thought of trying to move of my own accord did not even seek to cross my mind. I suppose should someone have been subject to a negative assessment, it would be all too easy of an escape if they had the choice to simply turn away from it. We are all due for judgement and our actions are our own so I do not think the keeper nor its organisation is unjust in making us face it. This is especially so considering all of the power and technology they have available to them, they could have chosen to conduct proceedings in a much more barbaric fashion. What is more, my assessment sounded relatively sanguine with all things given. I too think that the assessment was fair and considered many of the variable factors that I would have endeavoured to explain if it were asking me rather than just reporting it itself.

Eventually, the keeper looked at me. 'Well, do you have any questions which are pertinent to your assessment that I have just read before you?'

'I do have one question, actually.'

'I will grant you it.'

'At the start of the day, I nearly killed myself. You weren't there then, why are you here now? And as flattered as I am by what seems to be relatively constructive opinions, I really am not sure I agree with your determinations as much as I would like to and as much I would probably benefit should I do so. I may not have done badly during my life, or as you put it, not bad enough for it to have been mentioned when discussing the grand scheme of my existence in brief, but I also do not feel as though I have done much good. This is something that you ceased to have mentioned and I am curious about this matter, so much so that I risk bringing it up even with my own downfall at stake.' The keeper looked at me and seemed to manage something that was not too far short of a smile. Afterwards, he began his response, apparently without having to think about it beforehand.

'Earlier in the day when you attempted an act of suicide I did not arise because you were not to die at this point and of this, we are aware, for we can travel in a linear sense through time and all information of the happenings in the universe is readily obtainable. Should it have been the case that you were to die then, we would have scheduled your assessment long before it to ensure that you had one. We conduct these processes on a scale so grand your brain would explode if it tried to comprehend it even in the simplest sense. As duplicitous as it may seem to suddenly commit an impromptu suicide to avoid your reckoning by a keeper, I am afraid that this is not possible. We are, in every sense imaginable, far beyond that of your being, and as I am sure you can imagine, this must be the case in order for us to conduct our duties effectively. The conditions which bind yourselves, namely that of your mortality and all other things, whatever they may be and however they may materialise, do not even seek to present themselves to us because we have long since devised ways to avoid their every ensuing. Time is not a boundary to us, we see the past as we see the future and we can traverse through it at any time and by any length. Were you going to be run over or shot or crushed by a falling object, we would have known, and we would have been there.

As for the second part of your question, I presume you are referring to the situations earlier whereby you had the opportunity to help others but did not, of which I am aware you subjected yourself to great turpitude on account of this guilt. What concerned my judgement is that by demonstrating this, empathy is something within the bounds of your being. I might add that, a failure to act, in your case anyhow, is not an ailment and falls within the boundaries of minor actions which I do not include. Should it have been otherwise, rest assured it would have been included in the report. The reason for this is that the situations in which you did not act were not ones which were created or contributed to yourself in any capacity. Culpability in such scenarios only arises, especially so in a grave fashion, whereby the scenarios in which you fail to act are ones in which, by your own doing, an obligation, therefore, falls upon you to try and inflict a resolution. In your case, you were not prompted to act in any other way and your omission is justified because by acting you were putting yourself at risk that was unnecessary on a personal basis. It is not the job of an individual to rid the world of its failings. Indeed, only a fool would endeavour to do so. What is more, it would be entirely inequitable to judge those via a system that does not recognise this. In so far as the energy of the vessel is concerned, we only assess it based on what it is reasonably able to affect by its own doing and the inner motivations which inspire it to act in the way it does. What is more, deliberate acts which negatively affect others are deemed much more harshly than the failure to do what you would consider good. It is not necessary to be a hero, as your kind would put it, as the line between being a saviour and being foolish is a fine one indeed. Even if it were the case that heroism was favoured by our standards, or if such things were an obligation, you showed admirable bravery when you sought to make up for these failings by saving the doe. As if to illustrate my point, your life inside was, up until now, lacking in physical burden and it was only when you ventured to rescue it which led to you being outside, and being outside is what has caused you all of the subsequent mishappenings. It is clear that the remorse which built up within you inspired these actions and for this, I can only judge favourably because the reasons for which you felt sympathy were not ones in which you ought to.

I could continue onwards should you desire, but the outcome for yourself is positive. By my determination, you have conducted your life in a way which is overall satisfactory by our standards and as such, when the time comes your soul will be allocated accordingly. You should take pleasure in these findings, I have done this for many, many light years and I can assure you that some assessments have been much worse, in ways which you could not fathom (nor would you wish to).'

'I do have one last question before you go, please.'

'This final one I will also grant but that shall be all.'

'If you are here now, does that mean I am going to die soon?' I inquired.

'Yes, it does. Your expiration is to be soon but I would remind you that it is inevitable and indeed in this world's case, it is nothing short of a miracle (and perhaps also rather impressive) that you have survived this long anyhow. I appreciate that your being becomes sentimental about the consideration of death but you would be wise to surpass this and this is something which I believe you are capable of. What is more, your reaction is futile and changes nothing. Therefore, there is no practical need to have one. Unfortunately for your kind, you have not yet reached the point at which you can see past your current state. This is both a blessing and a curse because I can assure you that you have an eternity of traversing left before you encounter what you think the end actually is. The irony of it is that if your being were able to see past death then death would be the least of your concerns. This life you live is just the blink of an eye, it is a grain of sand on a beach, a singular hair on a child's head, it is the tiniest cog in a machine so grand it surpasses the boundary of the sky and all else beyond it (forgive me for the deployment of metaphors). There is much left for you to do and much less for you to see. It is only the wise man that seeks death because he knows that it is not all.

What is also important is that you still have some time left here before this time arises. During this time, you will suffer adversity and conflict and you will also have an opportunity for thought and reflection, so do not concede just yet. It is relevant, however, for you to know that this time is still subject to my judgement and will be considered duly when your time has expired. It may not feature in my report, but we bear witness to all and should something occur that warrants inclusion then the changes will swiftly be made in due course. You have not become immune to our procedures officially until your life has met its end. Unfortunately, we are busy entities and have much to deal with. Therefore, visits cannot always accommodate individuals in the way they often desire nor can they be at their very final moment. The last thing I will impart to you is this; the world in which you occupy is soon to be experiencing some innovative work, the process of which has already begun. I cannot disclose any more than this. Just know that all beings time to come is soon and in the next world and in the one after, things will be different for you and all else.'

The man stood up and walked a few steps down the road before disappearing entirely.

CHAPTER IX - SOMETHING OF THE MARVELOUS

After the keeper had departed, I remained seated on the bench for what must have been at least an hour. I cried a little, cursed a lot, and spent much time deep in thought. I tried my best to digest the keeper's words and all he had told me but it proved laborious and no matter how much I tried to replay his report it felt like it continued to disappear from memory. He had told me so much it was difficult to process it although I presumed this was typical. I too contemplated whether or not it was even real, or if it was just a symptom of madness that I had brought to life in the aftermath of the trauma I had experienced. As unlikely as this may seem, particularly on account of how in-depth and vivid an experience it was, it was still not an idea I wholeheartedly rejected. What I was sure of, however, was that my recollection of him and the words he spoke appeared to become more and more vague the more I considered them. It seemed as though his existence in my thoughts was deliberately trying to escape them for reasons I could not be sure of.

One thing which became clear was that I was not helping myself sitting here any longer. My mind just wandered around and around and nothing got resolved. It felt as though everything was spinning and I could just not manage to stop it no matter how hard I tried. I felt the urge to cry and grieve as the culmination of all the drastic things I had experienced began to catch up to me. I tried to fight it off, but I could feel it as it tried to consume me. The thought of crying was one I actively intended to avoid as I could not be sure I would ever be able to stop. I knew this feeling all too well and without thinking about it any further, I rose to my feet and left Kingfisher Walk at a fast walking pace. Still, the sense of panic just would not go away, so instead I began to run. It was only after I had taken the first few initial steps that I realised I had not actually run at all in years. In fact, I had not done any exercise whatsoever and even the most minor exertion that began after the few strides took a strange effect on my psyche. It felt as though my entire body was made of glass and my feet felt like they had lead weights attached to them that got exponentially heavier with every stride. My knees cracked with each step and the bottom of my back began to strain in ways I forgot were possible. My muscles, especially those in my upper and lower leg became instantaneously weary. My shoulders began to throb just from being required to hold my arms slightly upright. I could feel my skin get warmer and the sweat as it began to pour down my face and back in a matter of seconds. I had to gasp for the deepest of breaths with every passing moment and soon my lungs felt as if they were on fire. A strange sensation also began in my head as it felt as though my brain had expanded and was pushing against my skull and with it, became a sort of tunnel-like focus. It was exhilarating, wildly terrifying and exactly the kind of catharsis that I needed. Therefore, I just continued to pick up the pace until I felt like I was going to collapse. Then, I carried on some more.

I had no sense of direction or desire as to where I wanted to go, I aspired simply to be anywhere other than here in every sense so I just ran and ran. I did not look in front of me as one does when assessing their surroundings or trying to avoid obstacles, I just stared down at my feet and watched as each past the other with increasing difficulty. In doing so, I must have run beyond many desolate streets and buildings without even taking a second to assess them. As soon as a corner approached, I glanced up for a second only to turn and then continued looking down once more. On my journey, same as before, I could hear nothing – no noise made by humans or otherwise, the only sound I could hear was my heart as it began to beat harder and harder along with the sound of my heavy breathing. Although, this time around my heart was beating so hard in my chest that I thought it was going to burst and I was quite hoping that this would be the case as the thought of my stupor returning should I have stopped was most detestable.

After many minutes of running and perhaps even a minute at a sprinting pace, I reached the bottom of a fenced area that had survived the effects of time quite impressively. Having reached it, I fell onto my knees and rested my hands on the ground. I had completely extinguished the limits of my endurance and my collapse was not one done voluntarily. I stared at the concrete floor and heaved air into my lungs aggressively. Beads of sweat rolled down my face and dripped from me. After the effects of the fatigue had become almost controllable, I took the opportunity to look around and see where I had ended up.

A couple of metres past the beginning of the fence I noticed a large sign on my right. It was covered in moss but the writing was still visible, on it in large bold writing said 'Castle View'. Castle View was a large open plain with a hilly peak that overlooked the city. I remembered going to it a long time ago and a strange sense of nostalgia resided within me although I could not place precisely how or why I remembered it. I did not know who I went there with (if I did at all) even though I was somehow sure I had, at some point in time, done so. What is stranger is that although I could recall this location in some vague fashion, if one had asked me to navigate there from my front door I do not think I would ever have been able to locate it. Something about my arrival here felt much more than a coincidence and almost wandered into the remit of the mystical. What is more, I had looked up at just the right moment to notice the entrance, whereas everything before I had just ignored without a second thought. Yet, something about this area gave rise to a demand; a need to observe it, it was as if I was compelled by some external force to recognise its existence. Subsequently the fact that I was here did not appear coincidental.

I looked upon Castle View's stretch into the distance. The gated entrance was wide open and looked as if no one had walked through it in a long time yet it remained inviting to anyone who wanted to. After the entrance, there was a narrow path that led in a curved fashion up the hill and until the peak before continuing back down on the other side. It was clear that it existed in a forgotten world as the grass was overgrown and a small man-made lake which was near the entrance had since dried up and the floor was occupied entirely by leaves and rubbish.

Without considering any further, I hauled myself to my feet and continued through the gate. It felt as though the lactic acid in my muscles had already set in and I dragged myself up the jagged path with enigmatic conviction. The park was sealed by fences all around it in a rectangular fashion. There was another entrance to it over on the far side a few hundred metres away. The highest peak was at the centre of the park and it had an incline on either side to reach it. On the further side was a child's play area that I could recall from memory but that was pretty much all. I must admit, it was rather therapeutic to be in a natural area, albeit a superficial one, for the first time in a long time. The tall trees, most of which sat around the perimeter alongside the fencing that sealed its borders, stretched high into the sky and swayed ever so slightly in the wind, as did the grass which was waist-high in the patches where it continued to grow. The path had shrunk so much on account of the surrounding greenery traipsing into its vicinity that there was only just room for me to walk up it. Once I reached the top, which did not take me as long as I thought it might, I collapsed onto all fours once again, panting in a way only the wild know. I do not think I had yet recovered from my earlier sprinting session and my body pleaded to rest. Fortunately, this gave me time to take in the surroundings.

Although it did not seem like the peak was that high up when looking at it from street level, the extent of the view was impressive by all means. It was after the exhaustion had subsided slightly and I recovered control of my senses that I was reminded of how picturesque it used to be. I had spent years staring at a wall a few feet in front of me so staring at a panorama was most unusual, so much so that I almost felt slightly agoraphobic. It was almost as though I were looking at a painting had it not been for the breeze and the distant rustling of the trees.

The view stretched for miles around but most of what could be seen was dull grey ruins of the old office blocks and apartment buildings and other human makings that had since been forsaken. These were interwoven by many tattered streets which looked to be covered in litter and dirt and dejected in every visible sense. Abandoned cars and trucks that had rusted were scattered all over the streets, often with missing windows or tyres or laid upon their sides. The occasional tree or hanging basket which had been planted long ago amidst the dying metropolis had no leaves left and hung bare. Some buildings had even collapsed entirely and a vast amount of rubble and brick had been cascaded over the accompanying streets. In one of the distant squares that I could just about make out, a statute of an old politician had turned green in its decay and was also missing its head and an arm. The occasional corpse could also be seen, often on the steps outside of an abode or even laying out in the middle of the street. Most fixings, such as lampposts or signs or overhead electric pylons had been knocked down, eroded, or bent over at an unshapely angle. A hollow gust of wind that pushed powerfully through the space seemed to echo as it worked its way in between the buildings. There were still birds around, some of which perched on building tops or flew high around them in groups. Occasionally, I could make out what looked like a deer wandering through the street. Other times, small beings like foxes and hedgehogs subtly worked their way in and out of openings.

However, the faded colours of the forgotten conurbation were not the only things that I was able to make out. In the distance, right upon where the horizon sat and just a little before it, a surprisingly bright blanket of emerald green could be seen to form just as the city began to come to an end as if the natural world was forming an army and was preparing to invade the city. Tall and conspicuous trees stretched for miles around and the healthiest of vivid green foliage enfolded the expanse of the skyline. The contrast between the meeting of the two worlds was stark and it seemed to take place drastically over the course of a mere street or two. It almost looked as if it was slowly making its way towards me, like a tide that seems tranquil and distant from the beach at first glance but soon begins to wash over your feet.

For the first time in a while, I felt a wave of calmness descended over me before lifting me up and carrying me off to another place. I cannot be sure from what this sensation came. The only thing I could put it down to was the drastic effect that seeing so much of the world in one go had upon me. The words of the keeper, especially those having highlighted the insignificance of my own life in the grander scheme of ethereal existence no doubt too had an effect, as did what I had witnessed on Kingfisher Walk. At first glance over the tract before me, I did not think too much of it, but having sat here for some time observing my environment, I felt myself drift into some kind of existentialist diversion that was both calming and perhaps somewhat mawkish. However, it was not necessarily the view itself that I had fallen into a trance with but rather how the view had impacted me. Simply put, in admiring the resplendence of the opening before me, I was afflicted by how carried away I had gotten with my internal feelings, my own complexion and the idiosyncratic happenings of my life. More importantly, I was struck by how inconsequential I felt in this spot, overlooking the rest of the world that I had somehow still managed to exist in, despite everything else having died long ago. Having been indoors for so long, and within a small space at that, it becomes very easy to feel as though you are the centre of the universe; as if nothing else exists or matters because you are separate from all else and resultingly, you are everything. I suppose I underestimated how much this imprisonment had affected my own psychology and now, having seen a world that I had long since forgotten, a barrage of thoughts began to subdue me that were hard to come to terms with but also violently insistent.

It was not within the personal history of the spot that caused the arousal of this passionate expansion of the mind, nor was it its ravishing expanse that had been available to all others. Rather it was the ineffectiveness of my presence upon it that I was attempting to come to terms with, albeit an ask of a monumental adversary. One day, in another toil of time, be it past or future, some other man or being unknown to man may have occupied this very spot in which I sat. What they would have seen may be exactly that which I was witnessing, or perhaps a dichotomy of it. And yet, as they positioned themselves here, conceivably imitating my stature and mortality or without any of either, it would not have made an ounce of a difference; nothing shall be any the wiser - unimpressed, unwavering. The earth will not move nor care whether I rose at that moment and disappeared or rested there until I returned turn to dust. Nothing I or any other could ever do in this infinity would provoke it to regard us in any capacity no matter how small, no matter the man or the nature of his being. Here I was in its current state of turmoil gasping for breath, whereas perhaps once upon a time here a proposal was made before a sunset, perhaps here children played in their innocence, laughing and dancing as they left boot imprints in the grass. Despite all actions and thoughts, no matter how complex or deeply felt, nothing around would respond and there is nowhere we can place this frustration nor any formula that can change the outcome. I could have sat there for a thousand years and this perpetuate state of ignorance would always prevail.

Perhaps it is within this frustration that I have identified and can wholeheartedly relate to that lies the reason for the destruction of ourselves. Perhaps our human disposition and the development of non-existent ideals surrounding meaning, purpose, and entitlement compel us to be known, to be wanted. The expanse before me, indicative of a distant advancement of a new world, suggested that these are just notions built from the foundation of an inherent need to be recognised in subliminal acceptance of the fact that ultimately we are nothing. A thought that I had earlier glanced over, albeit only for expository purposes and no other, was that people in the old world seemed to develop the idea that we matter - that the world owes us something just because we exist, just because we are, but now I know concretely that this is not the truth. Once upon a time I too believed this even when deep down I had my doubts. It is much easier to believe in a lie than it is to accept that it is one and I cannot blame anyone else for falling victim to this duplicity.

I did not advocate this idea to upset those who enjoy the affordances of thinking that we are, by contrast, something to some degree. Rather, I think it not to be true only because it cannot be and the truth exists regardless of how we feel about it; it is entirely insistent and wholly uncompromising. To believe on the contrary would be an entitlement to a force incapable of granting us such a privilege. We always should have sought to come to terms with the fact that we do not matter, not because this would have driven us into the ground in existential angst. Instead, we should have sought such profound knowledge because sitting there at that very moment, my eyes were opened to a new perspective; an emancipating perspective, a philosophical vantage point of sorts, because I now realised that within the subscription to this idea is the ability to be free. That is the beauty of it all - in being nothing, we too are everything and as such, we are free... Free from everything that binds our damned pneumas to the mud. We are ancient forms of energy, manifested in ways beyond our comprehension, living on borrowed time not owed to us. We are flying on a large rock in a void through infinite space and time, we are stardust and that is all.

The world does not care for us and more pertinently, why should it? Look at what we are. I think of the former world and every aspect that we developed: space travel, science, medicine, technology, economies, democracy, law and order. Admittedly, all of such things are achievements of grandeur. However, even for those men who were not capable or did not seek to change the world, for the most, there was still clean water, warm homes, nice meals, comfortable jobs, safety and the right to be equal. Whatever we had seems as though it was never enough, and no matter the luxuries that we created, none of it changed what we are – what we have always been. Maybe nothing will ever change it and looking over the world we made and have now died within, it seems that this is most likely going to be the closing case. War, genocide, nuclear weaponry, corruption - no matter what we have ever had all we ever did with it was demand more. We could not live in harmony because this is not what we wanted, harmony is boring and it does not satisfy our greed nor the ugly part within that urges us to trespass into the omnipotent realms of the Gods. We elevated ourselves into a higher realm beyond that of self-preservation and we decided that we do not merely want to survive and breed but that we are owed it and much more. As such, our capacity for gratitude and complacency died too. There was and may never again be a species that is fortunate enough to be able to obsess over things which are not tangible. Perhaps I was wrong, or perhaps this was all just a spur-of-the-moment conjecture. Unfortunately, I cannot help but think otherwise. No matter the condition of the given world we continue to search for our place within it and from all I have seen and felt I cannot help but wish we didn't. We did not need a place, we did not need meaning or reason because without one nothing could ever matter, how could there be any more affordances than this? To hell with meaning, to hell with being exhibitions of metaphysical idleness, to hell with thinking and praise be to being, to running wild, to not letting anything dampen the fire that made us.

Whatever brought the world to be, I cannot help but admire it because it is abundantly clear that none of the human way is its fault; it is dignified in its apathy, it bathes in its ignorance. Even if it were, ultimately, who am I, or who are we, to say anything about anything? I am a by-product of distant origin, of energy which works in ways I do not understand. How dare I be ungrateful when the very existence that allows to me feel such a thing is one which is infinitely unlikely... Everything in this moment and all that had led up to it had felt hopeless but within it was a strange wonder, a rare sense that when we accept all that is before us without seeking anymore we are liberated from the very things that bind us.

Sitting on that peak in Castle View I came to terms with a lot of things, many of which I did not fully understand but why did I need to? It is a big joke, told by a very grand person on a very grand stage, a big joke of cosmic proportions and at this moment I am its only audience member. I thought back to the conversation that I had on that fateful night with Frank when I first met him in the bar, almost humoured by how relevant it still felt, even now.

I concluded that through acceptance, we could have transcended the boundaries of our mortality and become more than we ever ought to have been. There is, and cannot be, anything more marvellous than that. Whilst sitting before the old world and what is to be that of the new, I am humbly reminded of what I am - distant stardust. Simultaneously, I am everything and I am nothing. That is just how it is and that is the way it always will be. How silly, how beautiful and how tragic it is.

CHAPTER X - STAND A LITTLE OUT MY SUN

As my thoughts continued to wander without resolve, it was then I noticed something whilst on the hill's peak. On the ground below, just a few streets over from the opposing entrance to the one I had come through, I began to see a few figures moving. Normally, it would never have been noticeable but everything was so still it was impossible not to. I doubted what I saw at first but after a minute or two it was clear - a group of shadowy figures traversing across the street in a lethargic manner, seemingly looking for something. As I focused, I began to hear the faintest sound of voices fade in. They were sporadic but abnormal enough that they stood out. The figures must have been heading in my direction as they got ever so slightly louder over time. I had my suspicions at first and after watching and listening for long enough I could be sure that it was the crazies. A rage came over me that was hard to describe - I never thought that I would see them again, let alone have them practically stumble upon me. After all the monstrosities they had committed, including what they did to Frank and Hera, they still just ambled around like nothing was awry, as if they were not accountable for any of their sins. They must have felt like they were God, like they were untouchable. Someone had to do something and it seemed that no one other than me was going to be forthcoming. I heard Frank's voice in my head as it reread the final line of his note over and over;

'Send him to hell for me, I will see him down there. Send him to hell for me, I will see him down there.' There was no doubt in my mind that I needed to kill not only the Cyclops but all of them. If not just for Frank, but for everyone else they had brutalised and failing this, to balance out their callous effects on this world and tip it in the favour of the righteous.

Without considering any further, I ran down the far side of the hill along the path which was similar to the one from earlier and towards the bottom of it. It was probably over two hundred feet, but I could be almost sure I ran it in seconds. Before I knew it, I was at the bottom and had reached the gated perimeter which separated the park from the street. Over on this side, the gated fence was not only closed but bolted shut, for a reason I could not understand. I tried to pry it loose but I had no chance. However, I noticed that over by the side of the fence, hidden somewhat beneath some bushes, was a set of tools in a ragged bag. I searched through it, looking for a weapon, and managed to find a foot-long thick metal wrench. It was swamped in rust, so much so not of the mechanisms worked but it was sure to pack a fierce blow. I put it in the back of my waistband and vaulted over the fence which led back onto the street.

Not more than a second had passed from when I placed my foot back onto the concrete I felt completely lost as if all my sense of direction had vacated and I could barely visualise my own position compared to the surrounding area. I was frustrated that I had not kept a better bearing of the bandits' location when I could see them from above. It made me wonder if they had all seen me as I sprinted down the hill and were preparing at that very time. It seemed unlikely as I was so far away, but the silhouette of a human, albeit distant and vague, was a rare commodity and it was one that the crazies traded in.

The adrenaline at this point was much too overpowering and it rendered all of my capability for rational thought useless. The more I stood still and thought about what I was to do, the more it felt like a terrible idea and the weaker I felt. I tried to shake this sensation off and without thinking about such things any longer, I ran to the end of the street that I had arrived at, then around the corner of that one, then through an alleyway, trying to picture where I was and where I was going to end up as I went. It seemed that I ran a great deal of distance but did not really get anywhere although a sense of vigour and strength had instilled itself within me. I felt as though I could have just continued running forever and I was certain that nothing was going to stop me from finding them. It was prominent at this point that my need for vengeance had become dire and the concern for my own fate nil. It seemed that in hindsight, my tactic was that if I covered enough ground and made enough noise in doing so, I must at some point encounter the group that I was looking for. After all, they were hunters themselves and no doubt had the sole purpose of finding someone or something that they could eat. The irony would have it that perhaps it would be easier to find a hunter if you were actively fleeing them as opposed to pursuing them. Nevertheless, all of these more cogent thoughts were not ones I had the luxury of at this fleeting moment in time.

I had reached the end of the alleyway and turned left onto a wide main road. There were two lanes for traffic here, including islands and bollards in the middle of the street and shops that used to be scattered along it. It was before I even had the time to look around that I could hear the distorted sounds of the crazies emanating from the distance. They were loud, distorted voices. The dialects were most peculiar. The sounds were more akin to barbaric, animalistic grunts rather than well-enunciated words and phrases. The noises were just as I remembered them sounding the last time and once you heard the crazies you could be sure that you would not forget how they sounded. I looked around but could not initially locate them. The sounds got slowly louder but it was hard to understand the general nature of the conversation, let alone any distinguishable words. They could have been angry, sad, or ecstatic, it was impossible to tell, assuming they still had the human capacity to render such emotions. I tried to listen in case they were talking about finding me but any efforts for it were in vain.

I stood dead in the centre of the wide road and made myself as tall and wide as I could. There was enough space on either side of me for a car to pass by. The white road marking on either side of the island signalled the middle of the street and could still be made out in some places. However, the long-served disruptions to the road and lack of maintenance meant that it was an uneven surface, filled with cracks and craters and bumps of tarmac. On either side of the road was a paved curb on a higher level. To the left of me was an old convenience shop. To my right was a morgue. The road only continued straight for another fifty feet or so before it began to bend as it sloped off to the right. Not long after this bend commenced was it impossible to see any further around the corner. Then, the crazies appeared.

They caught sight of me just as they had traversed around the corner's angle enough for me to come into their peripheral view. Once they had done so, they stopped in their tracks. They became oddly still and stared at me confusedly. It took me no time at all to notice that it was there - the Cyclops, standing at the back of its pack like he was earlier. There were five of them in total but I could not tell if the rest of the descendants were the same as the ones I had previously encountered. The two at the congregation's rear were slightly taller, whereas those who stood at the front were much smaller in size. The front three looked like they were a completely different species entirely. It was only now that I was able to see them so closely and in good lighting that the horror of their appearance transcended.

They certainly were some sort of human, or something not too dissimilar from it. They wore old tattered clothing, most of which looked like something that a human from the old world would have worn. However, the garments were so ruined that the scraps of them hung loosely from the body. Most of the material looked like it had been ripped off, so much so it did not actually seem there was any point in them wearing it all. One of the crazies was wearing a grey t-shirt that was no longer anything other than ribbons of cotton. One of the others was barefooted, but his feet were shredded beyond belief; the skin pulled back or ripped off revealing the bright red tissue beneath. Some of the toes were missing, and the remaining part of the limb was battered into an unusual, club-like shape. One of them still had some sort of boot on, but this was also torn and its feet protruded through the end where a material in the flap formed. Their arms were nothing other than long, bony extensions of which they seemed to have very little control from below the shoulders. Their arms were hoisted up in an uncontrolled manner. Most of their fingers were either broken or severed. It seemed remarkable, based on what was left of their bodies, that they were even still alive, let alone functioning and seemingly pain-free. The fact they were even able to walk around and conduct themselves in their usual manner despite the endless amounts of serious injuries that they had sustained seemed impossible. And yet somehow, even though logic dictated that it would make them weaker, in my mind it made them even more frightening.

What was most disturbed, perhaps, was their faces. Their features were distinctive enough, with eyes and noses and ears for the most part. However, it was the state that these features were in that caused the horror; one of the smaller crazies at the front had a face that was covered in mud and dried blood, which was smeared across its lips and cheeks, so much so it was hard to see anything below it. One of the others was missing its nose and instead had a wide, torrid crater in its face where features once presumably lay. It looked like a bear had pulled the facial skin from it and in the crater beneath a greenish sort of puss had formed, no doubt from an infection that it had sustained. All of their eyes possessed an almost entirely colourless shade as if they had been blinded in some way a long time ago by some kind of bleach or poison. It was clear that this was the status quo for them as none of the crazies seemed even slightly concerned about the worsening state of the next.

All they seemed preoccupied with was me - their next meal. At least, I assumed they were infatuated with my presence because they were hungry. However, there was nothing to suggest that this was the reason, perhaps they just loved to kill. I almost felt an intrusive sense of empathy as it was clear that whatever nutrition was sustaining them was something that they had not eaten in a while. This was self-explanatory enough; there certainly were not any more corpses readily available that had not already begun to rot. Aside from the odd badger or fox or where lucky, a deer, it did not seem to be much of a landscape for a carnivore. The thought occurred to me that had I not pursued them, the likelihood is they would have died very soon of their own accord regardless. This was a conflicting thought because a part of me wanted them to suffer at my own hands, but another part of me was not convinced that putting my life at risk was worth it.

I could also now better see the Cyclops, and more specifically, its face, which was as repulsive, if not more so, than those of its followers. The deformed eye socket in its heavily scarred face looked as though the missing eye was torn from its head by something with superhuman strength. It was hard to imagine exactly what had the power or the will to do this to it. A ghastly, thick scar started in the middle of his forehead and extended down past his eye and to the corner of his cheek. Although this was greatly apparent earlier, it too struck me how tall the being was, especially when exacerbated by the shortness of the hunch-backed freaks before it.

It was once again discernible that it was, in some capacity, the leader of the group, for it appeared calm and composed like a military general. The creature stood straight, with its shoulders back and head held high. Unlike the rest of the crazies, it did not react when the group first caught sight of me.

For a while, the Cyclops stared at me through the sharpness of its one remaining eyeball, whilst those in front fidgeted and bounced around on the spot in barbaric amusement as if it were Christmas day itself, just like they had done before. It was hard to tell if they recognised me from before but I doubted they had the capability. They circled around each other, hunching over and traipsing their hands on the gravel as they groaned and shrieked enthusiastically. There was a noticeable amount of arrogance, or perhaps mere stupidity, in their actions - a definitive lack of rational and tactical thought. They celebrated their finding of me as if I had already laid down and surrendered myself to them. Most of them were not even looking at me whilst they bounced around excitedly. For all they knew, I could have fled on the spot and it seemed highly unlikely they would have been able to catch me given all of their physical ailments. Likewise, they did not seem to even consider the possibility that I was going to fight back against them, let alone be victorious. This only sought to make me more angry; their disillusion about finding me was clearly based on the history of interactions with humans, most of which probably ended with them crying and pleading for their life, only for this group of monsters to devour them anyhow. This was not going to be the case this time. I did not care if they killed me, I did not care if they ripped me apart. I was going to challenge them; I was going to remind them that they are ordinary mortal beings subject to death and suffering like the rest. The decision was made in my mind, as clear as any decision that I had ever made; I was going to put the fear of God in them. I pulled the wrench from my waistband and gripped it tightly in my right hand.

'Fresh blood', the front of the pack grunted before another repeated it, only in a more giddy and child-like manner. They continued to bounce around on the spot excitedly like an ape does when you dangle a banana in front of it. The thing spoke in such a disturbing way it suggested the motor-skills needed to speak were rapidly evading it. The utterance was more like an impulse rather than the vocalisation of conscience thought, like they were unable to control what they were saying. It seemed the ability to be rational, to think of their own accord, had long since retired from their being.

'Blood, fresh blood... Human blood' another grunted to itself whilst sniffing vigorously. It looked at the cyclops as if it was seeking approval. It was plain that they were obedient and did not act without its approval. Still, the Cyclops did not shudder. It appeared as though it was assessing me as a foe and although the others did not seem to care, the Cyclops was tactile and proficient. My fist clenched involuntarily and sweat began to seep from its pores. My wrath began to subside and a fearfulness began to take its place as I fought against my own emotions. The first of the crazies, who stood at the front of the pack, abandoned its more upright pose and leaned forward on its arms ready to attack. It looked up at the Cyclops from its position, which was as if it were to begin an Olympic sprint, and it nodded subtly at it.

No time at all passed before it charged at me whilst the others watched on attentively. My first thought was that it was uncanny how only one charged at me as opposed to the entire group, which would have made my position much more difficult. It almost felt as though I was a gladiator in a ring as individual opponents got sent out one by one to see who would reign victorious. It made some sort of noise that appeared to be a battle cry, as it fought its way uncomfortably toward me. It ran at me on all fours, grunting aggressively as it exerted, clearly expressing difficulty at the physical strain but convicted enough to brush it aside. The thing's body seemed like it was beginning to adapt to its newfound mode of travel but not so much as to be convincing. It propped itself up on its bloodied hands and used them to propel itself as its legs kicked out from under it. However, it did not seem as though the rest of the body, including its legs and shoulders and neck, was fully aligned so that it could operate with a proficient sense of unison. This resulted in a clumsy and ineffective movement.

As it approached, it began to adopt a more upright posture, seemingly so it could wrap its arms around me in a hugging sort of fashion. It yelped viciously before lunging and attempting to clasp me with open arms. It was a predictable move and easily avoided, mainly on account of the fact that it moved so sluggishly and began its attack from such a distance. I swiftly stepped to one side, cautious to make sure I did not trip over the curb, in order to avoid it at the last (and most optimal) second. The crazie missed me completely and stumbled clumsily to my left-hand side. Unbalanced and in the process of rising to its feet, it turned back around to face me, seemingly quite surprised at how easily I had just evaded the ambush, which was ironic because I too was surprised. I caught a glimpse of its unsightly face for a moment, which gave me enough time to decide where I was going to aim. I clung to the wrench in my right hand that I had equipped earlier and fiercely swung it in the area of its face, just as it had rotated to be facing me head-on. I thrusted the weapon with all my might and yet it was so long and heavy that its weight seemed to carry the force itself. Indeed, I put so much effort into the movement it felt as though the wrench was going to carry me forward with it. I just about caught sight of its hideous eyeballs as they made contact with my own. With a dull, almost anticlimactic thud, the wrench hit its lower chin area just as I had fully extended my arm. The force of impact vibrated the wrench violently in my hand, almost to the point where I was unable to hold it any longer. After this initial thud, the wrench continued to convert its momentum to no resistance. Its chin and jaw area shattered into a bloodied mess and spread across the street to the sound of a gentle wail. Teeth scattered the floor alongside a clump of mashed bone and muscle. The crazie, missing the lower half of its face as what remained of its now opened jaw protruded from its head, collapsed to the floor, seemingly still conscious. Once it had landed, its hands attempted to seize what was left of its face seemingly in an attempt to hold it all together. From where the chin begins just below the bottom of the earlobe, the entirety of its lower countenance had been obliterated. Its tongue, no longer having a place to reside, obtruded out of its mouth area and stretched all the way down below its chin. Lumps of dislodged tendon and bone and muscle seeped out of its head and down onto its upper chest area. A pool of blood began to form on the ground below as it gushed from its wounds and dripped down its neck and face. It began to writhe and fidget in pain as cups full of thick blood then began to spew from its throat. It made a grim gurgling sound, followed by a dire choaking one, seemingly as its body tried to breathe through all the tissue it had inadvertently swallowed. After a while, I saw its eyes roll to the back of its head and come down once again before its final agonising breath vacated.

Mortified at what had just occurred, and more so at what I was capable of, I turned my gaze to the rest of the group who looked on impassively. Adrenaline was coursing through my veins at such a rate it felt as though my brain had its own heartbeat. One of the smaller crazies which too stood at the front quickly pivoted on the spot from which stood and began to sprint in the opposing direction. It continued onwards until it had disappeared back around the corner from which it had emerged, chanting an illegible noise of panic as it went. The rest of the crazies who remained had become noticeably less animate and looked up at the Cyclops, seemingly in anguish, awaiting for their concern to be rectified or dismissed. As for the Cyclops, it continued to peer at me with the same blank expression and did not seem even remotely concerned having witnessed me decimate one of its followers. Rather, it seemed like it was accepting of the provocation. The remaining crazies eventually continued to circle around each other with growing intensity. Seemingly aware that its actions were dictating of their strategy, it spoke:

'I smell fear upon you, I detected that erotic stench from around the corner.' The Cyclop's voice rang out. It was deep yet hazy. It became clear to me exactly what the crucial dissimilarity between it and the rest of the cohort was; the Cyclops was conscientious. Most importantly and perhaps most concerningly, it was right; I was terrified. 'A creature like you should not be on these streets. Feeble, weak, emotional. This is our world now, ours to take from and do with as we please. There is no one to tell us what we must or cannot do. Your kind belongs in your home, where you should have stayed.' He continued in the same tone.

'You and your minions killed one of my friends. You killed his daughter, too. They were inside their own home, they never once wandered into this wasteland and yet you still killed them, no doubt without hesitation or remorse,' I said shakily despite my efforts to not sound so. I was not entirely convinced that replying was the right thing to do but I simply could not help myself. Furthermore, my response seemed to satisfy the beast somehow, as if it played into its generalship.

'I have killed many friends and many daughters. Your sentimentality and pathetic notions of vengeance aid you none. We are not in the old world, we are not bound by anything, least of all you. Animals roam the streets now, and animals hunt. No one and nothing, including you, is an exception.'

'We are all hungry, the rest of us do not do as you do. You are not an animal, you are as human as me. Your rationalisation is as pathetic as it is insincere. What is more important, I came here to stop you, and stop you I will, on God I swear it.' For the first time, the Cyclops smiled.

'Poor human, that is where you are wrong. I do not hunt so I can eat. Only these minions before me pull the scraps from the corpses.'

'Then why do you do it?'

'Because I love to watch the life drift from their eyes as I pull their hearts out. Because I love to listen to them beg and plead and whimper as they cry and shiver.'

'So you do it because you enjoy it?'

'No, I do it because I can.'

This time, two of the remaining crazies ran toward me at the same time although one was slightly behind the other. They wailed and screamed as they approached. The crazie at the front also moved in the same gorilla-like fashion but was much quicker. Its technique was more refined and it was clear that he wasted less energy moving this way. As the first one approached me, I took a step back to compensate for the speed it was moving, only to realise that it was not long enough. Once more, I swung the wrench, now dripping in blood, towards the oncoming attacker. As my arm had become almost parallel to me, the crazie had already grabbed it. In doing so, it used its other arm to hit me with a closed fist. The force was so surprisingly strong that it knocked me over to the ground and as I fell, the crazie landed on top of me and pulled the wrench out of my hand. It strategically landed with its right knee placed directly onto my abdomen, with its other knee on the concrete next to me. Its body was positioned slightly over to my right for reasons I did not immediately understand. All the while this happened, it did not let go of my right arm and I felt it grip my right wrist with stark power. It took me a second to come to terms with exactly what had happened. However, I did so just in time to watch the crazie tear a piece of my right bicep out with its jagged, yellow teeth. Then, I began to feel the force of the other crazie who was pinning my legs down with its arms. It then proceeded to pull a small chunk of my calve out with its mouth. As I observed, paralyzed in fear, the immediate force that was pushing down on me seemed to render me helpless. It was only when the first crazie began to slowly pull away, with a sizeable chunk of my arm in its mouth, that I felt the abhorrent burn as the tendon was pulled away from the muscle. At the same time, I continued to violently kick and flail my legs, trying to force the one below me from its position. Instinctively, I picked my left shoulder off the floor in a swift motion and threw a punch towards the crazie's mouth that sat on top of me, which seemed temporarily distracted by the piece of fresh meat it had in its mouth. I made solid contact with its chin and it tumbled over to the floor on my right, taking the contents in its mouth with it.

As the crazie on top of me fell to the floor in both pain and shock, I managed to use my uninjured leg to repeatedly kick the other one from its position as it clung onto my legs, trying to take another bite as I writhed. I kicked it several times to little avail until eventually I used a forward prodding motion that seemed to knock the air out of its lungs. Disorientated, it fell onto its backside and began to slither away from me as it clung to its upper chest. Having wounded them both, I managed to work my way onto my feet, albeit dumfounded, with blood dripping down my arm and my legs and a sharp pain shot throughout my body.

The crazie I had punched was still on its hand and knees to my side, cradling its chin and shaking its head as if it were trying to fight off the affliction, even though it did not feel like I had inflicted that much force upon it. The crazie that I had kicked also rose to its feet relatively quickly and looked at me with fierce rage. It still had my blood and muscle dripping down its chin as it stood directly opposite me. It glared at me and caterwauled in a high-pitched tone before charging at me once more.

I held out my hands and placed them flat on its chest. It swung both arms at me in a windmill fashion, around either side of my arms, whilst attempting to bite and continuing to scream furiously as I pinned it back. It proceeded to push back against me and no matter how much I resisted, its strength was overpowering and it succeeded; I was forced to take numerous, clumsy steps backwards in order to compensate for the fact it was almost breaking my defence. Eventually, I slipped over a ridge in the perturbed road and fell over once more.

The crazie landed on top of me and I grabbed its shoulders as it attempted to push against my outstretched arms with its face, seemingly in an attempt to rip my nose or anything it could manage to get a hold of off with its teeth. It thrusted down harder and further still until it was so close to me that saliva flew from its mouth and snot began to drip onto my face. It bit and snapped ferociously using an open mouth and bringing it crashing down time after time. I could see its bright green and yellow gums and teeth in snippets as pieces of blood and mucus flew out of its mouth.

In a desperate attempt to gain an advantage, I abandoned my two-handed grasp and propped it up against my forearm using the strength of my elbow and forearm so that I could search for something on the floor next to me. I rubbed my hand over every patch of concrete that I was able to reach but I found nothing. As my weaker stance began to give way, the crazie got closer to me still. It had shifted its body position further up my torso to gain more leverage and leant down over me more directly. As I glimpsed up into its merciless eyes, I saw a small, refracted reflection of my cowardice as I lay helpless on the floor, physically impeded and unable to retaliate. Just like earlier, I could hear my father's voice begin to echo inside my head.

'What the fuck are you waiting for! Go for its eyes, hit it where it hurts. It is going to kill you. Do it *now*!'

It seemed like this was the only possible option, and as horrid as it was, I placed both open hands on its cheeks, with my forefingers gripping over its ears and my thumb either side of its eyes. During the time it took for me to adjust my hand position, the crazie had managed to get just an inch or two from my face. I was able to barely hold it off by grabbing its head in the palm of my hands. I propped my thumbs backwards slightly and just as it was about to reach my nose with its mouth, plunged my thumbs as harshly and deeply as I could into its eyeballs. At first, they were met with a more dense resistance than I had anticipated. However, this did not last long. I only needed to apply a bit more pressure and it felt as though they had popped. My fingers proceeded many inches further into the sockets of the eye as a soupy clump of mush began to form and spilt out from its face and onto mine. I continued onwards until I could feel the skull behind it. The crazie shrieked the most horrendous shriek that I ever could dare to hear. It was so loud and blood-curdling I almost felt the compulsion to stop. I yanked the thumbs out of the sockets and a series of blood and a further amount of tissue fell onto my face.

It quickly got off me as it wretched in agony and clung to its face. There was no doubt that it was blinded as it stumbled the course of the road in a lumbered zig-zag fashion, yelping and screaming and flailing his arms in every direction. It turned back at one point and its colourless eyes that I earlier saw had been replaced by dark holes from which blood streamed out. I rose once more back to my feet which I was grateful for as at one point I did not think I would get the chance again.

When I felt confident that the blinded crazie was no longer a threat after watching it wander aimlessly in the dusk light, I retrieved my wrench from the floor. I walked back over to the weaker crazie from before who had put up not one ounce of fight since. The entire time that I had fought with its comrade, from the second time it knocked me down to when I blinded it, it had remained on the floor, wheezing and panting pathetically as if it had some kind of underlying ailment that I had exposed. Even I was shocked at how much cowardice and frailty it displayed, especially given that it was no doubt an experienced killer. I walked over to it impassively. I felt dizzy and lightheaded but my focus remained. The strange part was that it did not even appear to pay much attention to me, it seemed completely self-absorbed and bemused by its own suffering. It did look up at me at one point but did not seem to give me much mind. It proceeded to roll over onto its back and looked up helplessly towards the sky, continuing to gasp for breath limply. It sounded as if it were breathing through a straw and every passing breath got increasingly more wheezy. The thing that almost made me shed the slightest oddment of sympathy was that it seemed that it had accepted that it was going to die and was attempting to find a comfortable position to do so. I spread my feet to a wide position wits its body in between. I hauled the wrench high above my head with both hands and brought it crashing down on the crazies skull. The force that I achieved in doing so was tremendous, so much so it shattered into what seemed like a million pieces and in the same movement the wrench proceeded to make contact with the floor. Pieces of skull and bone and flesh sprayed themselves for yards around. The breathing ceased and its arms and legs became inanimate.

For a moment, I was so engulfed by watching a sequence of brain matter pour through the hole I just created that I forgot that the now insensate crazie was not the last one and that the ordeal was not yet over. After a brief inventory of the chunks that were missing from my body, and having taken a moment to wipe the liquified remains of eyeballs from my face, I looked back at the one which I had blinded. What I saw bemused me - the crazie had retired from its frenzied flailing and instead, began to walk slowly back over to the cyclops in a rather composed manner. It seemed as though the pain had subsided and an unsettling level of calm had come over it as if to suggest it was in the final stages of dying. The Cyclops had still not moved since it first arrived many minutes before. It had seemingly watched the entire event with an inscrutable look. Something made me feel as though it foresaw that this was going to happen. The crazie made an odd series of sounds akin to a soft cry, almost as if it were pleading for help, like a toddler approaching its parent after banging its head on something rigid.

As it arrived in front of the cyclops, it bent down onto its knees, looked down at the floor and continued the same weak, pleading noises at a greater volume. It was a disturbing thing to watch and what made it worse was trying to establish exactly how the crazie knew where it was. The crazie wrapped its arms slowly around the Cyclop's legs as it knelt down on the floor. The Cyclops looked down upon it without changing its facial expression. It watched on for a second before bending down swiftly, grabbing the crazie from the armpits and hauling it high into the air. It did so with such speed and power it was dumbfounding. The crazie's legs were a foot or two above the ground and they swung back and forth fiercely in rebellion, apparently in complete disarray that it was still to be subjected to further pain. This carried on for many seconds and the Cyclops did nothing other than stare at it disapprovingly. None of the motions that the crazie made had any effect and it proceeded to hold it there without difficulty or expression. The Cyclops swiftly removed one of its hands from the crazies armpit and before it became imbalanced in its grasp, the Cyclops gripped it by the throat with its other hand. As it did so, its legs began to kick at a lot slower rate. It was clear based on the crazie's reaction alone that it was grabbing it with a tremendous amount of might.

'For too long you have traipsed along with me. I have fed you, I have cared for you like you were one of my own, and you have followed me around living from my scraps and taking all that you can. And yet this is how you repay me? With weakness and cowardice? I have trained you like a warrior, and in the first battle you encounter you weep like a craven. You do not even have the good dignity to die well... So be it.' It said promptly, without any inclination of emotion. The cyclops' forearm appeared to tense as it grasped at the crazie's throat with increased conviction. It let out a weak, winded squeal as the Cyclops continued to increase the pressure to the point where the crazie slowly stopped resisting. It let go of its armpit with the other arm and placed this hand around its throat too. Having realised that it was to die, the crazie seemed to have some form of adrenaline-fueled response that came from within, as if it were a final attempt at surviving the ordeal. It flailed its arms around violently, apparently in an attempt to grab the Cyclop's face and push it away. It slapped the beast's head, pushed fingers into its remaining eye, and up its nose, similarly to how I had just struggled under the crazies grasp just moments before. All of its efforts were futile and eventually, a loud cracking sound rang out as the Cyclops viciously snapped its neck over to one side. Following this noise, the crazie's feet became instantaneously motionless. It hung there lifelessly in its grasp for a few seconds more before the cyclops launched it over to the other side of the road. It rolled over once or twice before remaining still.

The Cyclops looked back up at me and we stood directly opposing each other as if we were about to duel. 'I am impressed.' It eventually spoke. 'It has been long since I have faced a worthy adversary.'

'Is that what you do to your followers, is it? Snap their necks when they get injured?' I replied, unsure what else to say but trying to postpone the inevitable.

'It had surpassed any of its use, I was doing it a favour.' Things went silent for a few seconds before it produced a bladed article in its hand. It seemed like some sort of hand-crafted shiv, with a small wooden handle and a large yet randomly shaped piece of dull metal, which indicated that the Cyclops indeed thought of me as a better opponent than he wanted to admit. 'Are you ready?' It asked.

'I am'. It was at this point the Cyclops began to charge at me. It was far bigger, faster, and better adapted. Rather than the gorilla-like walk of its followers, the cyclops moved just like a human would only in a more bulky and robust fashion. The beast marched slowly over to me which surprisingly was much more intimidating that the quicker approach of the crazies. The distance that it managed to cover even when walking at this speed was impressive and it arrived in front of me in what felt like an instant. I once again attempted to swing the wrench, still dripping in blood, in the Cyclop's direction. I could not be sure my technique was that effective and in all likelihood, it was a slow and energy-consuming movement but as it had worked before I decided to hedge my bets. I had to adjust the angle at which I stood and threw the blow as it was much taller than not only the crazies but also myself. As I swung the wrench towards it, the Cyclops instantaneously raised its arm and grabbed my wrist. My attack was plucked out of the air as if I had swung it in slow motion or disclosed prior exactly what I was going to do. The Cyclops grappled strongly onto my arm for a moment and looked at me with a sardonic grin. I used my left arm, which was at this point free, to hook the beast's jaw. On impact, its head moved only slightly and it did not seem to cause it any harm. In fact, I was quite sure that the punch had broken one of my own knuckles. It smiled at me as if to humour my attempt, before proceeding to sink the blade that it held in its free hand deep into my abdomen, around the area of my belly button. At first, I did not feel any sharpness nor did I feel it penetrate my body. All I felt was the dull yet fierce impact as it drove the blade into me and the strength with which it did so was remarkable. The puncture stole the wind straight from my lungs and I gasped in agony as my body tried to make sense of the foreign article that had just infiltrated it. After taking some pleasure in the pain it had inflicted, the beast slowly began to twist the blade. In doing so, the agonising, sharp and burning-hot sensation of the knife inside of me began to seep from the point of impact further around my lower torso. I grabbed hold of the Cyclop's wrist with my left hand in an attempt to stop the twisting motion but I was not strong enough. The only thing that I could think about was how to make it end and in doing so, I remembered something; it was the sharp piece of wood from the stool that had been in my pocket the entire time. It was so small and light that I had forgotten about it entirely. It was hard to know how my brain had managed to remember something so random, maybe it was a survival instinct or a signal from my brain that I was not yet ready to die. I released my hand from its wrist and dug around in my pocket looking to find it. Having released the pressure on its lower arm, the beast was able to twist the knife further still on account of having no resistance and the excruciating pain intensified further. I could sense in the Cyclop's movement that it knew something was awry as it tried to figure out exactly why I had let go of its arm. Just as it had rotated the blade around ninety degrees and so much so I could no longer give it the free reign to continue, I found the piece of wood and pulled it from my pocket. It happened to have the sharp end pointing downwards, meaning no adjustment was required. As I withdrew it, the Cyclops noticed at the last second and the smug look quickly vanished from its face. I plunged the sharp end into its lower neck, using all the might I could muster from my frail body. The Cyclops did not even flinch at the impact initially. After a few moments, it took its hand off the knife and took a few awkward steps away from me. I too stumbled backwards in sheer relief. The Cyclops looked at me in surprise before feeling around for the piece of wood protruding from its neck. It was the first time that it had displayed any level of emotion. The piece of wood had gone through the Cyclop's neck at an upwards angle, most likely on account of it being taller than me. Apparently, the wood had gone through its neck and penetrated the underside of its chin before coming out in the mouth. The Cyclops grabbed the wood firmly with its right arm and proceeded to briskly pull it out with a suppressed grunt. As it did so, a thick trickle of blood poured out of the hole that was now present. It threw the piece of wood onto the floor before spitting out a clump of flesh and a tooth or two valiantly. As the blood continued to pour out, a wave of shock seemed to descend over the monster and its range of outward emotions progressed from shock to what seemed like rage. The Cyclops cupped the wound with its hand and with a deep, almost sentimental tone, looked up at me and said 'No.' It was only then I remembered I too had been injured and looked down to see the blade protruding from my stomach, which shimmied slightly back and forth in the hole it had created as I breathed in and out. I made the decision not to touch nor remove it in case I bled out before I had the chance to kill it.

The Cyclops, which had let out a gigantic roar and proceeded to rush at me once more. This time, however, it did not march composedly like it earlier had but rather sprinted. I felt weak and dejected, so much so that I did not think I had the capability to fight back once more. Before I had been able to decide what to do or how to do it, the Cyclops was before me. Instead of grabbing me like before, it used open palms to push me in the chest. It did so with such vigour that I left the ground entirely as I was tossed into the air. I landed back first and the hard floor knocked the wind from my lungs. I looked up into the sky defeatedly and caught a glimpse of the clouds before the Cyclop's blood covered face and body appeared over me. It straddled me like a donkey and the blood from its injury continued to spew sporadically outwards like a leaking watering hose, covering myself and the floor around me. It grabbed me with one hand by my neck and pulled my head upwards, so much so that I was only inches away from its grievous face.

'You think you can kill me?' It hissed with venom and contempt through gritted teeth as blood began to seep around the gaps in between them. Its one remaining eye bulging from its unshapely head. It was allegedly more annoyed at the fact that it was to be me which was to kill it than it was at the fact it was going to die at all.

It grabbed my head by either side, lifted it from the pavement and plummeted back down onto it before continuing the process over and over again, yelling and screaming all the while. 'No, no, no! not *YOU*! This, cannot, be!' It bellowed sporadically between blows. As my head continued to make contact with the pavement, I felt the back of my skull seemingly turning to mush as my vision became blurred and impacted and everything started to appear fuzzy and almost unreal. Just as I was about to either pass out or die, the Cyclops let go of my head and leant over the top of me in exhaustion, placing its hand on the floor on either side of my head as it panted and groaned as it gasped for breath.

At this point, the Cyclops was sat on my lower torso, just below the knife which it seemed to have forgotten about in its frustration. In one smooth and powerful motion, I used all of what I had left to use both of my legs and heave it up and over me. To my surprise, the Cyclops was lifted into the air and collapsed over on the floor beside me with little resistance. There could be no doubt that its strength had dwindled and its injury was beginning to best it.

I managed to bring myself to my feet, although I could not be sure exactly how. I was so dizzy that it was hard to stand up at all and I could feel blood dripping down the front of my body and the back of my neck. My body felt weak and ailments of all kinds riddled me. I walked a few paces further down and picked up the wrench for the final time. I turned back to face the Cyclops, who was still on all fours panting. The blood from its neck was continuing to seep and what seemed like buckets full spilt over the floor.

I wandered back over to it and used the top of my foot to roll it onto its back. It followed the motion of my foot and toppled over with minimal force. The Cyclops lay in a starfish position on its back, looking upwards. As I looked down upon it, it began to laugh. At first, it was just a slightly audible giggle but after a while it was in hysterics, laughing in a way only the mad know, as if someone inside its head had told a joke. I put one foot over the far side of its body and the other standing foot remained on the other so that it was laid in front of me. My position caused a blockage to the light from the sun and yet still, the shadowy monster continued to laugh at me. After I had stared at it for a while it did something quite peculiar, it once more turned itself back onto all fours and began to crawl away from me slowly as if it were trying to escape. It was quite remarkable that it was still breathing let alone able to move given that it had lost many litres of blood at this point. As it crawled back towards the way it came, I walked behind it at the same pace befuddled. It seemed as though it were trying to work up the strength to get back onto its feet. One thing that I could not fault it for was its determination.

'What are you waiting for?' It gargled through the blood that was filling its mouth and being spat out in small spots over the floor as it spoke. In one motion, I lifted the wrench high above my head and brought it down with all my might. It landed somewhere in the lower middle part of its back. The wrench caused a muffled and bathetic thud but alongside it a light cracking sound emanated and it shrieked a bloodcurdling scream of agony. It yowled once more as I landed another blow on its upper back. It proceeded to convulse and jerk in anguish as much as its body would allow and in doing so rolled over onto its back. All the composure that it had earlier displayed as the brave commandeering officer of the unit had vanished and the once legendary Cyclops was reduced to a suffering, mortal mess.

At this point, there was no doubt in my mind that the beast's back had been shattered as it lay there in paralyzed destitution. It continued to twist and convulse slightly but was far less animated and its legs ceased to move long before the upper of its body did. It looked up at me vacantly with its remaining eye, as if it was trying to intimidate me, but it was impossible to tell exactly what the look's purpose was. Whatever the intention, it certainly was not a look of remorse or regret. I clasped the wrench in both hands, lifted it as far above my head as I could manage and brought it crashing down once more onto its head. I made contact so fiercely that the wrench shattered the top of the skull and sank deep into its brain matter. Its skull almost split in half. I pulled as hard as I could once more and removed the wrench from the boney mess. It had entered its skull around the centre of its forehead and cracked it open like an egg. A laceration went all the went down from the very top of its head and down to its eyebrow. If I had placed my fingers in the crack and pulled horizontally I think I could have split the beast's head into two. Just as I had heaved the wrench above me once more for the second blow, the Cyclops spoke;

'Is that all?' It whispered insidiously below its breath before letting out another wild cackle, somehow still able to vocalize as its brain leaked through the large opening in its cranium and blood filled its lungs. I stared upon the beast and brought the wrench crashing down once more. I caught a final, solitary glimpse of the Cyclops' remaining eye before the wrench made contact with the facial area, shattering all the structure and bone content from the upper lip to the top of its head. The wrench went through its skull entirely, hit the floor beneath it and ricocheted back up slightly, along with the latter half of the tool that had been shattered to pieces. Coils and springs and small parts of metal sprayed around the vicinity along with grisly pieces of tissue. All that remained was a mangled, bloodied mess. It was intact from the neck upwards but any part of its head that was above the chin had been transformed into a large gobbet of matter. Bone and tissue sank from the outskirts of the crater and fell into the centre before piling up and covering up the view of the pavement beneath it. Its arms and shoulders fidgeted uncontrollably for a short while. Soon after this, a weak sigh sounded and it went limp.

I rose once more to my feet, panting, delirious with exhaustion and adrenaline. I wandered a few steps over to the side of the street before it hit me – a piercing pain ascended its way through the side of my body. I looked down at the blade protruding from my abdomen and with it, blood streamed down my side. For the past few seconds, the sense of elation from my victory had prevented me from thinking about it at all. I grabbed hold of the flimsy wooden handle and yanked the blade from within me. It was painful as all hell but I do recall feeling a release of pressure that was somewhat satisfying. I sat there and tried to withdraw from the pain, to drift off somewhere in my subconscious. The agony grew and things began to grow blurry. Still, I could not stop thinking about the Cyclops. What bothered me the most was that ultimately, I cannot be sure that my need for vengeance had been satisfied as I drifted into an emotional void. I believe this was because, in whole or in part, the fact remained that the Cyclops, for all it did and was, died laughing.

CHAPTER XI - ALL I ASK

Some time passed when I eventually came back to consciousness and I was quite surprised that I managed to at all. I do not remember entering the sensation of passing out nor do I remember anything immediately before this happened. A horrid panic became instilled, similar to how it does when you oversleep from a short nap and miss an event. I sat up from my laid-down position with a thick head, and even such a minor movement was greatly arduous. It felt as though where my brain interpreted it to be was a few seconds delayed compared to where my head actually was. Everything around me was blurred and disorientating, so much so it took me seconds to recall exactly what had happened and what led me to be laid out in the street for the second time today. The first thing I did when I was able to focus my vision was assess the wound I had sustained. A keen and fierce pain swiftly reminded me of its existence. I lifted up my top which was soaked in blood but appeared to have reached the point where some of it was drying. I tried to inform myself that this was positive. The source of the injury could easily be ascertained. It was in the lower left side of my abdomen, a few inches down and a few inches left from my belly button. There was so much blood surrounding it, most of which had solidified in thick clumps, that it was hard to tell how deep or serious it was, but a large gash was prevalent and it did not appear the least bit pleasant. One thing I did notice was that when I inhaled and exhaled, the wound began to expand slightly and as it did more blood oozed from it. It was from seeing this that I realised how serious it was. I put my top back down and took a deep breath. Surprisingly, I was not in great pain at this moment and a sense of calm took its place. I did not feel panicked or scared. I almost felt a sense of satisfaction at finally knowing the conclusion to my story, something which I had spent a great deal of time over the years pondering about, none of which envisaged it would have been amidst such a blaze.

As I started to retrace the steps in my mind of what happened, I looked around the street. Only a few feet over from me was the body of a crazie, and not far from this one was another corpse. They had not moved since I had fought with them earlier which made it clear that they were indeed dead, something that I was not entirely sure of before I lost consciousness. They were scattered inanimately over the spread of the street and most were surrounded by chunks of flesh and bone and pools of blood. Looking at each of their injuries helped jog my memory of how the fight occurred. It was hard to believe that it had actually happened and that it was not just a figment of my imagination. I never thought I had it in me to battle in the way I did, let alone kill, but with the right motivation or lack of it, I came to the conclusion that humans are capable of extremes well beyond the parameters of what we would normally expect of ourselves. If in the old world someone would have told me this was to happen, I would have denied it possible to the death. And yet, here I was, like the final gladiator in the auditorium, albeit without any audience, surrounded by those who had become deceased by my own hand. I almost related, to some degree. what the Cyclops meant (or so I construed) about killing for power. I did not take this sensation gratuitously from the act itself, but rather from being capable of the effectual aftermath of having done it. It made me feel as though I was in control which too was something I had experienced very little of late.

The Cyclops too was still lying there on its back and facing upwards. I managed to fight through the pain it took to stand and walked over to its body. A stabbing pain did begin to present itself in my side but it was easy enough to ignore, especially by glancing around and reassuring myself that I actually got off pretty well, to which I do not suppose there would be much disagreement. It is hard to tell exactly why I wanted to look at its corpse; perhaps it was out of morbid curiosity, or perhaps I felt the need to gloat. I stood over its body and looked down upon it. Its face, or the little that was left of it, was blank and the blood in its body had clearly stopped flowing as it was pale white. A thick pool of crimson-coloured blood had materialised and I observed that blood was still slowly trickling from its open head and had flowed many feet further in line with the curvature of the street. It was hard to imagine what anyone else would think have happened had they walked across all of these corpses. If it was me, I would have been confused as to what had the power or the will to brutalize the most notorious group still left wandering. I had clearly underestimated what I was capable of doing, both physically and mentally. Even in my frail and malnourished state, I would never have backed myself to take down one of the crazies, let alone the entire group.

After having stood for many minutes by now, the pain in my abdomen slowly got worse. An occasional and acute wave shot its way from the location of the wound once again but this time it started to proceed further up my body and with it an autonomous flinch followed. What is more, I could feel the blood continue to drip from it and roll further down my lower body and down my leg. Unfortunately, I was not a doctor, so it was hard to make a prognosis, all that I could be sure of was that it fell into the remit of not good. I could not tell what was causing my calmness in the situation because no amount of thought or observation in relation to the grave injury appeared to unbalance this pacific feeling. Perhaps it was external factors such as the shock of finding Frank and Hera and the fact I had already been so close to death many times, for which it seemed I was subconsciously grateful in a way I did not fully comprehend. Perhaps the factors were internal; my hopelessness was powerful enough to undermine what should cause genuine and immediate concern. So much had happened in such a short period of time it felt beyond the remit of my consciousness to process it and its incumbent emotions properly.

* * *

The next question, and certainly the most pertinent one, was what to do next. It seemed as though I did not have much time left and this was the biggest and most likely the last decision I would have the chance to make during my lifetime. The simple restoration of power that I now had over my fate was enthralling enough regardless of the dire circumstances, so much so it felt as though it was one which overrode the simplicity of my mortality. This was not a conscious decision, rather it was the resulting effect of my varied emotions and the subsequent sense of existential realisation, whereby I was able to set aside all matters relating to my human limitedness given their insignificance in relation to the grander scale of matters that I was now exposed to. To this end, I mean that no matter how much I considered I was soon going to die and no matter how much I pondered the considerations associated with such, it did not matter because a deeper and more powerful sensation was only interested in the contrary.

Here, I tried to implement a more pragmatic thought process as time was a virtue. There was clearly no point going back home as I was now free to wander and probably had been all this time since, which only provided further motivation for an adventurous finale. Moreover, what seemed to be the largest threat on the streets had been taken care of and the final person on earth who I ever cared for was dead. The most sensible and logical thing left to do, indeed the only thing that was left to do, appeared to be spending the very little time I had left exploring what remained of the world, only in doing so could my death be more noble, having experienced all of those things available to me despite the obvious adversary I was experiencing. Although I may have been risking the chance of having a less comfortable death, I envisaged that the closure it would offer made it worthwhile and little else argued opposingly. As elaborated upon, my imminent death was not something that gave me much concern and such a feeling only grew as time went on. In fact, an odd, perhaps masculine and heroic element of my character, which had long since been oppressed, felt satisfied at the fact I was ultimately going to have died in battle; like an old warrior or a stoic man of hardened proportions. I had always envisaged that I would have taken my own life or that I would have choked on my own sick or fallen down the stairs drunk. Haven had a final showdown and having finally stood for something, I felt comforted and as though I had achieved something in a deranged sense; as if my conclusion had made my feeble life all the more honourable.

I did not deliberate over the matter any longer and I began to walk to the bottom of the street where I killed the crazies, turned left and continued onwards, leaving them to perish naturally or be mutilated by whatever wild animal wanted a meal. Should the latter be the case in any regard, it was no doubt more deserving than the crazies ever were.

There was nothing overly spectacular or interesting about the first ten or fifteen minutes. Indeed, everything looked rather similar to how I had anticipated. The houses looked the same as the ones which I could see from my windows; boarded up and decrepit but still managing to stand. Houses that had been bricked or painted over had worn so much so that they were stained the colour of moss or faded granite. Gardens were overgrown and unruly. Most of the vegetation planted by man had long since turned brown, black, or become completely ruined. Everything on the streets was all but destroyed. Bus stops had been torn down with the exception of a few rusted green seats that retained a standing position limply. Lamposts, or the ones that were recognisable anyhow, had either collapsed, titled over at a precarious angle, or were so weak that they were a mere gust of wind away from collapsing, which made it difficult to understand how they had not already. The tarmac on the roads had clearly surpassed a state whereby repair would be possible by reasonable means of maintenance. It was cracked and dried, filled with holes the size of men, or covered in bumps where the heat had made it expand and grow unshapely, making it difficult to traverse and even more grotesque to look at. Most of the road signs and markings were faded beyond recognition. There was a lot of graffiti on the walls and on some of the houses, although even some of this had begun to wane and it was clear it had been done a long time ago. Some of the signs read; 'The *crazies* are out there, stay indoors' or 'Do *not* leave: you will be shot!'. The majority of these signs were done in a somewhat more official manner as if they were done with some kind of supporting authority and professionalism. This was not particularly surprising given that both hypothetical cautions were things I could attest to having witnessed their actuality. They were often in bold letters and done relatively neatly. With some of the other writings, this did not seem the case. These read 'When will this end' and 'GOD help me'. Others read 'We cannot stay inside forever' - if only they knew, or so I thought. One of them, which looked like graffiti at first but at second glance appeared to have been written in blood said 'Death is never at a loss for *occasions*'. This one was by far the most daunting, perhaps because it was not asking for anything and expressions of such a kind are those that belong to the most desperate and depraved. Everything was eerie in a way beyond comprehension, let alone documentation, to the extent I almost felt obligated to cease doing so due to the fact that any attempt, no matter how genuine, would be wholly unrepresentative of those who knew much more of it than me. So much had happened and so much suffering had taken place, and there was nothing left to experience it viscerally; no one left to see it or take it in, aside from the meekness of my own senses. Thousands of years of evolution and development and achievement, all reduced to nothing; to ill-advised graffiti on walls and other such debauchery. I envisaged a foreign entity coming down to earth in a thousand years and walking somewhat nonchalantly in the way that I was doing now along the varied streets. If such a thing was to happen, their opinions on the human race would not be difficult to foretell. Most of the streets that I traversed in the town were similar, so much so I would not be adding anything substantial by documenting them. Even as I got more central and the grander buildings like hotels and banks were visible, these were in a familiar state. Everything contributed to, and as such blended in with the depravity of the next.

In the very centre of town, which I arrived at after a rough estimate of about half an hour, the desolation was far more apparent. The centre was marked by a large open square. It was one that I remembered only slightly from the times I had visited it in the old world. Its perimeter was supplemented with shops and banks and pubs that filled the outer lining. In the middle, a neatly cobbled square enjoyed the expanse upon which it rested, with the exception of what was once a wide fountain on the southern side. On the north-facing side, a hundred feet council house stood there still and was once the cultural and historic landmark of the town that occupied all of the pamphlets and such. A large clock sat on its highest peak, but one of the hands seemed to have been removed. It was possible that it had fallen but I saw no evidence that this was the case. Despite being the oldest building I had encountered, it was one of the better-looking ones. Its old granite architecture stood firm and maintained its dominance over the landscape with the exception of minor failings whereby small structural exposures had become decrepit and collapsed. As for the rest of the square, it was quite impressive how well it had maintained its dignity despite such a long time without any companionship that such makings so often seemed to demand.

What must be duly noted at my own behest is that there were many bodies around this area, some elderly people and some men in what seemed like official or unofficial military uniforms - at least these were the ones that first made themselves apparent to my vision from the corner of the square at which I stood. Some of them were leant over benches or scattered sporadically over the fountain or in the expanse of the square's floor. What is further, some of the corpses were unquestionably those of children or at the least, very young people. They were almost all devoured, their remains (which in were varied stages of decomposition) were open at the chests and the organs appeared to have been pulled from within with a grandiose lack of clinical precision. Most of them were missing limbs and heads although some were in such a state of degradation it was hard to envisage how what remained of them could have once formed an entire human. A lot of them were laid in bizarre positions as if they had been killed whilst running or crawling or doing something otherwise incomprehensible. Some had been there for such time that they had almost become skeletons on account of their being no skin or muscle left and no other substantial matter remained. There was a silence which sustained monumental authority, so much so that I felt nervous to make any sort of noise. The tension was so severe it almost felt tangible; as if something were waiting to jump out at any given moment despite any logical conclusions that such an occurrence was of the most unlikely kind. I stood there for a while and although some part of me pleaded to continue onwards with my journey, another more sensitive component of my rationale made it almost impossible to do so without at least sparing a thought to the kind of scenes that had once taken place at my feet.

In some of the places, I could almost paint a story of what had happened, not because of my intuition but rather because, by extension of the evidence, it was blatant. Perhaps the most noticeable area where there was the case and where I felt a morbid curiosity attracting me was outside one of the bars in the far right corner. On the floor, I could make out there were two military-aged males laying deceased on the floor next to one another. It was not so clear to make out what had caused their deaths but inscribed forcefully into one of their chests with some kind of sharp object was a message which said '*child killer*'. Next to one of the bodies was a gold lighter that maintained a small unrusted area on its surface that almost glimmered in the sunlight. A few feet away was an entrance to a bar which was still slightly boarded up and was no doubt more so at the time of the occurrence. Inside the corner, which I could just make out when I poked my head through the weak beams, there was a small tent set up with sleeping bags that had been reduced to thin sticks and burnt material. The entirety of the building within was black with soot and singed to a crisp, so much so it was incredible that it was still standing. Inside the tent, or what was left of it, it was just possible to make out the decimated remains of a family, two adults and two children, all laid next to each other embracing. No doubt they were laid this way as the fire engulfed them. Nothing else other than entangled bones remained. Their situation made me think of Frank and Hera and of all those sorts of military people I once watched wander up and down the street vacantly.

I did not linger for too long in the town centre, it was far too traumatic, much beyond what I was expecting, although I am not entirely sure what I anticipated to find in a world that that I had long since forgotten and been forgotten in. I suppose what was most difficult to fathom was how pointless it now was to witness their suffering; they had transcended into a better place and it was I who was left to ponder over the pain their mortality caused them.

I walked south as I recalled that this was where the nearest bypass which took one out of the town was located. As it turned out, I was almost right; there was a sign that popped up in the southeast corner of the square which directed one towards an A road. If one followed this, there was another sign beneath it which read 'Motorway: One-Way City exit. Nearest Town Thereon, 35 miles.' I continued to follow its directions without sparing much thought as to why. As I kept walking, the pain in my side continued. I began to feel dizzy once more but not so much in a burdensome way, but rather in the way one feels when pleasantly high on hallucinogens or anaesthetics, just before one passes out or begins feeling otherwise regrettable. All the images before me began to turn blurry as my head swayed from side to side. I kept putting one foot in front of the other and trying to focus on bringing myself back to my senses but to no avail. I outright refused to stop my momentum at any point I was sure even this would be enough for me to collapse to the floor and die. I kept drifting off into my thoughts and struggled to find any recourse for this diversion. The best way I can describe it is when one is on the point of falling asleep, particularly so when exhausted far more than is usual, and as one begins ever so slightly to gravitate off into the pleasant creations of their imagination, a myoclonic jerk brings back one to reality. However, no matter how hard I tried to fight off this sensation, the streets and buildings that I was walking past became illegible and before long I was in an area that was difficult to recognise. I could not be sure I had gotten this far even in the old world as where I was appeared unrecognisable in every direction.

In all my delirium, I became subconsciously aware that I was wandering past expanses without paying attention to my own position and yet I still seemed to carry on doing so anyhow, I was trying so hard to keep myself upright that all else faded into insignificance. It was as if I were being controlled by something else. However, I do vividly remember seeing the motorway exit sign, it seemed as though I passed it a thousand times and yet I was still in the town. For some reason, this one sign seemed to act as a staple piece or a strong representation on behalf of some kind of spiritual or otherworldly need to keep going. It felt as though some kind of external force beyond was trying to compel me forward as if I must keep going. Although I was never one to give any mind to such things, I could not fathom any other way it was possible that I was still walking and covering a considerable distance. I fought with all my strength to keep brushing this exponential incoherence off by continuing to walk quicker and quicker. I began to sweat, my legs ached and my heart began beating quicker and quicker and despite it all, I just kept doing the same thing over and over.

'Just keep it moving, one leg after the other. One leg after the other, just keep things moving. You'll get there soon, wherever it is you're going, you'll get there eventually.' None of the internal reassurance was any good, things just kept getting more and more confused. I walked for hours, maybe even days. The sun may have risen and it may have set, I had no way to be sure and no measure or means of time presented itself to me. In fact, it seemed as though it was actively trying to avoid me and it appeared as though I could not buy a rational thought with all the money in the world. I had no idea where I was or what I was doing, I was barely even aware of my own senses. I walked past the city's town centre, down the entirety of the A-road, and somehow found my way to the main bypass leading out of town. I had not seen nor heard anyone or anything the entire time, for which I was not surprised but still subliminally disappointed. Although, it may well have been the case that I could have walked passed an entire crowd of people and still been none the wiser.

'I really am the last one, aren't I? I always thought it possible, but never considered it to be fact, to really be true. Fucking hell, the last person left alive, the last one left. Me, of all people.' Unfortunately, such intrusive thoughts only sort to exasperate the sense of crushing and debilitating loneliness that was fighting with my hysteria for the most in-control aspect of my being. Although feeling such an extent of loneliness was not uncommon, the sensation I experienced as I wandered through a forgotten world in such a frenzied state was incomparable. There truly was nothing left to do and nothing left to see and yet, no matter how effectively I convinced myself as so, my feet just kept putting one past the other.

* * *

It was somewhere at the beginning of the motorway, where the A-road joins it so that cars can merge, where I began to feel a little bit sharper. Granted, I had no idea how I had got here or what I was doing, but the starkness of what was now my reality seemed to bring me back from the state of temporary dementia I had seemed to experience. It was an unusual progression of events, whereas before everything was faded and obscure, now my vision and my enfolding surroundings were crystal clear in the most magnificent sense. It was on this very road that I started to truly see the contrast of this world with that of the old. It looked as if this were the very place where the earth started to begin once more and left everything else in its wake.

Everything in all directions looked like it had taken on a completely new existence compared to the one I was akin to. It did not feel as though I was in a place that I knew whatsoever, it seemed more like I was a traveller in a foreign land. The sun sat high in the sky and beamed down onto me. There was not a single cloud above no matter which way I looked. The trees, which were remarkably tall, swamped the side of the road and leaned over into its vicinity from above. Thick clumps of foliage that began below appeared to climb up the side and peer over the edge of the road's railings where they still stood. I had no idea where they had appeared from as I surely did recognise them even a moment sooner. The trees and vast canvases of green were so densely packed together that it was hard to even see anything past them, apart from during the occasional opening. The road beneath my feet, although it still existed, was contorted in such a way it looked as though the very earth below had rejected it. The metallic signs, of which there used to be many on long roads like this, seemed to have completely disappeared and as such, there was no way to determine where I was or how far away I was from anywhere else. It seemed as though everything around me wanted me to continue walking down this path and whilst it would have been possible to turn around and go back the way I came, I just could not bring myself to do it. Something, some kind of force was pulling me further, it was not letting me go. I knew that I had to be here, that I was in the right place.

I continued to walk further and further, trying not to let the ludicrous nature of everything else distract me. As I progressed down this one-way road, the most incredible and otherworldly things began to take place, which were so dumbfounding I felt my senses completely withdraw from the distractions of my own complexion. The tarmac that was once driven upon by the weight of many a busy car, by many a busy person on their way to work, slowly yet surely began to crack and deteriorate at an astonishing rate. As it began to fade, lush foliage began to protrude its way through as if it had fought for the right to be there and stood tall and proudly in its place. Thick and vivid green grass which was almost knee-high had begun to replace all sense of road completely and I was wading through it before I had the chance to blink. Perhaps more remarkably, this was not the sort of dried and tired long grass that sits in a farmer's field during the drier months, it was grass that looked healthy and well-fed, like ryegrass of some kind. I watched as shoots of it grew inches every second, crumbling the concrete as it forced its way through. Eventually, after what seemed like only a few more steps, it faded even further and further still until the point where I was no longer walking on a road at all, I was wading through the grass as if I had become lost in a field. Around me, the tall trees started to become less dense but they still ran parallel to the general direction of the path I was on, seemingly leading into the distance. Only a few hundred yards away, I could see what looked like the beginning of a forest, with a large opening at the front that looked as if it had been designed specifically to allow me passage through it. I turned behind me at this point and what I saw only added to the confusion, the path and road which I walked down in a straight line to get to this point had been completely sealed off by thick trees, as if they had circled their way around to block it off. I could not be sure how this was possible. However, it made me feel somewhat at ease because the decision of what to do next had been taken from my grasp.

It seemed hard to comprehend how the industrial world was vanishing at such a rapid rate before my very eyes, but vanish it did, and this is a fact I would contest with my final breath. I continued to plough onwards, walking further and further still, watching as this natural anomaly occurred all around. Although I had begun to believe that part of what I was experiencing was due to delirium, such changes continued to take place on an even grander scale, no matter how much I resisted physically or mentally. As I continued further and my field of view expanded, the greenery did not shy away, quite contradictorily, it burst into life in every direction that I looked. I was now able to see past small openings in the trees that ran alongside the path. Over in the distance, I expected to find something which made where I now appeared incongruous. However, this was not at all the case. As far as my eyes could see, there was nothing other than dense, lime and Erin green foliage. Thick and flawless sheets of tall grass stretched for miles around and I could not see any roads or paths that had been paved. Mighty and healthy-looking white oak trees, huge weeping pillows and coast redwoods spread all around.

I blinked once more and I was just before the opening to the forest. There were no longer any signs of man having lived here or anywhere near here whatsoever; there were no railings, barriers or signs. The road had long since perished and the path which I was now on was completely incomparable to the motorway which I had started on. There was no litter or discarded items on the ground, there were no man-made objects in view whatsoever.

'What is happening? This is just bizarre, completely bizarre. Where even am I? I cannot have walked this far, I have only walked a few paces and I have been transported to another world. Look at this place, it's... it's remarkable. Everything is changing before me, look! The grass is growing ten-fold at its normal rate... I must be flying through time, I must be lost somewhere, what am I to do?' I thought. In truth, I did feel intimated, terrified and confused, but none of these emotions was as strong as the sense of complete wonderment and awe.

* * *

Another strange bout of forgetfulness descended over me and when I finally came around, I now found myself completely submerged in forestation. Upon turning, I could not see the path from earlier, it looked as though I had wandered into the forest's opening and walked for miles past it. Either that or the opening to the forest had let me in and then sealed itself as if to confuse me. There was nothing, save only for the boots on my feet, that represented even the faintest shard of human presence. It is the first time in my life that I could turn every which way and not see a single sign that human life was ever here - and nothing had ever looked more beautiful, more honest. I could have been lost a thousand miles into an unexplored rainforest for all I was able to tell.

Above me, the light was being blocked by a canopy so thick and dense that there did not seem to be any part of the sky uncovered, apart from thin absences in the leaves where thin beams of light shone down on the floor below. Birds sang and flew in between the higher sections of the forest playfully. These birds were not typical robins or finches, they were multi-coloured as if they were some kind of rare tropical kind. In front of me, five-foot-wide redwood trunks were dotted sporadically every couple of yards and climbed so high I had to lift my chin at a right angle to my neck just to see their peak. Even when putting my arms out horizontally as far as they could stretch I could barely even begin to take up any of the trunk's width. Plants of all variations grew out of the ground, some of which seemed to have the freshest of all small fruits dangling from them tantalisingly. The ground was uneven with heaps of mud and tree roots they passed by.

I continued walking further. As I did so, the birds continued to sing. The further I got, I could tell that I was not in a logical place. 'Well, to hell with logic anyhow, to hell with it! I have always hated it and now it is gone, to hell with it!' I exclaimed aloud, almost feeling the need to giggle. The tree trunks began to move as I walked as if they were once more opening a passageway up for me. This movement was not harsh nor violent, it was slow and smooth, as it was trying to be gentle so as to not frighten me. Branches removed themselves from my eye line either upwards or downwards or sidewards and I watched them retreat at my convenience. The mounds of dirt and uneven natural terrain below my feet levelled themselves just before my foot made contact with the ground. With every step I took I began to feel lighter and more peaceful. Strange, light-mannered voices began to call out, seemingly from the birds or from something higher up;

'If only you could see your face, you look bloody terrified!' A dainty and soft voice which was quiet and smooth almost sang in a melody. 'No harm will come to you here my love, you've left that all behind now. You are almost there, come on now.' The voice sounded like that of a human, I could hear its intonation and the effect of movement as it enunciated but it had a weightless and echoey quality. For some reason, something reminded me of my wound. As I looked down and began to lift my shirt up with my hand, another voice which too was soft and calming spoke. 'You don't need to worry about that now dear, You can't feel it, can you? Is there any pain?'

'Erm, no, actually no... You are right, there isn't any at all.' I responded, looking upwards to try and find the source of this sound which at this point I was even more fascinated with than the exoneration of my physical suffering.

'Well, stop dilly-dallying, we haven't got all day. Not everyone makes it to this place, you know. You are one of the special ones.' The voices finished in a jokey tone. Sounds of distant yet well-intentioned laughter rang out from seemingly different sources as if they were other sentient beings that were humouring the response from the first.

I obeyed the requests of these voices, as it did not seem as though any harm could come of it. Only this time, I was not walking for merely a few steps, I was walking for hours, perhaps even days. Whereas earlier, it was not long before there was some manifestation of atmospheric change or an unusual occurrence, this time it seemed as though I had simply been forgotten about. Nothing happened, and nothing seemed to change. I walked and walked and walked, so much so that I watched the rise and fall of the sun and moon, many times over. This was the only thing I had that I could use to measure some scale of time but I was not assured that ordinary rules applied in this place as it seemed time did not move in a linear, progressive state but rather unravelled itself from a tangled mess. It even began to rain at one point and it was a heavy sort of rain that is refreshing but powerful. I felt cogent and about my wits once more, I could hear the rain pour just as I would have been able to before. What is more, the sensation of the rain on my face was most typical. One moment I felt like I was in the real world, the next I could no longer be sure.

The environment began to start moving again once more but they were not rapid and drastic like before. Everything once again accommodated me as I walked, but there was no interaction as there was before aside from the occasional quiet laughing that sounded more sinister. Things began to grow increasingly harder, everything that I felt before I entered this place, including the pain and maltreatment, started to restore itself. The pain in my wound once again came back and with every step felt as though it were getting wider. The delirious yet pleasant high that I once felt had disappeared and instead my head began to throb with pain. My hair and clothes were drenched and even my bones felt soaked to the core, so much so I shivered in disdain. My feet ached drastically and I could feel the soreness in them manifest in blisters and cuts. I tried to put my hands out so that I could stop for a moment and lean on one of the trees but as I did so, it moved further still as if it were taunting me, and I fell onto the floor face-first into a thick pool of moist sludge.

'What do you want from ME?!' I screamed at the top of my lungs, spitting mud and water out of my mouth whilst bursting simultaneously into a violent cry. I tried my best to put a stop to it but I could do no such thing. Pain ingrained itself in every part of my being and would not let up. Tears streamed down my cheeks and snot began to make its way down my face. 'I am walking, aren't I? I am DOING what you asked of me, I am walking! How much further do you want me to go? Can't I just die already? Would that make you happy, I am ready, just finish it off. Haven't I suffered enough?' I continued to cry as sadness was revoked and by anger; 'Well, I have suffered! And I know you know it too - to hell with you, to hell with this damned place!' I partly hoped that one of the voices from earlier would have replied but they didn't.

Eventually, I saw something whilst lying in the mud that stopped me from my hysterics. About fifty feet away or so, a man stepped out from the cover of the trees and into the path that had formed ahead of me. He was a relatively tall man but also quite skinny. His head was bald and he wore glasses. His clothing was entirely black but smart and well-fitted. What is more, he was not wet despite rain hammering every inch of the floor space. I knew immediately who it was, it was my father. I abandoned my previous pessimism and rose to my feet before picking up the pace as much as my tired body could afford. Water covered my face and stung my eyes, blood dripped further down my side with every step, sending shockwaves of pain throughout. My feet were now so sore I could feel my thin skin having ripped and the matter beneath rubbing on my boot heels.

As I arrived before him, he put his arms behind his back and crossed them. Just as I was about to reach his personal space, some sort of force blocked me and I could not walk any further no matter how much I tried, as if an invisible wall had been placed there and somehow, he seemed to be aware of its presence and what it sought to do. He stood and looked at me, clearly somewhat disturbed by the state that I was in but with a reticence that suggested he was unable to do anything about it.

'Dad? What are you doing here, what is happening? Please, help me. I can't do this anymore, I am finished. What am I supposed to do? Just tell,

tell me how to make it end.'

'Hello, son. I'm sorry to barge in on you like this.' He said without responding in any way to my cries for help. 'There is just one final thing from me, that I have come to say to you.'

'I've been hearing your voice, all of this time. Just when I needed it, I could hear you. Just one last time, Dad, please. Just tell me what I have to do. I am suffering. Take me with you, take me anywhere away from this place, I cannot bare it any longer, I cannot bare it.' I cried further.

'I know you could hear me. Of course, I knew it... Listen, I don't have long, so I need you to listen to me carefully. I know you are hurting but please, just listen to me. I wanted to say how proud I am of you, for all you have done, and all you have achieved in your life. I know it has not been easy for you, it never is for men in that world.' For the first time I had ever seen in his and my lifetime, a tear began to form in his eyes. It was such a startling moment that I immediately withdrew from my caterwauling and hung from every word thereon. 'I know I didn't say it much to you, but I mean it. You've done great, and I am proud of you and of who you are. You were a man too good for that world and you don't need to worry about anything any longer.'

'But what do I do, what do I do now? I don't know what to do.' I asked pragmatically, trying to appeal to his senses as my pathetic whelping did not seem effective. I suckered up all the strength it took to fight back the pain and emotion. As I looked at him, he began to become almost translucent, as if he was being sent on a frequency that was beginning to fade away. The translucency began to get slowly but progressively stronger.

'Don't leave me, please. I don't want to be alone any longer.'

'There isn't much further to go now son, so keep moving. I know you are tired but you are almost home. You will be home soon, I promise. Keep going.'

'Dad?' I said, He smiled at me once last time before disappearing.

I kept walking with a vicious rage fighting to get out of me. I was so angry that it seemed to override all the other unpleasant sensations. 'Here I am, walking again!' I screamed aloud with my arms out wide and circling around as to gesture to all that could see and hear me. 'You pretending you can't hear me now is that it, you want me to be grateful that I am here? Do you want me to get on my hands and knees and pray and give all my thanks? Well, guess what I say to that, *fuck you* and all of your stupid moving trees and fancy fucking birds. Haha! Yeah, that's right. You heard me. You think you can scare me, you think whatever you throw is going to bother me, well I didn't care for the old world and I sure as hell don't care about yours either, so fuck you, and fuck this *place*!'

I continued to walk even further, cursing vehemently under my breath and venting mentally in any way I could. However, it did not seem as though I was walking for quite as long this time. The daylight had now returned but I was on the brink of collapsing. Every muscle in my body that was used to walk ached fiercely and the souls of my feet burned so much now that I could not bear to put my weight on them any longer. I was gasping for breath so much that it felt as though my lungs would collapse. Eventually, my legs gave way beneath me. It was an odd feeling, I did not physically stop walking nor did I choose to fall over, my legs quite literally just ceased to move, as if paralysis had instantaneously ensued. I lay on my back once more and turned to face upwards. I closed my eyes and just laughed. I laughed so much that I began to cry and after this, I laughed some more.

CHAPTER XII - ELYSIUM

It was only a few moments later when I opened my eyes and lifted my head defeatedly that I saw it; I was no longer in a forest at all. At first, it took a while for my vision to gain focus but once it did I noticed that I had been transported somewhere completely different and I didn't even know or feel it as it took place. A most bizarre happening that, before the events of the last few hours, would have perplexed me beyond words. None of the catharsis or anger or sadness from just a few minutes prior had carried over into this seclusion, as if something had rid me of it.

Before me was a quaint and well-sheltered clearwater lake enfolded in daylight. Behind it was a waterfall that fell steadily against a rocky scenery and this was all. The lake was only a couple of meters in any direction yet it was still quite deep. The rockery, which appeared to be a light-coloured limestone, stretched all around the back wall of this idyllic area. Around the edges of the lake was a smooth and groomed patch of grass that circled it unobtrusively. A tightly packed bunch of Banyan trees occupied the entire perimeter of this seclude. Beyond them, it was very difficult to see anything else between the gaps and it seemed no light was cast in the yonder. The closer I tried to look, the more I noticed that everything beyond was covered in darkness, whereas this little area bathed in vivid sunshine that shone from above between a large and almost perfectly rounded gap in the canopy. It was very obvious, even from an immediate inventory of the area, that there was no through-road, nor was there any way to leave. By extension of this, I assumed that this was not a place where one is required to do anything or act. Rather, it appeared to be a temporary waiting place of sorts. It felt as though, for reasons I cannot describe, something in the background was loading itself - as if something were preparing itself for me as I was awaited here in blissful ignorance.

There were not many sounds available, although one of which was the gentle whispering of the birds and the occasional fluttering of their wings as they danced and flew across the lake together playfully, lowering themselves so much they almost touched the water's surface before returning to the treetops on the far side. Sometimes, a chirp from a grasshopper penetrated the tranquillity of the waterfall's placid stream before tapering off. The timid and fitful gust of wind which brushed past the leaves in the trees created a slight ruffling sound as it worked its way into the opening before it waned. All the noises around, albeit soft and quiet, were harmonious and in sync with each other as if all the beings here existed as one. Butterflies fluttered around in random directions, seemingly appearing from nowhere, as they caressed each other and played in the air, creating a faint fluttering sound as they pirouetted by touching one another and then drifting apart. They flew high, so much so they almost reached the top of the canopy but I noticed that no matter how close they got they never left. Beneath the water, which was a bright Cyan colour and entirely transparent, large redfish and tarpon swam peacefully past each other, apparently without a need to hurry, before turning around and doing it all over again, each time as uninhibited as the last.

Where the dainty waterfall entered the lake over at the far side, a small but unintrusive trickling vibrated the otherwise continuous surface, sending out puny waves that worked their way calmly to the water's edge before evanescing. An occasional breeze that was stronger than the ones from before passed threw into the opening but it was light and refreshing and never sought to intrude. There was a large amount of space in the canyon above, more so than I had initially realised. This allowed the sun to pass into the retreat without obstruction. It beamed down with luminous amber rays that alit all things here in a golden hue and the angle at which the sun was positioned remained perfect. Everything was bright and colourful in its own right without detracting from any other; the limestone glittered as if it had diamonds set in it, the grass (which was greener than I had ever seen) glimmered as it moved in the wind and the water from the lake was a colour so effulgent it seemed almost unnatural.

I sat here for a while and just observed the surroundings. I was not panicked or scared despite not knowing how I had ended up here. After everything that had happened to me, I just accepted any further proceeds with complete impartiality. It did not seem appropriate to act in any other way. All of the pain I had experienced, which was not so long since unbearable, had completely vacated, and I felt no physical or mental impairments at all. I had probably sat here for what seemed to be an hour, but I could have remained for a thousand hours more had I been permitted but somehow I knew that this not going to be the case.

Just as I had accepted that I was the only mammal in this heavenly retreat, I saw a small deer creep from behind the limestone rockery. It poked its head around the corner as if to survey its surrounding before proceedings inwards. It moved with a grace and sense of familiarity as it had been here before. It wandered over to the far right-hand side of the lake and began to sip water from the lake's edge. It did so amicably as if it dare not disturb the consummate aura of this place that appeared to have been sown into every atom in its vicinity. The doe looked up from its watering and appeared to notice me over at the side. It looked at me with a sense of gratitude. It was such a gentle and decorous being it looked as if it were bothering or offending me, despite it doing nothing of the sort. Eventually, the deer approached me in a benevolent manner, presumptively to investigate the unusual notion of human presence. I cannot be sure that I was the first or the last human to have ended up in this retreat, but it certainly did not seem like many had been here before. At first, I felt fear, having accepted my place as a trespasser in this utopian seclusion. I offered myself defencelessly should it choose to devour all of me that remains. I did not think this to be the doe's intention at this point, but I gave her the option anyhow as it seemed like the right thing to do and she was by far the most deserving of all the things that had recently tried to do so. However, it slowly came close to my face, so much so that it breathed lightly onto me. I extended my arm to stroke the soft fur under his chin. Surprisingly, the deer accepted my outstretched arm and its incumbent gesture of hospitality. I am quite sure that we bonded for a few seconds, which was confirmed by an empathetic look that it gave me at some point during our interaction before it turned and wandered back into the woodland as if it had been scared by something I did not notice. It had only taken a few steps beyond the Banyon trees before it disappeared from view completely.

I changed positions so that I could lie on my back. I looked upwards into the distant sky and felt the sun as it warmed my face. There was nothing else in the sky, not even the faintest disturbance that interrupted the plain of light blue in the distance. I relished the offerings of this moment and this place as I drifted in and out of consciousness.

There was only one thing that I could think about in the ensuing moments. I cast my thoughts back to earlier when the bolt of light came crashing across the sky and in my fear, I envisaged what is to come next after we continue our journey into the next world. I believed that during this experience, the place which I optimistically desired was one which is extremely similar in nature to the one before me, albeit this seclusion appeared to be a microcosm of no perpetuity. I made this comparison because, within this place that I had temporary access to, I was finally able to effectuate a place that I had dreamt of; a place that is capable of sustained peace unburdened by the heavy hand of man; a place of paramount, natural beauty. A place where suffering is limited and harmony is plentiful. A place where people can consult their eternal destiny and deliberate over the higher purpose of their soul. A place where people dare to think so greatly beyond themselves that they realise what they are and in doing so, have all the more for it. Having seen both this world and the old, its people, the way of life and what they are capable of no matter the rest, I am no longer sure that the next place that now I await will be quite as idyllic as the one before me now.

If I had it my way, I would have stayed in this seclusion forever, but something made it seem clear somehow that my imminent transition was inevitable. This place, assuming it was making a statement, seemed to be a testament to everything that I wanted life to be and everything I knew that it never could. Therefore, having accepted in full and unconditional terms the actualisation of my fate, all else that was left to be considered was where I would end up next. I thought about what it would look like and how it would be. It was hard to imagine that it would be a place as perfect as the little cove before me, especially given that everything else that I had both regrettably experienced and imagined with intensity pointed to the contrary. However, for the first time, this did not bother me in the slightest.

In the end, I believe that my conclusion was simple; I did not need nor desire whatever is next to be perfect. In fact, I no longer cared for such ideals. I just hoped that, if nothing else, it will be somewhere better - somewhere easier. I spent my final few moments enjoying this place and smiling before being moved on.

AFTERWORD

Thank you for reading, I sincerely hoped that you enjoyed my first adventure, which has now reached its conclusion.

Please, if you have the time, do leave a review or/and a rating (they can be very important for indie authors on self-publishing platforms) whether good, bad, or anywhere inbetween. I would very much love to hear from you.

I am due to release my second novel by (hopefully, with all being well) the end of 2024. Please do check out my authors page or visit my website at www.danielcraigemery.com for regular updates.

ABOUT THE AUTHOR

Daniel Craig Emery

Daniel Craig Emery (he bears no relation to Mr. Bond himself, unfortunately) was born in the Beighton region of Sheffield, South Yorkshire in 1999 to a mechanical engineer and a counsellor. He subsequently moved to the Nottinghamshire town of Worksop, where he grew up and was educated at a local comprehensive school.

After sixth form, Emery moved to Nottingham City and went on to read law at Nottingham Trent University. He worked numerous part-time jobs, including one on a concrete plantation, one as a bar manager and as an SEN teaching assistant. He also interned at law firms, the Nottinghamshire Coroner's Court and did pro bono legal work. He ultimately became dissatisfied with the prospect of a career in law, especially following his final year during COVID-19 lockdown, and upon completion of his degree he decided to pursue his passion for writing, something he had been doing casually most of his life, and studied an MA in Creative Writing, also in Nottingham.

Emery studied prose fiction as well as screenwriting and wrote essays on topics such as the works and influence of Ernest Hemingway and the manipulation of narrative perspective. He also wrote numerous stories, including the submission of short stories and a contribution to the cohorts' anthology series. A shortened version of his debut novel, 'Where Life is Easiest For Men' was submitted as his dissertation thesis.

In his spare time, Emery is an avid Sheffield Wednesday Football Club supporter. He enjoys keeping active in the gym and drinking a beer (or two) on the weekends.

His second novel is due to be released by the end of 2024. For Regular updates, check out his website at www.danielcraigemery.com.